Only Fate Could Predict

Rick
To some creativity is hard to
come by. To others all it
Takes is a thought, a word,
or a friend. And friendship is
the Best thing to Have
Love Ab Laffin

Only Fate Could Predict

❖

H. L. Laffin

To order additional copies of this book, contact:
Xlibris Corporation
1-888-795-4274
www.Xlibris.com
Orders@Xlibris.com
51073

To my sister Tanya
If it wasn't for her asking me to tell her bedtime stories so she
could fall asleep, then I may never have found my talent.

I'll love you forever.
Cheers.

INTRO PAGE

As we are heading to the door, Mandy is waiting there for us because there are police with guns pointed ready for us. Michelle comes to and knocks me over sending both my son and gun out of my hands. I yell at Elijah to run for the door as Michelle grabs my hair and puts me into a headlock while pointing a handgun on me.

I watch as Mandy grab Elijah by the arm and pick up my gun. The blood drains from my face; here I thought Mandy was on my side, trying to struggle out of Michelle's grasp when I see Mandy put my gun to my son's head.

Feeling less pressure on my back, I scream at Mandy that I thought I could trust her. While Michelle feels like she won't have to kill the kid, she becomes more relaxed. But Mandy quickly turns the gun at Michelle and me, shooting.

Ryan was still at me wanting to have another baby, and every night he wanted to have sex whether I wanted to or not. This wasn't how I thought things would be with him home. I guess I always pictured the loving couple who missed each other.

I could see that I was getting under his skin with being obstinate, not wanting to make another baby or listen to him, and having an attitude toward him. And instead of being the wife who'd pine for her husband, I was being a distant and bitchy wife. I was fighting with him more than I was loving him.

With letting Mark into the house I casually ask, "What are you doing here? Where is Daisy?" I look around the porch for her but do not see her. "Aren't you and Daisy working on your missing wife?" I ask finally, trying not to let my anger arise.

Watching Mark fidget in his place, then break down, "I am so sorry. Things were going well, but Daisy wanted to go through with her crazy scheme. Having me hit her and then run out, so that a friend would find her and take her to where Sally was taken. It's been two days and I haven't heard from her, so I thought maybe she came home or her planned worked." He finished while lowering his eyes in shame.

PROLOGUE

"Hi, I want to thank all you today for joining me on *Chat*. With us today we have the famous and amazing Daisy Gaston." The audience applauds, "She came from Vancouver where she grew up. After a family tragedy, she left to attend college in Lethbridge, where she met her husband. Living a secret life, this woman became a huge success in the business world as well as a hero to our country. I want to welcome Daisy Gaston."

I heard Clapping from the audience as I walked onstage. I knew that Jill was trying really hard not to mention all the impressive things I had done with my life so that people would read my book. I took a seat on one of the couches onstage. "Thank you, Jill, for having me on *Chat*, it is a real honor."

"Thank you for coming, I know you are a very busy woman."

"Well I do like to fill my days. But I'm glad the book is finished," I say with a chuckle.

"Yes the book, *One Night of Fate*, when did you have time after being in another country?"

"Well after being wounded and needing to spend some quality time with my youngest, I thought I would write. And that was three hundred pages ago."

Sipping water, Jill said, "You are an amazing woman. You risked your life for many others who never knew you beside what they saw on the media."

"It was something I felt compassionately towards," I mentioned before we took a break.

After break Jill looked at one of the cameras then said, "If you've just tuned in, we are here with author, business mongrel, producer, family woman, and local hero Daisy Gaston. Daisy I know that you don't want me to reveal too much of the novel. But is there anything you might want to mention to get the readers interested?"

I took another sip of my water and smiled. "Sure thing. I was brought up with good morals and strong family values, with a brother who was my best friend. I loved to dance, and it showed while in college because I spent most of my time at the clubs. I always befriended people I felt needed someone they could trust, and I guess that's how it all got started."

I thought back to how it got started. The night I was getting ready to go clubbing with my friends, the night that changed my life forever, the night that caused me future pain but endless happiness.

9

PART 1

CHAPTER 1

I looked in the mirror and thought to myself Ryan Gaston is coming over to the house to pick me up soon since my fiancé, Mark Hodges, was getting ready to go to work. I don't know what it is about the thought of Ryan coming over, but I hurried myself up a bit more. Mark is a conservation Officer and rarely home, so Ryan being my best friend always chaperoned me when I went out to the bar with Shane and Tom at the Rock House. One of Mark's requests if I insisted on going out. The Rock House is like the hippest club in town, where they played mostly the top 40 hits and all the young adults went to have a good time and dance.

I go to give Mark a kiss good-bye; I'll miss him for the four days he will be away on duty. When Ryan comes to get me, I hear Mark telling him to watch out for me. Looking at Ryan, I wonder why Mark trusts me with him, with Ryan being way more attractive with his tanned skin and more chiselled features. Mark is taller than me by six inches and has fair skin, with soft features in his face. Might explain why he's so trusting and such a pushover. I pretty much get away with anything I want with Mark, but being Ryan's friend I don't get away with very much. It's like he is smarter and can read between the lines with me.

"Honey, I will be fine, I know how to handle myself, and Tom and Shane are my friends." I tell Mark while hugging him. Why he worries about me I'll never know. Tom is not very cute and never goes home with a girl when leaving the bar. Shane on the other hand always leaves with a girl and is fun to drink with.

*　*　*

Looking at Daisy Dime with her long silky strawberry blonde hair, and green eyes, with her gentle tan. Mark is such a fool to leave her alone all the time. If she were my girlfriend, I would never leave her alone and defiantly with someone like me. But since Mark is a great guy for her, I feel no reason for him to be threatened by me. I love dancing with Daisy and just having her in my arms. Why can't all women be more like her? Sweet, gentle, with a caring personality, a strong drive, and the will power to succeed. I understand Mark's fear when Shane is around her. I too feel something unsettling about the guy that I don't like either. Being that Daisy is my best fiend, I would do anything to protect her and keep people out of her and Mark's relationship.

She was the first one to befriend me when I arrived in Lethbridge, and she really listens and understands me. I laugh to myself as they argue. She always try to be the strong one, try's to win all the argument, and she does with Mark, but with me I will not allow her to think she is in control.

Deep down she has no idea what kind of pain a man can bring to her. They are so opposite, Mark and Daisy, but for some reason they make it work. He's always gone, and when he is home she is always going out with Hillary, me, or another friend.

*   *   *

"That's fine, but I don't trust them as much as I trust Ryan with you." And with that Mark gives me a final kiss good-bye before heading out the door.

We meet up at the bar with Shane and Tom; I go and dance with them on the dance floor while Ryan gets me a beer. I always flirt with these guys, but just friendly since I'm engaged to Mark and not that interested in them. But Shane is suck a hunk, being tall, handsomely broad shouldered, crisp black hair and green eyes. I defiantly would have gone out with him if I had met him before Mark. Tom is shorter, a little heavier then Shane, but has a great attitude, someone who is around for a good time.

Once Ryan is back with our drinks I dance with him for the rest of the night. Just being in his arms is weird, the sensation I feel, the warmth of his body and strong arms around me. Ryan is just a little taller then I, with curly black hair, deep brown eyes, and tanned skin. Being that he is Arabic, his accent is very heavy, but his English is very good, having been in the country for a few months and completing his college here in Lethbridge. We have been working together at Dooley's Restaurant since he arrived here in Canada. Most of the time our dancing is pretty provocative, with me dirty dancing in his arms. But that's is far as our relationship goes because we are attracted to each other, and I'm Ryan's boss; our relationship is strictly flirtatious friends.

*   *   *

Feeling Daisy's warm body against mine as we danced makes me want to never let her go back to Mark. I hate that the gods make it so I can't be with a Canadian. If I could I'd marry her before Mark had the chance. But deep down I know Mark has more to offer her, a home, security and he is Canadian.

While I, on the other hand, am still trying to move out of my sister's house and get my papers. I'm watching as Shane buy Daisy a beer; for some reason him buying her drinks make me feel sick. I trust myself, but this guy is always trying to sleep with some girl or another. I know she's known him longer than me, and she says to trust him. But I have seen guys like him in my country, and I know what their intentions are when they buy drinks for girls.

*   *   *

Shane comes up to me and says, "Daisy, I got you another beer since you were looking low." Ryan looks at me oddly as I take the beer.

"Thanks, Shane," I share my beer with Ryan while dancing with the group. Ryan goes to the washroom and Shane hands me another beer. I win the drinking contest the three of us are having. But shortly after I start feeling very tired and ask Shane to take me home since Ryan is no where to be seen. We are almost out the door when Ryan catches up to me and demands, "What is going on? I leave for one minute and you leave on me!"

I tell Ryan that I'm very tired and asked Shane to take me home. Ryan interrupts and says, "I'll take her home, if you don't mind." After putting his arms through mine, we go and he helps me into his jeep.

I feel really lose and relaxed, we park in a parking lot, I give Ryan a back massage and we talk about life. "Ryan, why haven't you found a girlfriend?" I ask him.

*   *   *

"Because I have to marry someone from my culture, and I don't want there to be difficulties with the girls in this country. And I'm looking for someone like you, Daisy." Ryan says with sincerity in his eyes. *God how if I had met you earlier, I would have been the one you'd be marrying, and if you were Arabic my family would approve of it more so.* Just thinking that she was going to get a ride home with Shane makes my stomach turn. As Daisy leans into my body, I pet her hair while she continues to talk.

*   *   *

"Hum," I say sluggishly as I fall toward Ryan. I look into his eyes and we kiss, a soft gentle kiss. Then the kissing gets heavier, and we start petting each other, me placing my hand on his hard manliness. He starts to play with my breasts and kiss my neck.

Waking up in my apartment with my head feeling dizzy, I whisper to myself, "Wow that was a pretty intense dream." Getting a sudden chill I relise that I'm naked, not wearing any panties or bra but a thin negligee. I head for my housecoat hanged on the back of the bedroom door, when I stumble over Ryan. He's in my bedroom on the floor with only boxers on. Why is he here at my house? And half naked?

God he looks so hot and sexy. If I didn't have any self-control I would attack him like a lion would its prey.

Thinking that rather strange, I wake him up. "Ryan, why are you here?" I ask him with a shaky tone.

I feel my body as I wake up groggy and look at Daisy. "What? Where am I? Why are you at my house?" Looking around I notice I'm in Daisy and Mark's bedroom

15

on the floor. My body hurts so much, especially my head, and I see my clothes are thrown all over the room. Daisy seems to be wearing a pretty thin blue see-through negligee.

Just looking at her turns me on, but remembering she is engaged brings me back under control. I know that if she were my wife, I would bind her arms and make endless love to her, claiming she could not leave the bed until I had my fill of her.

*   *   *

"I'm not at your house. You are at my house. And your not wearing much clothing, nor am I." I tell him with fear in my voice. Please tell me you just crashed at my house, and you didn't find me doing anything indecent." Heading for my house coat, I wondered why my head and body hurt.

"Oh," Ryan says and gets up off the floor.

Putting the robe on after noticing how see through the negligee I was wearing and looking at Ryan's hard but furry chest, I notice some scratch marks and taking light of the evidence I went to the kitchen to make coffee and break feast. Ryan walked in with his clothes on, and I ask him, "Do you remember last night?"

Cause I sure couldn't seem to remember much, just dancing, and the rest of the night is a blur. This is so unlike me; what did I drink or smoke, and why does my head throb? I thought to myself while flipping the eggs.

"I remember going to the bar, drinking, and dancing with you," he tells me while drinking his coffee.

Ryan leaves, and I mark the calendar due to this strange behaviour of mine. I feel this is very odd behaviour from me. I must have drunk way too much and should cut down. Maybe Marks being gone all the time is actually bothering me, like Hillary says, and I should lay off the hard stuff.

Mark gets back four days dater, and within the next two months we get married June 15 in his hometown of Vernon. The wedding is simple and cheap, with fifty people attending and a small wedding party.

Looking at Mark Hodges with his slick black hair and fair skin, I feel really blessed to be marrying this sweet, charming man. Since I met Mark in college, he has always made sure I was okay, well-looked after, providing me with anything a girl could want. Looking into those hazel eyes I told him, "I do," but felt odd when the part about being loyal came. For some reason my mind went back to April 5, the night I still can't remember.

After the wedding we head up to Edmonton for our honeymoon. Feeling a little tired and sick, we just cuddle most of our honeymoon. On our last night in the hotel I'm laying on the couch, and Mark has a rose behind his back. He kneels down, kisses me passionately, and shows me the rose. I smell it, and then drag it ever so seductively down my chin, down my cleavage all the way down to my belly button.

As Mark can't take it anymore for he wisps me into his arms and takes me to the bed. Gently, as he removes my clothes, I'm kissing him on the neck and lips, tasting him in my mouth while his tongue moves around. He starts kissing my neck and then focusing on my nipples, sucking them ever so gently, I moan with pleasure as he continues to suck and kiss my breasts. Mark inserts his hard passion into my wetness. With long slow pumps as he is trying to drive me further into ecstasy, I finally release.

Once were finished making love, we lie beside each other breathing heavily. We felt it was well worth the wait of three months celibacy so that it would be special on our wedding night and honeymoon.

When we get back to Lethbridge, my best friend, Hillary, who works at Dooley's like me but on different days than Ryan and I, asks, "So when are you and Mark going to have a baby?"

I look at her and laugh, "Not for a while, I'm only twenty-three and have many years left before bringing a child into this world. Plus I'm a manager at Dooley's, that's not a major career decision." What is she thinking a baby? God, that would ruin my perfect life of partying, and not to mention Mark is not around enough to be a great dad.

Hillary is a great girl, tall, slim body, with long red hair and oceanic blue eyes. She's my bar pal; we hit the clubs in this town every weekend and shake the place up. Ever since I came to Lethbridge she has been my best friend, sharing my dreams and keeping secrets. Although I can never tell her my desire to be with Ryan, she wouldn't understand as if I even understood. As well as that day he was at my house and we were both half naked; she'd think I cheated on Mark.

"Daisy, how is it again you two met? Cause I swear you two don't mesh!" Hillary kids, knowing how we met.

Mark and I met when I first arrived at the college in Lethbridge. I was carrying my books and bumped into him. We started to chat. Then we began dating, and after my first year we moved in together. He was older than I and had been in the college for a few years, so he was graduating and going into his job.

At first we were great together, but once he started to stress over finals and began his career, I started to see less of him and more of my friends.

At work Ryan tells me all about his girlfriend. "Her name is Runée, she's shorter then you, Daisy. But she's really nice, just loves to cuddle and talk. I really like her, she's a bit too possessive, but that's all right. I have told her that we're friends and to accept you, or else I'll dump her."

"Ryan, I'm very happy for you, I hope it works out, buddy. Cause I wouldn't want to have to have two husbands," I tell Ryan with a kidding gesture as I give him a very big hug, but it feels odd as if there was a static shock. I pull away and look at him strangely. He too is looking at me with a puzzled look. "Hillary and I are going to Rock House, you should see if Runée will come," I told him so I could meet this girl that he decided to try and get over me with while I got married. Why I can't be happy for him? I don't know, but I will try and put on a good face for him. I wish I can have both men in my life, but his religion would never allow us to marry, and it is too late for us.

*   *   *

I thought telling Daisy the news of Runée would have made me happy. I thought by having a girlfriend my feeling for Daisy would subside. She looked happy for me, but deep down inside I could tell she wasn't really happy and was a bit jealous.

She gave me a hug to congratulate me on finding a girl worthy of my attention. But hugging her felt weird, 'cause I got a spark from her.

*   *   *

Later that night at the club I start coughing and sneezing. "Great, I have a cold," I tell Hillary. We are on the dance floor having a great time. I try to drink but feel sick, so we figure I've outgrown beer. On to the cocktails and shots, we headed to the shot bar and bumped into Shane.

"Hey, man," we tell Shane.

"Girls, what are you doing out tonight? And where's Mark?" Shane asks with enthusiasm as this blonde is hanging off his arm drunk. Man, he does look good in his beige khakis and blue T-shirt. Why do I think about and admire every other man than my husband?

"Just out to dance, Mark's gone for a while at a conservation camp. Ryan's with his girlfriend," I tell him before taking a shot. *Damn, that was strong*, I think to myself as I try to hear what Shane is telling Hillary and me.

"Well I'm going home with this honey," Shane says as we look at the girl who's on his arm. She's the type of typical slim blonde girls that he always takes home.

"Well were going out next weekend, you should come," Hillary tells him before he leaves.

We finish drinking and head home. The next day I seem to be in love with the toilet because all I can do is throw up. Regretting eating from the Pita Shack and drinking those shots because I couldn't drink the beer, I call in to work sick.

Ryan has to open the restaurant for me the next morning 'cause he's my fill-in when I'm sick and can't doing morning prep. But I will still come in and manage the place if I feel better. My cold is getting the better of me lately, causing me to be cranky at my staff and neglecting some of my jobs.

Two months later I was shocked that Mark was nice enough to be home around my birthday but left the bar early cause he had to work the next day. I'm not sure why I married him at times since I spend more time with my friends than I do with him. I have also been spending more time with Ryan. I don't mind, but that guy has to spend some time with his new girlfriend.

18

As we go out to one of the lesser-known clubs, Hillary and I are dancing with Mark and Ryan, having a great time drinking and doing shots only to have Mark leave at the stroke of midnight.

I love that my birthday is in August with the sun and the beach parties. My brother and I used to have great parties with all our friends down at the beaches, with fires going to keep us warm. When I got older and before I left home for college, Matt and I would go to the clubs and spend the whole night out making Mom mad.

The next week I ask Ryan if he wants to come out to the bar with us, but he tells me that Runée wants to stay home and watch movies. I've noticed that since he's been going out with her, Ryan and I are only able to talk at work because she always has some reason we can't talk at his house or why he can't come out with me. I put my concern aside for tonight so I can have fun with Hillary, Tom, Shane, and Krissy. Krissy is one of Hillary's friends. She's short, has brown hair, small eyes, with a cocky mouth, and a terrible smoking habit, but a blast to party with.

Since Ryan isn't here and Shane was my original dirty dancing partner, I dance with him to the music, bumping and grinding with him. He's not as good as Ryan, but lately with being sick I don't really care, and I can't get my mind off of the jealously I'm feeling toward Runée. Shane buys me a drink after I get back from the washroom. I dance with my girls, and a few strange guys come up behind us, so we dance with them. We continue to dance with them till Shane and Tom comes and kicks the guys out.

*   *   *

Getting a phone call from Mark as Runée and I were about to move one-step further in our relationship didn't bother me as much as it bothered her. I would have been able to get to the Rock House faster if I had not gotten into an argument with Runée. She is so jealous of my friendship with Daisy that I'm feeling about ready to dump her. She won't let me talk to my friend on the phone and harasses me at work even though I have told her that Daisy and I were friends before she came into the picture, and if there is anything my friend needs, I will always be there, and that she has to understand. Because no sex is worth the loss of friends and freedom.

Getting to Rock House and seeing Daisy dancing with Shane, especially after the fight I just had, made my blood boil. I could see that she looked tired and worn out. I grab Daisy by the arm and twirl her into me as I look at Shane with rage. *I know you up to something, buddy, and I swear to god I'll figure it out*, I ponder silently.

*   *   *

I put my arms around Shane and dance slowly and rest my head on him, feeling dizzy and tired. I'm thinking that I should get checked out about my cold. My thoughts are interrupted as Ryan grabs and twirls me into him. I look at him strangely as to why he's here and not with Runée. I notice that he seems to be very angry. Wondering why, I turn away from him and put my back against his chest just as a good song comes on, and then as if instinctively we start to dance provocatively. He places his hand on my belly and I feel the tightness, and that same electric spark, after which he pulls his hand away just as fast as I push it away.

"I have to go to the washroom," Ryan tells me with fear in his voice and leaves me on the dance floor. *Why is he acting so weird? Did he and Runée break up, and why do I keep getting an electric spark from him?* I think to myself as I go back to dancing with Shane and the girls.

*   *   *

Why is it every time I touch her I get an electric spark, and why did her stomach feel so tight and swollen. I did not want to be here in the first place, but nore did I want to go home either. Heading to the bar for a drink was a better idea, then the crowded washroom. At the bar I order a drink and overhear some girls talking about how they can't trust guys to buy them drinks anymore.

There is too much date rape going around, and one of their friends woke up not remembering anything, but her body hurt. They also mention that it's not fair that guys can't pay for their drinks without trying to drug them.

Hearing this shocking information, my gut goes numb, and I immediately think of Shane. I can't get this sick idea of out my head that Shane has been going around drugging girls and having his way. I head back onto the dance floor to look for Daisy so I can get her out of here. My mission is thwarted by some chick who wants to dance with me, and being polite I dance with her but keep my eyes out for Daisy, hoping it's not too late.

*   *   *

I go to the washroom with Hillary and Krissy, and some girls are talking about a new drug that guys are using to make their dates sleepy and forgetful. They then take the girls home and have their way. Feeling creeped out after hearing that, we head back to the dance floor and dance some more. Shane offers me some of his beer; it tastes weird but nothing these days seem to taste right. I see Ryan dancing with a pretty redhead, but they have some space between them, and I laugh to myself.

Dancing with the girls, I start to feel queasy and dizzy again, getting mad at myself for drinking the beer when I know it seems to be having an effect on me, and being sick isn't helping.

Shane comes back and tells me that we should go. I agree after feeling the spark when Ryan had touched me and now feeling dizzy. I let Shane lead me out of the bar, after telling Hillary I'm going home. I don't want to bug Ryan; he seems to be having fun, and lately he has been looking drained.

I put more of my body weight on Shane, feeling very tired. Once outside Shane leads me to his truck. I faintly hear Ryan yelling at Shane to stop where he is. We stop, and Ryan catches up, "Where are you going with Daisy?" he demands of Shane.

"I know your up to something, I have been watching the girls who hang out with you, and they're all sleepy or overly drunk when they leave with you. I have heard about this date rape drug that makes girls sleepy, and I bet your using it!" Ryan yells at Shane.

"No I'm not! The girls are just tired when we leave. You have no proof! Same with Daisy, she hasn't been feeling well with her cold and all the stress at work," Shane replies with determination in his voice.

The bouncers have now gathered around the guys in case a fight breaks out. My legs get soft, and I feel my body go down, but luckily Ryan is there to catch me. The bouncers detain Shane as Ryan rushes me to the hospital.

*   *   *

Seeing Shane almost leave with Daisy just about killed me, but intercepting at the right moment felt good, especially when Daisy collapsed in my arms. After the bouncers had restrained Shane and helped me put Daisy into the jeep. I drove as fast as I could to the hospital. Carrying her into the emergency room, I yelled for a nurse. I notice some cops enter just after I did, and they look at me like I've done something wrong.

A nurse takes Daisy into an emergency room, and when the doctor comes to see her, the nurse comes back out and asks me information about Daisy. "Your wife, is she pregnant? How much has she had to drink? And when did she go unconscious?"

I try to answer the nurse the best I can, giving her my name and the information to her questions. The doctor then comes up to me and asks if I'm her husband otherwise, I can't see her. I tell him yes and out of the corner of my eye see the nurse write my name down for the husband. The doctor me tells that the tests show that Daisy was indeed drugged by Rohypnol. A drug that guys use to make the girls tired, rape them, and the girl has no memory of the event taking place.

Feeling sick to my stomach and wanting to kill Shane, I continue to hear what else the doctor says although I don't hear much except the part when he says she's pregnant.

*   *   *

I wake up in the morning feeling like crap, my head hurts, and my body feels tight. The doctor comes in an hour after the nurse checks my pulse and vitals. The doctor tells me that I suffered no damage from the date rape drug and nor did my baby. I look at him with shocked eyes. "My baby?" I say to him. The doctor then proceeds to tell me that he'd like to run some more tests, then my husband can come in. Mark is going to be really mad coming back and finding out I'm pregnant.

We never had any plans to have children early and so soon in our marriage. At times I'm not sure I still want to be married to him; he's always gone and never does anything with me when he does come home from his trips. Dreading Mark's entrance, I'm surprised to see Ryan come in when the doctor leaves.

"Where is Mark?" I ask Ryan with skepticism.

"I never called him yet, and they think I'm your husband. I wasn't allowed to see you otherwise unless I was, so I just allowed them to assume," Ryan said as he approached my bedside and kissed my forehead. "Congratulations, Daisy, Mark will be so proud."

I look at him oddly, and then the doctor comes back in, and tells me that I conceived somewhere around April 4 to 7. Cause I am four and a half months pregnant. Feeling the blood drain from my face, I feel ill. Mark and I had gone celibate about three months prior to the wedding because we wanted to make our wedding night special. I tell the doctor I was also on the pill, so getting pregnant isn't possible. But then the doctor informs me that the drug used to rape girls can also destroy what the birth control pill does to protect them.

I hate that I can't remember what happened on April 5 and knowing Shane had drugged me last night, I was pretty sure he had done so in April. I put on a brave face so that Ryan wouldn't see my fear; I'm hoping it is Mark's. The doctor schedules me for an ultrasound and tells me the date so I can leave.

When I get home, I go to bed without hearing the report of Shane being arrested for using date rape drugs on many girls as well as me. When I awake, Hillary wants to come over. When she does we watch the news, and chills go down my back; to think I could be carrying Shane's baby.

Ryan calls, and I tell him I just want to stay home, but I ask, "Do you have any memory of April 5? 'Cause that is about when I conceived, and I know I was hanging out with Shane."

Ryan tells me no, but he got a headache when he was driving me to the hospital that night. I tell him that I had some dizzy dreams while in his jeep on the way to the hospital, but they were fuzzy. It was like I got a small flashback to something every time I drive with him in his jeep, but nothing that triggers a memory.

When Mark gets home from his latest stint on conservation, he informs me that he has gotten a pay raise. I'm so happy for him and decided to tell him the good news. He takes it very well, a little shocked that it happened so soon. He's shocked that the birth control didn't work when it should have but guesses it must be God's will. We tell both our parents, and they are very happy to be grandparents and plan to come up as soon as the baby's born.

CHAPTER 2

For the next four months, I continue to open Dooley's and manage the odd night shifts. I've not been going out to the bar very much and have been spending a lot of time at home either with Hillary or alone. Ryan has been put on a tighter leash after the whole incident; Runée seems very jealous and suspicious of me.

Granted I see Ryan often now, he's been scheduled for the same days as I. That way I don't lift anything heavy or hurt myself. Flirting at work makes the quietness at home when I'm alone seem more bearable. And with me tickling him or hugging him, giving him back massages, and just cuddling whenever we have the chance, has made the last four months go by faster. But for some reason every time Ryan does touch me, or I touch him, I get that same electric shock and feel a strange connection.

* * *

Daisy has become more beautiful as I have watched her grown into her pregnancy. She glows and seems so happy. Yet sometimes when she doesn't know I'm looking, I feel I can see pain in her eyes. I wish I was able to be around more, but Runée has gotten even worse. We have finally made love, but it just doesn't feel right, and I swear she is trying to get pregnant even though she says she can't, which I don't believe 'cause I know she hates Daisy.

Mark is gone so often on jobs; it's a good thing Hillary and Krissy go and see Daisy to keep her company. I enjoy the times I'm able to sneak a call her and every day that we work together. I feel as thought Runée is now coming to work and spying on me. For the last two weeks she has shown up at work at the strangest times and wants the weirdest things. If I weren't so concerned about Daisy's welfare I would have dumped Runée a long time ago.

After hugging Daisy today, and having Runée come in through the employee door which was unacceptable. I have decided to break up with her, but I can't let Daisy know or she will think is has something to do with her. All she has wanted since she got married was for me to be happy. But I can't be happy with how things are going with Runée, and I don't believe what she's trying to do to me. I will be happier as soon as I tell Runée off and knowing its going to be a bad argument, since she's been up to something lately.

*　　*　　*

Being that it is January and really close to the due date, Mark is once more going on another camp out. I begged him not to go since I could go into labor anytime. He tells me he will be gone two weeks, and then will have a month off to help me with the baby.

At work I hug Ryan, and a few tears fall from my eyes, but I wipe them before he can see. I'm just so tired of being alone; pondering if this baby's Shane's or Marks has been very stressful. I place Ryan's hand on my belly, and I feel the baby kick it, as well as the sparks.

"Ryan do you remember anything about that day you slept over at my house and were almost naked?" I ask him while his hand is still on my belly.

"No, I have faint memories but nothing clear, I don't know why," Ryan tells me and then goes back to prepping.

"Ryan, why is it when ever you touch my belly, you get an electric spark?" I ask him.

"I don't know, but I'm sure Mark does too, it must be the baby likes us," Ryan says while cutting celery.

I look at Ryan then say, "Actually, you and I are the only one who seem to get an electric shock when touching the baby. Mark says I'm crazy 'cause he doesn't get one. He thinks it might be a side affect from getting pregnant on the birth control pill."

I hurry up with my work in silence so that I can get home and think about how I need to deal with this problem. Once at home after my shift, I decide the best thing to do is leave Mark and go back home to my mom's.

Mark is still away, and his parents are on vacation in the states, so if I'm going to make a move, I best make it now. I pack up some clothes and write Mark a letter telling him that the baby died, and I can't live with him any more. I have everything in my hand and go to open the door, when who should be standing there but Ryan.

"Where are you going, Daisy?" Ryan asks while walking into the living room. He sits down and looks at the folded letter on the coffee table.

"I'm going nowhere, just to my prenatal class." I tell him with my voice being shaky. Why did he have to come here, today; I could be on my way to the airport, give birth to my bastard child, and live alone and not have to hurt anyone.

After reading my letter to Mark, Ryan puts it back on the coffee table. "I can't believe you'd tell Mark his child died and run away. I can't let you do that." Ryan stands up and takes my bag from my hand and closes the door.

What is he up to? It's my life; he can't take over. The child isn't his; it most likely is Shane's—a convicted rapist. Just because my baby has a connection to Ryan means nothing. I pout away and ignore Ryan, but it seems he's not leaving.

He spends the night at my house, and I can't sleep very well because he makes the baby excited. I hope that he'll fall into a deep sleep, and when I think he has, I try to make a break for the door, but am cut off by him. Not helping my situation, Ryan decides he will sleep with me in my bed.

We go to work the next morning, and there is so much tension between us. I'm exhausted and feel very weak. I can't think, keep getting weird flashbacks. Ryan tells me that he broke up with Runée a week ago. I ask him why, and he tells me she was getting to possessive and other reasons, but he's not going to discuss them with me. I tell him that I want to lie down. He tells me to rest in his jeep while he works some more on the prep.

So far, being that it is the middle of January and that I am feeling wiped out along with the fact that I may have to go through this pregnancy with out my husband makes this month already feel like eternity.

*   *   *

Going to Daisy's house was just so weird. I was driving around town and ended up at her doorstep, and good thing I did 'cause she was going to run away. I know she is stressed, and I know it has to do with if she had slept with Shane, and why she can't remember that night I stayed over. But it doesn't bother me to the same extent it's bothering her. I wish she would just open up to me. She looked even more stressed when I told her that I broke up with Runée.

I wanted to tell her more why I ended the relationship, but for some reason my instincts told me now was a bad time. Letting her rest a little might help; she needs to not stress the baby out or possibly go into labor.

*   *   *

As my head falls to the cushions of the jeep, I fall asleep immediately, or so I think. I dream that Ryan is kissing me, and I'm pulling my shirt off, and he gently kisses my breasts, then moving my bra, he nibbles on my succulent cherries. I moan with pleasure and start massaging his hard cock. We start kissing intensely but pull away as fast as we started to tell each other we have to stop. I cry in pain, for I have dreamt this for as long as I could imagine.

We pull up to my house. I'm mad at him so I immediately get out of the jeep and run to my front door. While I am stumbling to find my keys, Ryan comes up behind me and unlocks the door with my keys, which he found. Once inside he immediately kisses me and finishes pulling off my shirt. Since I never did my bra back up, it falls to the floor. We make our way to the bedroom. I fall onto the bed as Ryan kisses my neck and collar bone. Moaning with pleasure, I slide down the bed to his crotch; I unzip his pants and pull them down to find his hard, strong masculinity ready to bed me. I start to pleasure him as he caresses my hair and breasts.

Suddenly he places me on the bed, and after taking my skirt up to my waste and removing my undergarments, he starts to suck and nibble on my most precious treasure. I moan and arch my back for more, after which Ryan gently moves up my body to start kissing me again, but slowly inserting himself into me. I allow in his swollen member as we make passionate love. We roll around, nibble, kiss, work hard and slow down. But in the end he explodes a river into me and then collapses on me.

The last image I see is of us falling asleep in one another's arms. But the last thing I hear is Ryan telling me he loves me, and I tell him that I truly love him.

Abruptly waking from my dream, I felt like it might have happened. I'm in shock that I might have made love to Ryan in my house and cheated on Mark. I started to cry because I knew Mark would never understand or forgive me.

Maybe the baby was Ryan's and that's why we share a connection. But then what would happen? Should I tell Mark, and how would Ryan take it? Because from what he told me of our talks, he didn't want a baby unless he was married, and he wasn't looking at getting married anytime soon.

Would I still be able to go through with my running-away story and get away with Ryan not finding out? I had a feeling he wasn't going to claim the baby. Deep in thought, the door to the Jeep is thrust open.

Ryan opens the door to the jeep and asks in a stern voice why I'm shaking and sweating. I tell him nothing; my stomach hurts all of a sudden as I walk past him back into the kitchen. Ryan tells me that he's going to take a nap for a few minutes since he wasn't able to sleep having to make sure I didn't run away again.

As I'm chopping tomatoes for the salad prep, the pain in my stomach are becoming more unbearable. I feel I won't be able to come back tonight to close the restaurant. I feel sick and run to the toilet, but throwing up just makes my back pains become more intense. I manage to get it under control for now, I think; when Ryan comes back to work and I can instantly tell something happened to him too while resting in the jeep.

"Ryan, do you remember that night?" I ask, my voice very shaky with a hint of pain.

He looks down to the floor then up and tells me, "Yes, just now while I was taking a nap. I dreamt that we started to make love in the jeep then did so at your apartment." He tells me with sadness.

With tears breaking through and running down my face when Ryan walks up to me, wipes them off my face, and I tell him that I too now remember us making love twice that night I thought I was raped by Shane. Ryan places his hand on my tummy, feeling his connection to the baby; we now both know the answers to each one's questions.

"The baby is mine, Daisy, you know it is. We were both drugged from the drink Shane got you, and we made love the day the doctor said you conceived," Ryan tells me with compassion.

I turn away from him and feel more pain. Cringing in pain I think to myself, *Yes it's true. Buts it's not fair, I wanted this baby to be yours, but I'm married to Mark. Why has fate been so cruel and yet Ryan, you wouldn't let me run away? Its like I've always known, you touch me and the connection is undoubtedly there.* Feeling the pain come faster and sharper, I break the thoughts and cry out in pain.

"Come on, you're in labor. We are going to the hospital," Ryan tells me in a sharp voice as he escorts me into the jeep.

On the way to the hospital Ryan calls the boss, telling him I'm in labour and to find staff to cover our shifts.

Once at the hospital, the doctor asks Ryan again if he's my husband, and the nurse who recognises him from before answers before he has the chance. Now in crucial pain, I can't hear what the doctor says except that I'm going to deliver this baby right now. Ryan is told to scrub up to help his wife. When he comes back, and after fifteen minutes of pushing, I deliver a perfectly healthy boy.

Ryan looks at the baby with his little fingers, black curly hair, and deep green eyes with only the tears of a father. I look at my son and cry; he looks so much like Ryan it's unbearable. I rest up after the doctor takes the baby away to be cleaned and weighed.

*   *   *

Wow I can't believe this beautiful boy is mine, his skin is as fair as Daisy's. Looking at her crying, I just can't imagine what she is thinking, but I bet she is feeling pain, love, and uncertainty. 'Cause I know I too am feeling uncertainty about what our future will be like. But one thing I know is for sure: Mark will not raise my son.

"Doctor, I want a DNA test down on this baby, to know if he's DNA matches with mine, my wife wasn't sure," I ask the doctor with as much authority as I could muster up since I was so emotional after seeing my son being born.

"Congratulations, Mr Gaston, have you and your wife decided on a name? And I need you to fill out some papers." The nurse who put me down for the father tells me as she hands me a clipboard with tons of papers on it.

*   *   *

I wake up and ask to see my son, the nurse tells me she will bring little Elijah Gaston in. I look at Ryan and ask him who named my son, only to find out he did.

"Ryan you can't name my son, you are not the father," I tell him with a quiet voice of authority. But right before Ryan has a chance to give me an answer, the doctor walks in and tells me that indeed baby Elijah is both Ryan's and my child. I just close my eyes and weep silently to myself. How I'm going to handle this situation?

The next day Ryan takes Elijah and me home. Tells me that we have to talk about this and how to handle the situation. I tell him to go away and leave me alone because I just want to sleep and forget about all this, but I'll call him later. I feed the baby and put him to sleep in his crib.

Sitting in the living room I cry and wonder why I had to marry Mark and get pregnant with my best friend's baby. Mark would never understand, and he would hate me forever. Sure I always dreamed of being with Ryan, but deep down I knew it would never happen and that it was a dream. I had to run away and leave a note telling Mark the baby died. It would still work, and then he wouldn't be as hurt. But as soon as that idea was completed, Mark walked into the apartment early. Feeling my color leave my body, I stood up with weak legs and allowed Mark to place a kiss on my cheek undeservingly.

And then he noticed my tummy was no longer big. And asked when I had the baby and where it was. Taking him to the nursery I asked God why he had to come home early. I told Mark I had him yesterday; I could see the smile on his face, and my heart went out.

I watch as Mark pick up Elijah, looking at him with happy eyes. But then I saw his eyes go sad and the many undeniable questions running through his head. "Why is his skin darker than ours? Why does he have dark hair? Why does his ID bracelet say Gaston?" Mark asks with anger in his voice as he handed me back the baby.

I put Elijah back in his crib and start crying. "Because he is Ryan's and my son, he's not yours. There was a DNA test done, and Ryan named him, and the birth certificate was drawn up." I go to reach for him, but he pulls away as if I'm dirty.

Mark leaves the nursery just as fast as he had given me my child back. I slowly go to follow him, but am cut off when he comes up to me with a paper in his hand. "Is this why you wanted to tell me my child died? You though it was easier then to tell me you had an affair with your best friend who I trusted?" Mark yells at me as he shoves the letter in my face.

Damn, I wish he had not come home so early. "It's not like that, it happened April 5, when I went out with the gang, Shane tried to rape me, but . . ."

"So because Ryan saved you from Shane, he thought that was his reward to make a baby with you? I don't believe you. You never stay home, you're always out to the bars with your slut girlfriends," Mark said with such rage and pain it made my spine shiver.

"No, Ryan drank from the same drink as me, and we both got drugged and made . . ." I say with a little voice as the chock back my tears.

"Right, so you feel using this is a way to soften the blow that you and Ryan have been having an affair behind my back? How long has it been going on Daisy!" Marks yells at me while I try to squirm out of his outstretched arm as he grabs my shoulder with force.

"We've only ever flirted. You know that, it was an accident. I swear and you can ask him . . . ," I tell him with a tinny voice. Mark then smacks my face and walks out of the apartment, slamming the door behind him.

After wiping my on flowing tears away, I call Ryan to warn him that Mark knows and was very angry. "Did he hurt you?" Ryan asks, but I deny telling him the truth. Elijah is screaming in his crib, which I finally hear, having no clue how long he has been crying. I go to feed and comfort him. I fall asleep with my son in my arms but am suddenly awakened when I feel Mark's shadow over me.

After putting Elijah back in the crib, Mark drags me to the living room and shoves me to the couch. He then goes to tell me that we will be divorcing tomorrow, and telling both families that the baby did die 'cause it would kill his mother if she found out. I swallow the lump in my throat as he continues on. Mark also tells me that if work or his family ever find out, it would be a disgrace and embarrassment to him. We are to tell anyone that the baby died a month ago, and I have been trying to get over it. Plus we were trying to find the right time to tell them about the baby, but our marriage fell apart at the same time.

The tears run down my face that I can't see him. Why is he being so nice and taking this to well. I don't deserve this, and nor does he. I look up to him as I hear him say, "You and your son will be moving out tomorrow or as soon as you can. I have been posted to a new town, that is why I came home early."

I cry and notice his hand is bandaged and say to him with some compassion, "Why is your hand bandaged?" Mark goes to tell me that Ryan ran into him at one of the coffee shops, and they got into a fight.

Mark walks toward the bedroom but turns around like a devilish cat, and say, "And Ryan was telling me that if a girl in his country gets pregnant, they kill her and the baby. Or else the man has to claim his mistake, and I don't think Ryan would like you dead or his son. So I hope you enjoy being married to him." And with that he went to bed.

I sat back down on the couch and was breathless; I never had time to think what might happen. Ryan had talked to me about the girls in his country and how they or the baby died. He had mentioned to me that we could never marry 'cause I was not from his country, and his family would disown him. I can't marry him, not like this. I always dreamed if I were ever going to marry him, it would be because he loved me. Not because he got me pregnant and felt he had to marry me so I wouldn't die.

*   *   *

I felt the pain in Daisy's voice as she told me Mark came home early and found out. I was trying to figure a way for her to tell him and wanted to be there for her. It wasn't all her fault; we were drugged and our hearts took over. I had to go looking for Mark to tell him not to be so hard on her.

Finding him at Timbers, I wasn't able to sit down, when he grabbed my jacket and forced me outside. Before I knew it he hit me, so I fought back but knew that this wasn't going to solve the problem, so I surrendered to him. I told him I was sorry.

"You're sorry, that's all you have to say. You sleep with my wife, your best friend, and get her pregnant. You expect me to raise your child because you aren't man enough!" Mark yelled at me as he put distance between us.

"It's not like that, it was a accident. We were taken advantage of—," I tried to tell him before he walked back into my face.

"Right, you also got drugged and were forced to have sex. I think something has been going on the whole time," he said while breathing down my face. I could see the pain and anger in his eyes. And I guess if I were in his place, I'd be mad too.

But he didn't understand. We never planned it, just always sort of dreamed it and talked about it. "We're not getting anywhere, it happened. What would they do in your country if you get another man's wife pregnant?" Mark threw it in my face as if to cut me down to size.

"They would kill the women for cheating on her husband. Either give the baby away or kill it too," I told him wondering where he was going with this.

Mark looked at me with wide eyes, and then chuckled. "Well, I guess you had better do the right thing. I wouldn't want Daisy or your child to have to die." He walked away from me, but then walked back as if to say more. "She will no longer be my wife and living with me as of tomorrow." And with that he walked past and left me in the street to think about what had just happened.

*   *   *

I woke to an empty house. Mark had left with most of his things. I wept silently, and continued on with my day, but yesterday's events came back to me when I heard my son crying. After packing some of my possessions and what little I had bought for the baby before he was born, I headed out to find an apartment for us.

Finding one was easy although trying to get all my stuff there would be a bit of a challenge, so I call Hillary. "Babe, I need your help, can you come over to my apartment?" I ask her as I start to ball.

The apartment I rent is two bedrooms, with a cozy living room, spacious kitchen with a dinette, and a small but renovated bathroom. It was on the fourth floor and had a balcony overlooking the coolies, with a fireplace in the living room.

Hillary meets me at the old apartment, and I gave her the rundown on the last few days' events. She hugs me and tells me she is so sorry and doesn't blame me. After helping me move all my possessions to the new place, she tells me she'll watch Elijah as I go to buy some more furniture and deal with some business.

When I get back to the new apartment, Hillary asks if Ryan knows I had moved and if he's going to help with the baby. I tell her no then go back to the old apartment to wait for Mark with my son.

Once at the old apartment, I'm rocking Elijah to sleep, and there is a knock at the door. I answer it only to find Runée crying. She pushes through into my home and demands to know why I broke her and Ryan up when I have the perfect life, a husband, and a child. I tell her I never broke them up; she must have made him mad by overstepping a boundary. Runée then looks at Elijah. I can see she sees the similarity between Ryan and him, but then she tells me to say away from Ryan. I yell, "Gladly!" as she leaves my apartment.

Mark comes back to the apartment. "I see you have taken no time to move out, that's good. I have gone to the landlord and cancelled our contract, completed some business, and of course gotten our divorce papers." He hands me them, and I can see he has already signed them.

I hold the pen and sign them as tears fall down my face. I know there is nothing I can say to stop this from happening. I look up at him, and then he tells me to take what I want and have a good life.

After sitting for a few minutes I finally get up and walk around the apartment. I do take a few things that were ours. As for the rest he can sell or throw out; I can't keep it for there are too many memories, and I have to start my new life with my son. I leave the key and a short note reminding him that I still love him, and am deeply sorry.

I look back once more to my old life and close the door.

I call, and call her. Why is she not answering? I know she has moved after checking her old apartment. Mark told me as he was moving out. Not that he was chivalrous about it, but he did inform me. I wanted to see my son; I had only seen him the day he was born.

My sister took the news better then her husband, Daisy's and my boss. Of course, they asked me my intentions, which were what any normal man should do: I would take care of Daisy and our son, make sure they had everything I could provide them with. And my sister told me that I needed to do whatever it would take to do the right thing.

When I called my family, my mother scolded me but asked me if I loved her. Shockingly I said yes, and then my mom said I had to do the right thing. My father was irritated, and so was my older brother, who called me a disgrace and told me not to ever come back home again, for it would be the last thing I'll ever do if I wanted to live in this world.

Do the right thing. First Mark, then my sister, and now my mother. I wasn't so sure Daisy would go along with doing the right thing, but I had to try. I know she'd protest, but if she were going to do the right thing for our son, she would learn, and it would be hard.

*   *   *

Over the few days of my new life, I noticed Ryan had been desperately trying to call my cell, but I ignored his calls. I continued with my life, including shopping at Velars for toys and clothes for Elijah when I run into Ryan. He looked at me with annoyance and rage, but then hugged me and asked with concern in his voice, "Where have you moved? Why don't you answer my calls? Is everything all right with Elijah?" But to answer his own question he picks up the baby.

"I have been getting on with my new life. Mark and I have gotten a divorce. I have had to move out, and we are fine. Now please give me my son back, and leave us alone," I tell him while trying to reach for my son. But I notice this was not the best thing to say. I could see the hurt and anger in his eyes, and fearing the Arabic wrath I allow him to hold onto the son I had deprived him of for four days.

Ryan then went to tell me that we needed to go somewhere alone. He paid for the baby clothes and toys I had in the basket. I try to protest but oblige as he put his credit card down and gave me a disapproving look. The whole time he holds on to Elijah, we head toward a little coffee shop in the mall where his sister is.

She embraces me, and I can tell she knows what has happened. She tells me everything will be all right and to let Ryan be in charge. Not sure what she means, I stand back and watch as he gives her our son and tells her something in Arabic.

After that he grabs my hand and pulls me out of the mall. "I'm not going anywhere with you Ryan. And I want to go home with my son," I tell him with as much strength as I can summon.

He demands to know where my car is, and after giving in I take him there, but he decides he is going to drive. I sit alongside him as he drives us to the courthouse. I try to stay in the car and wait for him to do what he has to do at the courthouse, when he comes to my side of the car and pulls me out. "You are coming with me, this will be quick and painless." Ryan puts his arm around me, and guides me into the courthouse and into a courtroom. Not liking the feeling I'm getting in my gut, I let him lead me to my fate.

Having no resistance when I'm in his arms being that they're so comforting and hypnotizing, I follow. Ryan goes up to the judge and after talking with him comes back for me as I'm seated watching him. Ryan asks me to sign the papers he received from the judge.

I look at them but am not sure what they say so I ask the judge what is going on. The judge informs me these papers are custody papers. I tell him I don't understand why Ryan should have custody of Elijah. "Ryan was at the hospital the day Elijah's birth certificate was made," I tell the judge feeling the ground below me weaken and my body start to shake.

The judge then tells me that since I refuse to marry Ryan, I have to sign over my rights to my son. Taken back by all this, I go find a seat. My breathing gets heavy. *What s going on? Marry Ryan? I just got divorced, and I'm not his religion or from his country. I have never been approached to marry Ryan. What was the judge saying?* Confused, I look at the judge and asked, "What, I don't understand?"

Ryan then sits down beside me and says, "Because you have given birth to my son, you have to marry me, or give me full custody. In my country an unwed mother or woman who has committed adultery is killed, and my family would no doubt try to kill you if you kept a male heir from them. They are not allowed privilege to their bastard child." He puts his arm around me, trying to make me understand what he was offering me.

What was he saying? Give up my son or marry him? They can kill me or take my son? "No, I will not marry Ryan to hold on to my son, and they cannot kill me, this is Canada!" I yelled at both the judge and Ryan.

Ryan looked at me with sympathy and anger. "Daisy, you know how sons are very important to men from my country. Don't make me hurt you anymore then you have been hurt. I will take him away from you. Please sign the papers for his sake." And with that he took my hand placed a pen in it, and looked at the papers.

I too looked at the papers and could read them clearly. It was a marriage certificate; if I was to hold on to my son and not die, I had to marry him. "How long do I have to be married to Ryan?" I asked the judge with uncertainty like I didn't want to know the answer.

Funny as it is, one point in my life I had dreamed of being married to Ryan, but now I loathed him with all my heart for forcing me to give up my freedom and threatening to take my son away from me. All the feeling I once felt for him had died right there in the courthouse, and there was nothing but rawness in my heart.

With no answer from the judge, I sign the papers. I had just lost my husband, had a baby with someone without conscious intentions, and might as well marry him to keep my son. Ryan slips a white and yellow woven gold braided wedding band onto my left ring finger, and numbly I slip one onto his finger. The judge finishes the papers and then congratulates us, telling me it is legal, because I was divorced from my ex-husband before my wedding to Ryan. He also apologises for it not being romantic, but that can wait till later. That solved the one question I was thinking, and I weep silently to myself as Ryan guides me back to the car.

Once we get back to the mall, I collect Elijah and head for the car. Ryan was talking to his sister, and I didn't want to try and figure out what was being said. Once at the car Ryan catches up to me and demands my new address. And like a zombie I give it to him.

At the apartment, I sit on the couch and look at the marriage certificate in my hands. The judge issued two copies to us, along with the papers to Elijah. I stare at them numb. Because of Shane I lost Mark, got a son, and was forced into marriage with a man I loved at one time but now despised.

I cry myself to sleep, but am awaken by a knock at my door. Feeling like it was all a terrible dream that I was forced into marriage with Ryan, I am quickly brought back to reality when I look at my wedding finger and notice a white-and-yellow gold ring on it. The ring looks to have the gold weaved or braided into the band and very old. As I get up to answer the door, I try to pull it off my finger, but it will not move. It's like fastened or something, and it will not come off. Giving up, I go to answer the door.

*   *   *

I sat in my room at my sister's house, ashamed of my self. I had just threatened, bribed and forced Daisy to marry me for the sake of our son and her life. I knew if I told her she would not understand, but being sneaky about it was not me, and I hated it. My sister gave me hell for my behaviour but helped me pack my stuff so I could move in with my wife.

Wow, she was my wife; I've always dreamed it, knew it would never happen. Yet now it has and she hates me, which I could tell by looking at her when she gave me her address and left. Looking down at the foreign object on my left hand, it felt odd, but oddly comforting. I know Daisy will be trying to get it off her finger. And if the myth is true, then she will not be able to get it off her finger.

When my mom gave me the rings when I left for Canada, she told me to find someone to love, and the rings would prove that when the time was right and I was with my soul mate, it would show in the rings. My ring was proving the myth right, and that made my decision easier to accept.

* * *

I open the door only to see Ryan standing there with boxes beside him, and suit case in hand. Closing my eyes and not believing this, I allow him to enter. "What are you doing?" I asked, already knowing the answer. I show him to what would be our room. The thought of sharing a bed with him made my skin crawl; funny how once I liked cuddling and holding this man. But now the thought appalled me, and I knew I did not want him to touch me. "Just because we are married doesn't mean I have to like it. And I'm informing you that you will not touch me."

As Ryan brings in his stuff, he casually says, "I will do as I like. You are now my wife! And will learn to live by my rules and obey me 'cause I will not allow you to do as you like, like while you were with Mark." And with that said he kissed my forehead and went to the master's bedroom.

I felt my blood boil and my freedom curtailed. I could tell this marriage was going to be hell. I was going to have to be a devoted, house-cleaning wife that would not be allowed to have fun. *What ever happened to the nice and loving Ryan I once knew?* I thought to myself while heading to the kitchen to make some tea.

After he seemed to be happy with putting things where he wanted them, he joined me in the kitchen. I looked at him with enraged eyes but could not hold my glare for he still was dangerously gorgeous. "Just because I am your wife doesn't mean that I will obey and do your bidding." I threw at him as soon as he swallowed his first sip of tea.

He looked at me with the slits of his eyes as he swallowed then said, "In my country a woman who is impregnated while unwed or by a man other than her husband, is killed, including her child, or sent to a prison camp to pay for her sins. And woman who disrespects their husband can be sent away too." And with that said he left me alone in the kitchen to heed his warning.

* * *

I thought moving into the place would make life easier, but I was mistaken. For some reason Daisy didn't welcome me with warm welcoming arms; instead she was sharp and cold. Not the Daisy I was used to or had grown to love, but what should I expect when I had taken over her life?

Runée has not stopped calling me, and I finally ran into her at work but not by accident. It seemed she'd been stalking me. "Ryan why don't you return my calls, I'm so sorry. Please give me another chance, I promise I can be friends with your friends who are girls. I miss you so much and can't live without you. I know you can't live without me too and you have to do the right thing because I'm not lying!." And with that being said she felt she needed to kiss me.

"Runée! I'm not interested in you anymore. I have married Daisy, we have a son together, and we are happy. I'm sorry but I was never in love with you. I have always loved Daisy, and you are too crazy for me to be with. You control me when I need to be the one in control. Please leave me alone, don't stalk me, move on, and I will never believe you." I warned her with a very harsh tone and then pried her arms away from me.

Over the next few months I went to work, came home, watched my son, tried to talk with Daisy, and went to bed with her either not talking to me or arguing with me. All actions coming from her were very cold and estranged. She was sitting on the couch reading another romance book, probably wishing it was her in the book. I couldn't take it any longer, this neglect to talk about what happened a couple weeks after Elijah was born. I walked up to her grabbed the book out of her hand and pulled her to me.

*   *   *

Early April the completed divorce papers came and I cried. I had heard from Mark once, and he moved to Toronto. He wanted to know how the baby and I were. But what he really wanted to know was if I had been forced to marry Ryan or was able to get out of it. I told him that I chose to marry Ryan so that Elijah would have a better life with both mother and father. I wasn't too sure if that was going to be true with the way Ryan and I were getting along. Ryan was trying to be nice, but I was still too angry that I kept him at a distance.

I could not look Ryan in the face; I felt betrayed and mistrusted him. I did feel his eyes looking at me, and they would burn my body. Even though I was mad at him, my body sure wasn't, and every time he came near or gave me a little peck, the hairs on my body would stand up, and my breasts would get tight with anticipation. Ever since my run-in with Ryan at the mall, the day I was forced to marry him, Sherri, Ryan's sister has been coming over to the house more to see her Nephew, and Ryan would take him over to their house as well.

I decided since Sherri wanted to watch Elijah more often when I would go shopping that I could go back to work sooner than planned. Not wanting to work with Ryan, because I felt I could not be civil toward him, I made up the schedules putting him on mornings and myself with another cook at night while I managed the restaurant. Hillary was of great help in these last few months; she put more shifts in and had coffee with Elijah and me almost every day.

After a couple months of being back to work, taking care of a small child, and avoiding Ryan at all costs, I lie on the couch and start reading one of my newest romance novels. Out of nowhere Ryan walks up to me, rips the book out of my hands throwing it aside, and pulls me to him.

CHAPTER 3

I look at him with fear as he places his neglected mouth over mine as I was about to yell at him for his behavior. My body still frozen, I slowly relax and kiss him back. Letting go of all my anger toward him, I put my arm behind his head and grab his hair. Our kissing gets more aggressive. He then leans me back to the couch and starts kissing my neck and down in between my cleavage.

I want him so bad; I kiss him back just as fierce and start unzipping his pants. Now I just realize that I can make love to him without regret or fear since he is my husband. All my dreams can come true; I can make passionate love to him and remember it the next day. As we have disregarded our clothes, I am under his body, and he slowly inserts into my wetness. The pleasure of just the slow motion drives me crazy that I scratch his back until he pumps me faster. The motion is fast paced that I arch my back with my orgasm being so explosive. Having not had sex or mad love with a man since Mark on my honeymoon has built up. And with my body wanting to be touched by Ryan for the longest time, I couldn't help but orgasm some more.

I flip Ryan over so that I am on top and I ride him so hard and fast that his eyes go large as he lets go of his pleasure in me. I collapse on him. While lying on him I mention to him how wonderful that was for me.

He looks at me in the eyes, the warmth I can definitely feel, and says, "I am sorry for the ways things had to turn out. Everything happened so fast, and I really wanted to marry you, but I knew you were confused over what Mark did. So I'm sorry I forced you, but I was scared my family might hurt you, with you being unwed. Daisy, I want you to know that I have loved you from the first day I laid eyes on you, but I accepted our friendship because it was all I could have. Please know that I still love you and never meant to hurt you or Elijah." And with that said, the tears ran down his face.

Right from the beginning I had tears in my eyes, but hearing what he said, the tears run down with out warning. I hugged him for a long time; I too had dreamt about marrying him. Granted never the way it happened, but after hearing what he said I understood better. I pulled away from him and looked into those sad but lovely, deep brown eyes and said, "Ryan I have loved you, always wished I could have married you, but knew it too would never happen. I was taken back by the events in the last few months, but honestly I'm not mad at you anymore." I told him while wiping tears off my face.

"I want to build a future with you not only for Elijah, but because I want to spend the rest of my life with you." And I hugged him again. We started kissing, first slowly but then it got more passionate and I could feel him get hard in me again. While I was still on him, he picked me up and carried me into the bathroom, and we made love in the shower, with the water trickling down us.

Ryan had gotten up earlier, and I felt I needed the extra sleep after last night's activities. I kissed him good-bye, brought Elijah to my bed, and fell asleep again.

Being that it was a beautiful April morning—the sun was shining so intensely with the light reflecting off the windows—and having the day off, I took Elijah to get groceries.

After having done that, I'm fastening him in his car seat when Runée comes up to me. I look at her startled and ask what she wants as I go to put the groceries in the Jeep.

She yells at me for interfering in her relationship with Ryan by getting pregnant and making him marry me. "Why did you take Ryan away from me? You had someone! You had Mark! But no you had to cheat on him with my man. We were suppose to get married!" Runée screams at me.

"I never forced him to marry me, it was the other way around. It didn't go like that you witch" I yell back at her.

She threatens me to stay away from him if I know what's best for me. I in turn tell her that I knew him first, made love to him first, and she could go to hell. This not being the best thing to say, Runée turns around and cuffs me. I feel my left cheek swell, and hear Elijah start screaming. I look at her in the eyes and say, "Leave my husband alone or you will deal with me." I then punch her in the face as she drops to the ground.

Getting into the Jeep, I drive home holding my left cheek. I call out to Elijah to get him to stop screaming. He calms down, and I look back at him in the review mirror, poor little guy has tears down his face. Man I can't wait to get home to put one of these steaks I bought on my face.

I'm stopped at a red light and I notice a car speeding up to my car, and they look as though they are not going to stop. I get my foot ready to step on the gas. Looking back in the mirror I can't believe my eyes. It's Runée, and she is going to slam her car into me causing an accident. She's totally lost it; I step on the gas and run the red light getting onto the next two-lane main road. Runée blows the light and chases after me. Elijah, as if on cue, starts to cry again.

I have to weave in and out of traffic to get away from her, but she pursues me harder and starts to bump into my rear end. Elijah starts to scream. I hear my cell phone go off, and I'm getting scared she's going to cause me to crash. I have to do more illegal moves by running lights. I think to myself while I flee from her, *Where the hell is a cop when you need one?*

Realizing that I'm close to Dooley's I try to make a turn for it. This way I can stop the car and Ryan can see what kind of neurotic he had gone out with. As I go to make the turn cutting off traffic, Runée speeds up the car and slams into my side door causing the Jeep to spin.

My side door is smashed in pretty good, and my body hurts more than my face did minutes ago. I look around and now see police cars, I can hear Elijah screaming, and I see the police pulling Ryan off of Renée. Shaking my head as I take my seat belt off, I turn to the back seat to tend to Elijah. I'm wondering where Ryan came from.

The fire department comes to help me out and take my son and me to the ambulance. I look back and see Runée is in a cop car, and they have Ryan handcuffed. With my head hurting so much, a cop asks me if the man in cuffs is my husband. And I nod as the attendant helps me into the ambulance.

Once at the hospital the doctors run tests on Elijah and me to see if we were okay. Elijah is all right and has no bruising or damage. I, on the other hand, seem to have sustained three broken ribs on my left side, a slight concussion, and a large cut on my left temple that needs stitching.

After resting for a bit, the police come to collect a report from me. I tell them the information they need. Since I'm not allowed to leave the hospital yet, Sherri and Renaldo come to visit; Ryan has been detained at the police station.

Because Ryan is new to the country, they want to make sure he had nothing to do with any of today's events, Sherri tells me. She also tells me that because of him beating up Runée, he could be deported. I honestly couldn't care; if I hadn't met him, my life wouldn't be so messed up. Just when I thought things were going to be better, I was sorely wrong.

I make a small remark about how my life is hell at the moment, and Sherri asks her husband to leave so we can be alone. After Renaldo leaves, she informs me that if Ryan gets deported, he will be taking my son with him. Because I produced an heir for him, he will take the child away. And the men in their country have more power than the women. I close my eyes—this is just getting better and better the longer I'm married to him. And I have to put up with his psycho ex-girlfriend who wants to kill me, great!

After Sherri leaves, the nurse brings Elijah in to be fed. I don't want to be in this marriage anymore. It will never be happy; I just was divorced, forced into a marriage, then almost killed. What's next if I stay with Ryan? After hearing from the nurse that I won't be released anytime soon, or at least not until Ryan is able to help me with Elijah, I decide I have to make a move. Leaving Ryan all but a short letter to account for my actions, I get ready to blow the hospital.

I make it back to the apartment after seeing the nurse with my son to pack some clothes and personal effects. I grab another cab to the bus station and catch the bus to Calgary. Once at the Calgary airport I make plans to fly to Mexico. Fearing that Ryan might figure out where my Mom lives, I decide getting out of the country would be best.

I had also read in the paper about something going on in Mexico that caught my attention, and I felt I'd be the perfect candidate. After arriving in Mexico, I pop some T3s to help subside the pain and passed out with Elijah in my arms from all the stress.

I get to the hospital and receive a letter from the nurse and a quiet sorry. I read the letter only to find out that Daisy has decided it would be best for her and our son if she took off.

Once at the apartment, I see she has been here to pack. I can't fathom it. I knew Renée was crazy, but I always thought Daisy was a strong woman. Maybe losing her precious husband, having her friend's baby, and being forced to marry was too much. But damn, why did she have to kidnap my son and leave me. There is no way I'm going to let her get away with this when I find her.

After calling the credit card company, I found out that Daisy was in Mexico, had been there since she left. It seems she thought she was sneaky, but grabbed our joint account card and was using it 'cause that's where all the money was.

A week later I thought it was time she could use a call, and when I called the hotel I found her in, I had them transfer me to her room.

* * *

After a week of relaxation, I am starting to feel better when the phone rings. "Hello, how are you my runaway wife?" My blood drains from my body. How did Ryan find us? "You were doing good, but you took our credit card, and that is how I know where you are" was the answer to my thoughts.

"Please, Ryan, just leave us alone. I need to recuperate from what your ex-girlfriend did to me."

"Well you see, my darling wife, I'm on my way to get you. And then we will talk about your behaviour of taking my child away from his father," he says with authority and anger.

Elijah starts to cry, and I tell Ryan that I have to go and can't talk long. He then slips in how he isn't closing the account but will be in Mexico shortly and told me not to move or else. I pace around the room while feeding Elijah. I don't want to go back to Ryan now that I have clearly pissed him off.

Once I check out of the hotel, the cab driver takes my to a small village about twenty-five minutes away from the resort. I use the washroom and buy a few things for the baby on credit, but when I go to get back to the cab I notice the driver has left. Since the resort is only a twenty-five-minutes drive and my ribs don't hurt so much, I chose to start walking back with Elijah in my arms. The pain in my broken ribs becomes unbearable after fifteen minutes of walking, so I take a rest.

A truck pulls up asking if I need a ride; I graciously take it. I comprehend as the truck turns around and heads back to the village that it was a big mistake. Once back in the village I take a better look at the people. It seems the women wear clothing to cover their faces, and there are more men in this village than women. Feeling my gut wrench, I get ready to have to fight for my son and my life.

The guy pulls up to a house, and once the truck comes to a stop, he comes around and yanks me out of the truck. While trying to free myself and run, I'm hit upside the head, and all goes black.

I wake to a mouldy odour and dim lights. Once I adjust myself to my new surroundings, I search for my son and find him in a basket asleep. As my heart settles a little, I take in more of the situation.

Here I am in a darken mouldy basement with no windows and one door to the main floor. I would have to wait till I was either brought up to the main floor to make a break. With my ribs still causing me much pain, this was going to be a tricky and slower escape then I could have normally made.

After trying to find ways of escaping, a man comes down but doesn't speak to me in Mexican. He speaks English and tells me that I have a phone call. It's Ryan and that he has found me, I go up to the main floor.

I notice there are four locks to the door of my basement cage and armed men at the top of the stairs. "Hello, Ryan? Please be you? Help me?" I quickly tell whoever is on the phone.

"Well I'm glad you decided to run away to Mexico, where the market for women is high. It seems you have drawn attention and are worth a lot to these men. But as for our son, they want less for him. So I figure I will buy him. He's worth more to me than you. You'll just run away again, and Daisy you were never happy. So if you ask for help, then yes, I'm helping our son. But at a cost. And as for you, maybe you'll learn to be happy. Hand me back to the men." And with that the tears were streaming down my face, I had gone and hurt Ryan so much that he didn't want me. I handed the phone back, heard my captor talk in Mexican or Arabic. I wasn't very sure cause my head started to hurt.

For the next few days I'm provided food and water, but not without a fight. It seems the men feel they have the right to touch me. I manage to keep them from touching me too much but with the pain of my ribs, I don't win too much. The day finally comes when Ryan is picking up Elijah. The men take Elijah away as he's screaming for me. I cry and fight my hardest, but with one good hit I go down. I watch the door close and faintly hear Ryan talk to the men about his son and how he could care less about the mother. Ryan then talks in Arabic, but not knowing the language better, I do not understand what he is saying.

Hours later, the head of the organization comes downstairs and demands, "Take your clothes off now or you'll be beaten." Looking at the whip in his hand and after some hesitation, I finally take my clothes off, leaving myself exposed in this cold basement. The man looks at me as my skin crawls and my blood goes cold. I turn around for him so he can see what I have to offer his buyers. "You are damaged, no good to me," the man snaps at me and then heads back upstairs.

H. L. Laffin

I gather my clothes and fall to the floor with tears in my eyes. I notice a letter on the ground that the man had dropped before leaving.

Daisy, I'm sorry for you're loss. I would have tried harder for you, but you didn't try hard for us. I do hope you go to a good man, one that will be able to protect you, as I was not able to. I do thank you for a beautiful child.

Ryan

I close my eyes, hold the letter to my chest, and pass out with fatigue and defeat.

* * *

After having Elijah checked out by the doctor, and him coming back healthy. I sit on the hotel patio and look at the ocean. I didn't see a trace of her. Maybe they had sold her, but my heart had told me no. The front desk clerk told me Daisy wasn't looking well, with her black eye and cut on her face. Damn that woman, she was become very much trouble. I knew I couldn't just leave her there, but the men had told me she wasn't for sale. But thinking of them touching her made my blood boil, and the anger in me was becoming uncontrollable.

After a few days at the hotel it seemed my sister had overheard some men talking about a Canadian woman who was very attractive and will be for viewing tomorrow. Just hearing this I knew I needed to be one of the men to view my wife, but I would not buy her back. No, I had far more things in store for the sellers and her. Trying to get Elijah to eat and behave had not been easy since he's been away from his mother. I could tell Elijah had some strong connection to her, which made my decision harder.

* * *

My captors came to me in the morning. "Put on this dress, and make yourself beautiful. Today we sell you to the highest bidder," one said after throwing the dress and makeup at me. I sat there in my dimly lit cage and regretted ever leaving Canada. My life with Ryan wasn't that bad; I had lost faith in him very quickly and taken him for granted.

What I would give to see his face and touch his warm body. To caress and make love to him one more time would be a blessing. Sobbing while I dressed in this elegant yellow sundress, I did my hair up high and my makeup very heavy. I felt no man deserved to see my beautiful blonde hair and soft-featured face. Once I was dressed the suitors were introduced to me; I was to take a walk in the garden with each one.

The first one was short, heavy and had an odour about him that made me sick. He placed his hands all over my body to see my figure, like he couldn't tell with this

42

dress on. It shaped to my every curve very well, but he felt the need to touch me. He placed his hands on my shoulders, down my breast, and squeezed them, then slid his hands to my waist, then down to my butt, where he rested them for what seemed like a long time. My body went tight, cold with dread that he might want to test the goods. He talked about what he expected from his wife or mistress as I observed my surroundings.

The courtyard was fenced and had guards at every corner of the property, which made an escape a bit difficult. I did, however, notice a spot where there was barbwire and red maple trees. I made sure to remember my surroundings so that I could report it. I was in thought about this attemptable escape when the man I was with turned me around quickly and placed a kiss on my face.

It was sloppy, heavy, and hot. I was trying to fight back and not kiss him. He managed to grab my left side more, causing extreme pain to my slowly healing ribs. I gave into his terrible kiss so that he would release his grip on my side and cried in pain, which was to his enjoyment.

The next few suitors were a variety of rich older men with either heavy colognes, terrible clothing, and made sure I knew sex was a big thing to them. The three men had kissed me, some touched me, and others questioned me to see if I was intelligent and would cause trouble. All I knew is if I was sold to any of these men, I would move heaven and earth to get back to Elijah and Ryan.

I just needed one of these men to like me enough, once he bought me, he'd regret the day he was ever born. I would do as I needed and then be back home to retrieve my son.

After being with what I thought was the last suitor, I was hoping to make my escape very soon. My face hurt, my ribs were killing me, and I knew at any moment my captor would show me my buyer, and I would never see Ryan or Elijah again, but not if I could help it. Being informed there was one more suitor before I was to be sold to the highest bidder, I tried my hardest to look happy.

I look up to my last suitor as he came into the garden. He's wearing something over his face, so I could only see his eyes. I notice him to be taller then I, slimmer then the previous men. His eyes were so daunting that they remind me of Ryan. Instantly I hope that this suitor wanted me more then the others. "Please walk with me," he says in a husky voice as he precedes me. "What bought you here, may I ask?" this man states while I catch up to him.

"I didn't have much choice, if you hadn't noticed this is a black market for women." I sarcastically say to him as I am walking along side him. "Why have you decided to buy a wife rather than find one for free?" I throw back in his face with annoyance.

We talk more about my days at the camp as he calls it. The more we talk about my future and life in general, I start getting sharp with him. "Why don't you just do like all the other men, kiss me, touch me, and decide if I'll be the one you want. Your wasting my time, I need to get on with my new life!" I yell at this man. Damn why can't he be like the others, not ask many questions, just gawking at me, and then walking away. I need to get back to my husband, and as were getting closer to the edge of the property, I could easily do so.

"What is on your mind? I sense something terrible. And I don't want a troublesome woman who will have to be tied down." And with the way he said it, it sent chills down my spine.

"Look, what is on my mind is none of your business, and you have no idea what kind of trouble I could cause." I glare at him and quickly regret my words.

"I'm willing to bet you ran away from your husband and would be a problem for any of the men today who have shown some interest in you."

Right on the button, as if he'd heard or knew I had caused pain and heart ach. I looked at him, seeing anger, hurt, and betrayal. This man stopped and grabbed my hand; the warm sensation that went through my body made my breasts tingle. I stepped closer to this man, breathed in his lingering smell and was confused.

There was something about him; I just needed to see behind his mask. "Yes, I was married. I did cause lots of pain to a loved one. I was recently in an accident by my husband's ex-girlfriend, who tried to kill my son and I." As I step closer, I could see his eyes change and compassion enter.

The man steps back as if my closing in on his space is a problem. "So where is this son of yours?"

I look to the ground and mumble, "My husband came to fetch him, more like bought him and left me for sale. Said I was too much trouble." I wandered closer to the fencing, seeing that the guards were busy. My chance for escaping was getting better; if only I could get this man to just leave. I knew if I ran, he would chase me down and tell on me. But for some reason running from him seemed like the wrong thing to do. As I'm heavy into thought, I don't hear the man yell "run", but he grabs my hand and pulls me to the fence.

Once at the fence, I can't get over with my ribs killing me. "I can't," I cry in pain to the man, and then he helps me over and run to this black car. I try to run but collapsed; the pain is too much to bear. The man comes back and picks me up. I look back once outside and see the guards trying to shoot the car down before falling into obscurity.

Waking up in a hospital room, I'm greeted by the doctor who explains to me that my ribs are not healing well. I need to lay off doing strenuous activities, and should not be lifting my baby. "How do you know I have a son?" He then explains the amount of lactating I have been doing since I was brought here. I close my eyes to try and forget what was my life a week ago.

The nurse comes in, and I break down crying. She sits with my while I sob about what I have done. The lady sternly tells me to go back to my husband and fast. When I can't reach Ryan at home, I worry he has taken Elijah back to Lebanon, and I'll never see my son again. I'm wondering who that man was that rescued me, and how I will be able to thank him. As soon as I can leave this hospital, I will be gone on the next plane out of this country.

Being released from the hospital wasn't exactly a welcoming thought when two big burly men grabbed me to take me to the hotel I was once registered in. Not bothering to fight, I just let them lead me to one of the room. "Sit here, the man who you were with will be here shortly."

They leave me in the dark where I am to think. So I did not escape so easy, this man did have plans for me. I figured if I told him how happy I was that he rescued me, and then maybe he'd left me go and not ask for a reward. The thought of having to sleep with this man was too much to bear. He seemed too nice to be the type who demanded sex from his women.

*   *   *

What was I going to do with her? my sister had asked. I wasn't too sure. My son refused to eat or sleep. Daisy seemed to be the one to comfort his cries, and yet she betrayed me. I felt letting her go easy would not teach her a lesson well deserved. Just being near Daisy made me want to yell at her, but at the same time seeing the hurt in her eyes, I just couldn't yell at her or harm her, for all I wanted was to hold her and never let her go again.

*   *   *

"So what will you do now that you are out of the prison camp?" I could faintly see his shadow as he approached, with my nerves on the verge of breakdown.

"I would like to find my husband, and beg for his forgiveness." I just managed to whisper out. I watched as he took a seat, crossed his legs and could only see a small glint in his eyes. "I thank you for helping me escape, now that I think about it. My plane would have worked if not for the fence." That gives the man a small chuckle.

"How did you meet your husband who you felt you needed to run from? And if you didn't love him, then why marry him?" He stretched out his arms, flexing his fingers on which I could see a beautiful gold wedding band on. Intently playing with my wedding band, I remembering when the men tried to take it off but couldn't. How thankful I was; it was the only reminder that maybe Ryan might still love me. Realizing that this man had a wife, and maybe was a knight in shining armour, I figured I'd amuse him a little.

"He was my best friend, I got knocked up and was forced to marry him or lose my child. The rest is personal if you don't mind." I said with determination not to answer any more personal questions. Looking into those dark eyes, I could see he was amused with my answer.

"I have just one more question and a favour to ask you. Do you love him?"

I close my eyes and see Ryan burned into my eyelids as that is all I could think of. "Yes I love him. I loved him the first day I met him, but I was involved with another and could not have him. I never stopped loving him even when I took off. It was hard to leave him, but I had to protect my son from his crazy ex. I just hope he'll take me back." I am sobbing like a little baby, and the man hands me a tissue and holds my face.

"The favor I want is a kiss for gratitude." He leans into me as I close my eyes. Gently he kisses my lips, but opens his mouth for a more passionate kiss. At first I protest but the taste of his tongue is too familiar, the way it moves in my mouth. I inhaled this mans aroma and am taken back by the familiarity. Pulling away from this man, I open my eyes only to see Ryan. The whole time it was my husband; Ryan rescued me wanting to know if I truly loved and appreciated him.

"Ryan, I'm so sorry" was all I could say as the tears broke through, and I hugged him like there was no end. I didn't want to leave him again; I would have kept hugging him if not for him pulling my arms off him.

"The doctor said not to put pressure on your ribs. And someone else needs to be held by you more than me." With that Sherri walks in the room carrying a crying Elijah.

I held him tight, talking to quiet him as happy tears fell on his face. Ryan sits me down, placing a pillow on my lap so I can feed my son better. After Elijah falls asleep, Ryan takes him to his bed so we can be alone to talk.

PART 2

CHAPTER 4

It has been twelve weeks since that dreadful day that Runée tried to kill me and I fled to Mexico. I'm still getting nightmares about the accident and almost being sold on the Mexican black market. Ryan insists that I seek help for my troubled mind because even though I am happy, healed of my wounds, able to work again and lift Elijah, the nightmares are starting to show on my face with my pale complexion and weariness of my body. I tell Ryan I haven't seen my brother or mom in a very long time, and that maybe going for a visit might be just what the doctor ordered to help me.

Ryan is shocked to hear about my brother. "What, a brother? And why did you not feel the need to tell me this!" he said since I had never mentioned it before.

"Matthew was my best friend, and when I met you my life got a little complicated that I forgot to mention him," I say remembering just how close I was with my brother and all the fun we had at school functions.

Since I had moved to Lethbridge, I had completely shut out my brother and mother, except the occasion calls. It was as if to remove a bad part of my life, like a child does a nightmare.

With Ryan being unable to find time to come with me to Vancouver, he permits me to go but says, "Elijah is going to stay home."

No liking the feeling in my gut and the lack of trust from my husband, "I'm not going to run from you again." I tell him with as much sincerity I can find while trying to comfort him, and still seeing the fear in his eyes.

At the airport it becomes a whole other story, because as I'm starting to board the plane I hear my named called by security. Getting there I see Ryan and my son who is screaming his head off. "I made a mistake, Elijah has to go with you because he won't stop crying, and I don't want put up with this while your gone on vacation," Ryan says to me in a defeated and frustrated manner, with pain and fear running through those eyes as he hands me our son.

"Babe, don't worry. My mother will be happy to see her grandchild for the first time. Look I love you too much and regret that I ever did what I did. Trust me I will not make that mistake twice." I leaned into him with my son in my arms and gave Ryan one last hug and kiss before boarding the plane with my now happy quiet son.

Driving up to the old home, looking at our yard in full bloom, I'm reminded how I always did love July. It was my favorite time of the year and the warmest. As a family we had designed the yard and planted all the trees including Dad's rose garden, my Japanese garden, Mom's special veggie garden, and Matt's cactus garden.

I pull up in front of the garage and walked into my moms house, and before I had a chance to put my luggage down my mother was at me and pulling her grandson out of my arms. "Gee, Mom, you don't even say hi?"

With tears still in her eyes and a smile from ear to ear, she says, "Sorry, dear, but you have not let me see this child. And I am so happy to finally meet him for the first time." With that she goes back to hugging him making him giggle.

I take my luggage and put it outside my old room. Gathering Elijah's dipper bag, I hand it to my mother. She goes to the washroom, and I go make a spot on the carpet for Elijah to play. As I wander into the living room the scents of Lilic popery, and the soft colors of the walls, cream carpet, fill me.

Just as I thought, the furniture was still the same rich red oak. The black grand piano in the corner opposite the fireplace and the pictures of Matt, Mom, the family and I. But most importantly all pictures containing dad and our family.

"Oh, Daisy, I see you have made a spot for this little guy to play," Mom says startling me in my thoughts. Turning to her, she see's my tears and puts Elijah down on the blanket I put for him. As she wrap her arms around me, hugging me tight, I let it all out. "Baby, I know you miss him, we all miss him."

"I just wish he was still here, I made such a mess with my life," I whisper at the same time as I try to wipe the tears away.

"Dear, you have not made a mess. Ryan still loves you and will forgive you. Just give him time to understand and show you he trusts you." Mom said as she kissed my cheeks.

As I manage to clear my tears off my face, I chuckle, "But he's Lebanese, and they are very possessive men and don't trust easily once they have been lied to."

Mom finds some food to make and tends to Elijah as I go call Ryan to reassure him that we are safe, telling him that I'll be spending some time at home with my mom, which isn't a lie until my brother comes home.

As I'm at the dinner table eating supper with Mom, I hear the sound of a 1964 Mustang GT. Dropping my fork and running to the door, I open it to see Matthew getting out of his red hot classic Mustang that Dad used to drive. I run into his arms giving him the biggest hug and kisses. How I had missed my brother; it has been four years since I last saw him. "So you up for some clubbing, little sis?" He winks at me like a devilish cat.

"If Mom will babysit, I was born to club." A smile forms on my face so big, and excitement burns in my body like none I had felt in so long. As I go to get ready in my old room, left just the same as the day I went to Lethbridge for college, I look at the pictures of Matty and I dancing or doing some crazy activity. We always went

50

to concerts, on ski trips, clubbed, and hung at the beach and house parties. Most of the pictures had other friends in them, and there were only a few of them with just Matt and I.

Mom was happy to babysit; she felt like it was a blessing to have Elijah just home with Grandma.

I look in my full-length mirror at the Australian-crystal-beaded straps wrapped around my neck to keep this beautiful red Spanish-style dress clinging tightly to my breasts and upper body; at the waist the skirt fans out with ease as I twirl. I add a small amount of jewellery and a touch of makeup to finish my look.

Before leaving the house I had Mom take a picture of Matt and I. I kiss Elijah once more before heading out with my bro to cause havoc on the town. Once I recognized we were at one of our old favorite clubs, we start to dance. Ryan always thought Shane was my original dirty dancing partner, but in all honesty it was Matthew. I had taken dance as a little girl, and Matty just loved to move his body. So once I was of age, my friends took me to a club, and the dirty dancer was born.

Dancing up against my brother was great; it wasn't sexual as with Ryan, but driving other people crazy with envy made doing what we did more enjoyable. After finding some other people to dance with as well, the night seemed to go by so fast. Once the clubs had shut down, Matt and I decided to walk along the beach and catch up. Since keeping my promise to stay away from home, I've only e-mailed him a bit of my life and less in the last couple months.

"So, sis, what has been going on in your life? I see you're not with Mark anymore." Mat goes to squeeze me tightly around the waist.

"Well, I always loved Ryan, just had to get drugged to actually make love to him." I laughed to myself.

Stopping with concern in his eyes, "What? Who drugged you?"

"It's all right, the guy's in jail. Ryan and I both got drugged. Let our hearts take over and made love. Then Mark found out the son I gave birth to wasn't his and divorced me only to have Ryan marry me immediately." I walk to the wall of the beach walk and looked at the waves as they crashed against the rock wall.

"I'm sorry, you are happy aren't you, Daisy?" Matt placed his arm around my shoulders and I leaned my head on his shoulder.

"Yah, it couldn't have worked out better if I had dreamed." And with that we just stood and watched the waves while the sun rose.

* * *

Letting them go was a hard thing to do even though I knew I could trust her. But the fear was still there; I couldn't help but worry what kind of trouble Daisy might get into. When she was with me I had more influence over her, and she behaved better, but out of my sight I knew she would revert to the wilder days, like when she was with Mark.

I called Daisy's mom's house later that night after Daisy had called to tell me she would be staying home with her family, only to find out that she had indeed lied and gone clubbing with her brother.

I was angered beyond belief. As I tried to get someone to cover my shifts for the next few days, I was told to ask the boss. I couldn't comprehend it since Renaldo was the boss and wouldn't have had a problem. I asked, "Why I should ask? My brother-in-law is the owner, and if I want time off, I need not ask!"

But to my shock I was informed that no, Renaldo did not own Dooley's anymore; now my wife was the proud owner. Feeling more betrayal by and anger toward my wonderful wife, I told the staff to find a replacement.

After arriving at Daisy's mom's house later that same night, I was greeted by her mom, Susan. I saw my son asleep in a playpen and picked him up to kiss him. I came to the conclusion that Daisy figured her mom can be her personal babysitter. Susan and I sat in the living room while we chatted about her precious daughter.

"She is such a lovely girl, always helping others and just loves her brother," Daisy's mom started off.

Looking at Susan with her blond hair and strong bone structure, I could see where Daisy got some of her features. "Where is her dad? And how close is Matthew and Daisy?"

I could see pain behind those beautiful hazel eyes and regretted asking regarding Mr. Dime. I found out that Daisy's dad died in a terrible bank robbery, and that after that fateful day Matthew became Daisy's protector. The two became even closer to one another since Daisy was at the bank with her father when he was shot.

Hearing that she had witnessed her father being killed in front of her eyes at fourteen years old almost ripped my heart out. That would explain why she rarely talked about her father. But hearing from Susan that Daisy was very close to her father was the added knife I needed to my heart.

After enjoying a long-awaited sleep over at Matt's apartment, we head to the beach to tan and shop. When I got home I headed for the shower, but my attempt was diverted by the fact that my husband was here as he came out of my brother's room stopping in front of me. "Who's covering your shift? And why are you here?"

But just looking at Ryan made me wish I hadn't asked those questions and hugged him instead. Seeing that he was enraged and not going to answer my questions, "Fine, I'm taking a shower, and I guess well talk later." As I head to the bathroom my heart starts to race.

While in the bathroom showering, I hate the fact that he is here. I just know he is going to try and control me. Letting the hot steamy water run down my soar underworked muscles, I moan with frustration.

As I'm in my room changing, Ryan walks in. "So why did you lie to me about staying at home, when clearly you went out partying while leaving our son home with his estranged grandmother?" I could see the anger and hurt in his eyes.

"My brother came home to see me. Matt and I are really close and love clubbing. He asked if I'd go out with him. So how could I pass up a night out with my brother, and I never really lied to you. I was intending to spend time with mom." I could see that this satisfied him, but this wasn't why he was angry with me. "What really is the problem?" I turned around to face him instead of looking at him through the mirror.

"When were you going to tell me about the restaurant!" Ryan demanded with rage. Here was the real problem: I, a woman, had a business in my name, and this was degrading to him.

"I was going to surprise you when I got back. But I needed to get away and forgot to tell you. Since I have been gone from Lethbridge, I have not had one nightmare." I placed a kiss on his face and wrapped my arms around him as I tried to be sweet.

Dinner could not have gone better if I planned it my self. Sitting at the table with Mom, Matt, and my new family made my heart do flip-flops. Ryan sitting at the head of the table reminded me of dad, but I did not let on to Mom that I was thinking of dad. I didn't want her to be sad at this grand time. Ryan complimented her on the lasagna; he also offered to help with the dishes. Matt and I went into the living room and reminisced about our days at summer camp or hanging out at the beach. I could see Ryan was a little unsettled, but he adjusted very fast.

"Matt and I are going clubbing, so if you want to stay home with mom, I'm sure she'd love that." I told Ryan around seven o'clock when I got up to head for my room to get ready. Instead of him sitting with Mom, he got up and followed me to my room.

After closing the bedroom door Ryan commented, "Your room gives me more insight on you and your childhood." He put his arms around me and kissed my neck ever so softly.

*   *   *

Seeing her princess's bed, blue walls, and pictures of friends and family all around her, I could see that my wife had more love and compassion then I thought I knew. Seeing the pictures of Matt and her touched my heart. I knew she would protect our family with her life.

Then it came to me, she was doing that when she ran to Mexico. Pulling her close to me, I felt the need to not let her out of my arms again and placed gentle kisses on her neck.

*   *   *

I hug Ryan back and start playing with his hair. As he massages my back and guides me to the bed, I fall back on it. I can't remember ever making love with anyone in my bed but who better than with my husband. I start kissing him, and the kissing becomes more intense. As he started kissing my neck and unbuttoning my blouse, I moaned silently, with one hand playing with his hair and the other unbutton his pants. Once we were naked, caressing each other, I start stroking his hardness.

He grabs my hand away from its task, and holding my wrists above my head, Ryan slowly inserts his hard penetrating instrument into my wet and ever-so-dying need for him to make sweet, passionate to love to me. We rolled around making tense, passionate love on my bed for the first time in its life. After our joint explosion, we lay there quietly till I hear.

"Daisy, are you ready? Is Ryan coming? If you are not ready I'm coming in to tickle you." The door knob was turning, and I yelled, "Give me four minutes and then you can come in while I get ready." I shouted to my brother praying he would not open the door to see two naked people.

The both of us quickly got dressed in some clothes, then I let Matthew in so he could chat while I put on my bar clothes and got ready. Once we got to the Twisted Edge, I tell Ryan that I'm on a mission to find Matt a girl and ask if we could pretend we are friends, and if he'd help Matt with the girls. After a small argument from Ryan, a conclusion is met.

I find a girl for Matt as he is dancing with Ryan and some girls they hooked up with. I wait for a pause in the music before introducing Matt and Ryan to the girl. Unfortunately, she takes a strong liking to Ryan and is all over him on the dance floor. As my temperature rises, I see that Ryan is just going along with my plan as I had suggested with a devilish grin on his face.

While the boys are dancing with women, I meet a young athletic girl who seems to be bored sitting at the bar. "Hi, my names Daisy. You look bored."

"You could say that, I was here to meet some friends, but they cancelled. Oh sorry I forgot my manners. I'm Montana," the young lady says to me as she sips her cocktail.

I can see she works out by the muscle in her arms, or else she works for a company that lifts heavy stuff. Her long chocolate brown hair was swept up away from her hazel eyes. Looking into her eyes as we talk I can see this lady has sincerity and compassion. Matt would be smitten by her.

We start talking about our lives, things that we did as children, how we went to the same high school, but because it was so large fate would have had to intervene in order for Matt and her to have met. Releasing there are lots of similarities with Matt and her, I ask if she would like to meet my older brother.

"Hey, Matt, I want you to meet Montana," I say to him with a quick wink of the eye. Catching on quickly he excuses himself from the group.

As Matt takes Montana's arm and links it with his, he leads us to the tables where it's a little quieter so they can talk. We all sit at a booth, they start talking and noticing how they take a liking to one and other. I look back to the dance floor where Ryan last was and the previous girl I tried to introduce to Matt but took a liking to Ryan are still dancing together.

Feeling the need for space, I head to the top floor where I can look over the balcony keeping an eye on Ryan and the bitch as well as my brother and Montana. While I was enjoying a martini, a few men try and make a pass at me, but one in particular decides to make conversation.

"Hi, I'm Dan, you look like you could use some company," Sitting down Dan explains how he's a basketball player for the Vancouver Grizzlies and thinks he's met me before. We talk for a long time, and I see Ryan is still dancing on the floor with that same girl. Matt is now dancing along side him, so I ask the Dan if he'd like to dance.

While I dance with Dan, he invades my space and is all over me. I can see this bothering Ryan, and he try's to come to my aid until Matt stops him. "Get your hands off my sister or I swear to god, buddy, you'll pay," Matt warns Dan.

I have told Dan no and backed away from him many of times. Knowing the rule that no man beside Ryan is able to touch me, I have tried to put distance between Dan and I. Since Dan is either too drunk or ignorant to understand, I turn around and slap him. He doesn't take to me slapping him very well, but seeing both Matt and Ryan enraged, Dan makes the right choice and leaves the dance floor with the bitch following him.

For the rest of the evening I dance with Matt, Montana, and Ryan. But dancing up close with Ryan, I can feel his tight grip around me as he whispers in my ear, "You are in trouble, I'm not happy with you. Do not leave my sight again!" As I was warned I continue to dance with Ryan until Matt and my favorite song came on.

Interrupting Matt and Montana wasn't very hard since I could see that Matt was already telling Montana that he'd be right back so that he and I could dance. As we danced I can see the astonishment on Ryan and Montana's face; they seem impressed with how we dance. While Matt and I danced to this Latin salsa song, there was a crowd forming around us. After the song was over, we received applause from the onlookers. Matt and I returned to our partners. I saw intensity and confusion in my husband's eyes.

All of us leave, heading to another bar down the street. Dan approaches me from my left side. In doing so I can see what is on his mind, clear as it is on his face: that he is hurt and humiliated that I slapped him and that I wont be coming home with him since that was his original plan.

He grabs my arm, pulling me away from my family and friends. "Who do you think you are, bitch!"

Holding both my arms while yelling at me, Matt comes up to Dan and Says in a stern voice like my father's, "Let go of my sister now!"

He lets me go, and Ryan yanks me into his tense arms while Matt is quickly there with a fancy kickboxing move. Dan goes down like a ton of bricks.

At last we are at a quiet sports lounge, and we really get to know Montana and muse over about that fancy move Matt pulled.

Montana goes to ask Matt when he learnt to fight like that. But before Matt could answer I jumped, "You see, our father was Latin, so he had taught us a few moves."

"All right fair enough, Daisy. Well how come you and Matt are like Latin lovers on the dance floor?" Montana asked.

Looking over to Ryan as my face blushed at the comment, I said with pride, "We have Latin blood in us, and I took many different styles of dance classes, then one day Matt joined my dance classes." Remembering the times when the girls would talk about my brother in his tight jumpers made me laugh. "So Matt and I became dance partners in class because we were the best and loved to dance together." I finished with my eyes starting to tear.

Not only was it a memory of dancing with my brother when I was young, but some nights when I couldn't sleep, Dad and I would dance to his country's music and some of the music he found appropriate for me. I as well loved to watch my mother and father dance together.

Matt placed his hand over mine and said, "Yah, but then Daisy moved to Lethbridge to go to college. I had no one to dance with, and now she's back for a visit with her new family. And since she's only here for a couple weeks, you can see why I want to spend all my time with her." Matthew looked at Ryan.

"I see, but what you did, when defending your sister, that wasn't a new move? Where'd you really learn that?" Ryan remarked with his gorgeous eyes. I could see that he was hurt not to have come to my aid and suspicious of Matt's talent.

Looking at my brother and seeing him decide whether to tell Ryan or not, I intercept. "Once I left for college, Matty took up kickboxing since I was no longer here to dance with. He pretty good ah? I always told him to enter competitions." I smiled and patted his thigh. If Ryan found the true reason to why Matt learned kickboxing, he would be furious with me, feel less of a man, and would never understand.

I see that Ryan and Montana are impressed with Matt. And noticing it was five in the morning, Matt and Montana talk briefly in the corner before he helps her into a cab and gives her a night's kiss. While waiting for our cab, I bug him for a bit until Ryan tells me to stop. Heading home, I tell Ryan, "I'm going to sleep over in my brother's room to catch up on life." Seeing the hurt in Ryan's eyes, I tell him that we will spend time together alone.

Once home I head into Matt's room, pillow and blankets in hand. I look at his pictures on his desk. Some frames of the two of us and one last family picture.

Remembering that day and being around dad brought tears to my eyes, and I wipe them away before Matt could see, but It was too late. Coming up behind me, he wraps his arms around me. "Don't cry, Dad wouldn't want you to pine over him any longer. I miss him too, Daisy, but we'll be with him again one day."

Feeling my brother's love, I wonder why I moved to Lethbridge. The only good thing was meeting Ryan and marrying him because of our affair that resulted in a child. I have missed my family and my friends. I really could have gone to college here. Why did I need to get away when I should have been strong enough to be here for my family?

Then realizing why I moved: it was Mom threatening to disown me as her daughter if I didn't leave and get out of the business. I wasn't willing to lose Mom over a job, especially since I had lost my father to that same job.

Both Matt and I sat on his bed across from each other. Looking at him with intensity and love in his eyes. He looked so much like Dad, with his deep brownish red hair, emerald green eyes, beautiful tanned olive skin, and now with age his features more defined and body hard as a rock. I now could understand why Montana was not sure if he was interested in her at the lounge. He's way too good looking for most women to be with.

Shaking my head while I look around at his room again, I asked, "Why have you left this room the same? You have your own place."

"I like to feel at home when I stay at Mom's, plus I didn't think it was fair for her to have both kids moved out and no memories to look at. She has never complained, I think it makes her feel safe," Matt said, throwing one of his old stuffed-animal bears at me.

Moving out of the range of the flying bear, I laughed. "Do you remember when we were at John Lawson Bay and had that kick-ass party with Bobby and Jenn? And those punks came by and thought they'd start a fight with us?"

"Yah, I was so shocked when you got up and kicked their ass. There was no way I was going to let them hurt my little sister," Matt said while remembering the old beach days.

I sip some water from the glass I got when we all got home. "I miss you guys, and I really miss Dad. I just wish I knew what I know now . . ." Tears well up in my eyes.

"Daisy, don't go there. You know there was nothing you could have done, you were just fourteen. What happened did. And Dad wouldn't want you to still be mourning him." Matty moves to give me a big hug. We continue to discuss life and the past memory, and then we pass out only to be awakened by Mom.

"You kids going to wake up or what? I want to take Ryan and Elijah to the market." She tossed cold water at us, and we groggily respond.

"Mom, it's too early, and my head hurts, plus we have a concert to attend tonight." I sit up and wipe the water off my face. Damn woman, always trying to be a smart ass in the early morning. I fall back to bed and roll over.

Then 8:00 p.m. rolls around, and Matt and I are at the concert with front-row seats and afterparty passes to a local club that's throwing a rave. With these passes, there is enough room for the first two rows to dance comfortably. The music is great, the lights spectacular, and we are dressed to kill. Ryan even gave me a look of disapproval before we left the house, which let me know that I was dressed just right for the concert. Ever since being married to Ryan, I had to learn to tone down my style. Matty was dressed in black slacks and a blue silk dress shirt and smelling of Hugo Boss.

I was fashioning an black angle-cut satin dress with spaghetti straps, stiletto heels, sparkling jewellery, and vanilla fragrance.

The singer finally comes onto stage and starts singing. Matt and I are dancing and enjoying our self too much to notice the music suddenly stops, and the artist suggests people from the audience come up on stage and dance. The bouncer points to me letting me know if I'd like I can go on stage, so I ask if Matt can come up on stage and dance too. The music starts up again, and Matt and I forget where we are, except for the fact we were having a blast.

The singer hands me a microphone and wants me to sing along with the band. I start singing and dancing with Matt and her at the same time. After a few more songs, we are escorted off the stage and given VIP back stage passes.

"I can't believe we got to dance on stage, that was so cool," I yell over the music and hug my brother.

Later that night, the musicians and the band ask us to join them at the afterparty they are having at the Vancouver Royal Hotel. Once there and given our drinks, Shelly, the lead vocalist, asks me if I have ever danced professionally.

After chocking back on my wine, I answered, "If you ask have I ever stripped, the answer is no. But I did take dance lessons years when I was little. My brother and I were in many dance competitions."

Chucklin "Well both you and your brother are excellent dancers and should never give up the art. And your singing is not too bad, have a little more faith." Shelly leans on to me and gives me a hug. "If my band or another band needs you to help with choreographing, would you be interested?"

Shocked, I look at Shelly and respond with "Yes, but why would you want me to choreograph for your band or music videos? I'm sure there are better people for the job than me."

She fills me in on some of the competition and how she sees talent that would bring me lots of money.

After mingling and playing pool, Matt and I finally head home to sleep. I know I will be in a lot of trouble with Ryan, but I just don't feel like getting into it tonight. I pass out in my brother's room again but only after chatting with him till four in the morning.

I awake suddenly at 12 noon when Ryan storms into the room and tells me that I have to be ready to go out with him at 4:00 pm before slamming the door. I fall back to the bed. "What was that about?" my brother asks.

"He's mad at me for being out all night and not spending any time with him. Ryan has not seen me like this, if ever. Don't worry about him, his growl is louder then his bark." I put my arm around Matt and fall asleep only to be awakened at 3pm.

Working with a hangover and trying to look my best for Ryan, I manage to make it out of the washroom quarter after 4:00 pm. We drive to one of the famous beaches, took a long stroll with the wind blowing my hair.

Holding my hand Ryan asks, "So how close are you and Matt exactly? I'm not sure since the fact that you have slept in his bed every day you've been home. And not to mention the fact that you have ignored our son as well as your mother."

Not liking the tone of his voice, I let go his hand and walk faster from him to put distance between us. I turn around on him in rage and say with harshness, "There are things about me you will not understand, and I wish not to disclose them. But my relationship with my brother maybe stronger than yours with your family. I love my brother like my father." Ryan approaches me. I put more distance between the two of us and continue, "Mom understands that I miss Matt and need a break from Elijah.

"Matty was my whole world before I left. Sure I had boyfriends, but they were all afraid to approach me cause they would get their ass kicked if they hurt me. Matt and I got closer after Dad died, but only 'cause I didn't want to loose another man in my life."

There are now tears in my eyes and Ryan has gotten closer to me. "Elijah is enjoying being with his Nana, so don't lecture me. Cause frankly you weren't supposed to be here on my vacation!"

"Baby, I am so sorry, it's not what I mean. I guess I'm jealous how much time you spend with Matt. I love you and want you to be happy, and if that means spending your time with your brother, then I will enjoy my visit with your mom. But can we spend today together like a second honeymoon?" Ryan then embraces me, wipes the tears from my eyes, and kisses my cheek. With a hug so tight I wince in pain.

After our little chat, we stroll farther along the beach walk. We finally stop at a bench and watch the water lap against the rocks, I rest my head on Ryan shoulders. He wraps his arms around me and whispers words of love to me.

After what seemed like eternity of being in Ryan's arms, we finally leave and head for the dinner reservations. Ryan orders for me lobster with pasta, and for himself a medium rare stake. While we eat, I explain what life was like while my father was still around.

"He was always home for dinner and hated to be away from Mom and us kids. Up until his death, he would always read me a bedtime story or talk about how his day was and what he had planned for my future. Dad never missed being around me. I know he spent more time with me then Matt. I know it hurt Matty, but he never showed it. They had a special relationship. They'd go to the ball diamonds and do guy stuff while I was at dance." Pausing to sip my wine, I think about the last time I saw Papa dressed up.

He was taking Mom out for a night in the town. Wearing his black slacks, maroon silk shirt, and black matching sports jacket, he smelled of Hugo Boss and was clean shaven. I had hugged him that day as if it was going to be the last night I saw him.

How silly I was that it was not going to be the last night, because the next day I was the one who was there with him when he was taken away from me by ambulance cover with a white sheet. If it wasn't for his stupid job he would never have gone into that bank that day. We never did any banking at the Royal Bank, but Dad had gotten a feeling and saw one of his targets.

"Babe, where were you just now?" Ryan asked while grabbing for my hand.

I looked up at Ryan not realizing I had stopped talking, "Sorry, I was daydreaming." I finished my dinner and waved away the dessert cart; I was much too full from dinner.

And I really missed my papa. Looking away from Ryan out toward the ocean, I smiled to myself. It was like I could still smell my dad, and feel his love that night.

There was a violinist playing in the far corner. I noticed the man slowly walking toward our table while he played. The melody was very soothing that daydreaming became easier. The man stopped at our table and Ryan stood up walked around to my side. Pulled my chair away from the table and put his hand out for me to take. Stepping to my feet, he embraced me, held my hand, and we danced a waltz near our table. The other guests had stopped and were watching us, and we danced slowly to the music. He pulled me close to him, and I rested my head on his shoulder as we swayed and moved over the floor.

I thought back to Mark, and he was never this romantic. He would be afraid of what others thought. Being with Ryan was so far the best thing I could have done in my life. After the music ended, Ryan dipped me and we kissed very passionately. He then turned to the violinist and paid him a handsome tip.

I went to sit back down, but Ryan still had my hand in his and wasn't going to let it go. I looked at him oddly as he dropped to one knee. Feeling my face go flush, I placed my other hand to my face. There was no way he was going to do what I anticipated.

"Daisy, I know I wasn't man enough before. But I want you to know that I have loved you from the moment we met. It just took our son to make our life happen a little faster. Please do me the honour of being my wife, and the mother of my future children?" Ryan held in his hand a box with a two-karat princess-cut diamond in platinum and gold to match the wedding band he had given me. The wedding band that I could not for the life of me seem to take off.

I felt so overwhelmed. What was I going to say? No? Yet I was married to him. If things were different, would I have married him? Unlike Mark, Ryan had made me feel beautiful, special, loved, and needed. "Yes, I will be your wife and marry you."

He then placed the ring on my wedding finger beside my wedding band. It matched so beautifully. Now it was complete: he had proposed to me, and now I'm married to him. Ryan stood up, and we kissed with a long and deep kiss as the other guests in the restaurant clapped in celebration. After hugging we stat back down at the table. I was in shock still 'cause I did not hear Ryan speaking to me. "What . . . ?" I asked puzzled.

"Were you not paying attention? I asked you when you wanted to throw our wedding."

I looked into his eyes and saw the sincerity. If I was to get remarried, it defiantly was not going to be big and expensive. "How about October fourth, but just a small ceremony with a few close friends. I really don't want to go through the whole big fuss." He seemed to agree with me on the date and with having just a small guest list.

We took another walk along the waterfront. "You know I was thinking, Elijah was a surprise and not planned. I know I didn't do the most honourable thing when I forced you to marry me. But you know it was because I care about you. So, Daisy, I was thinking we should plan a proper honeymoon since we are remarrying and maybe try for another baby to complete the start of our new life together. I promise this time things will be better, and you will be happy."

I looked out the ocean, and yes, this marriage was not the way I'd have wished it to go. Getting divorced one minute and then forced to marry or lose my son the next. Now Ryan was trying to make it up to me by offering a fresh start, a proper wedding, a honeymoon, and wanted another child.

But I was just getting my life together. Elijah, how I loved him, but after being around my brother made me realize how much I wanted my life back. My son took up all my time and never wanted me out of his sight. I shivered at the thought of another baby; true I loved Ryan more then anything. Now to have another baby after I just acquired the restaurant, which need all of my attention.

"Ryan, I would like to have another baby . . ."

He pulled me close to him and hugged me so hard that when I tried to pull away from, I couldn't. "I love you so much. Maybe we could try for a girl this time."

Freeing myself from his strong arms, I look into his happy eyes. "Ryan, I want another child as much as you do, but, babe, I just bought the restaurant. Let's wait till Elijah is older because he still needs a lot of my attention. I haven't the time for the world. And where do you fit into this equation?" Seeing the hurt in his eyes, I regretted saying no, but I had to take control of my life. I knew I owed him for the stunt I pulled in Mexico, but he was already dominating my life too much, and it had to end or be curtailed.

"All right, a little later then." As if it was that easy, he just squeezed my hand, and we walk back to the car to head back to my mom's house.

Parking outside, Ryan leaned forward to place a gentle kiss on my lips; the kiss lingered a moment. I returned the kiss with the same amount of intensity. His kisses got a little stronger and more passionate. I placed my hand behind his head and returned his kisses with more passion. It had been a while since we last shared intimacy. Except in my bedroom. Placing my hand behind his head I pulled him into my bosom, and wanted to feel his lips and tongue on my chest. As he gently nibbled and sucked on my peaked nipples.

I moaned with pleasure and sucked on his neck while I undid his shirt. Oh it felt so good as he sucked on my breasts and placed his hand down my pants. I just wanted him so much that I could care less that I was outside my mom's house making out.

He moved my body so he could better place his hands on my pelvis and into the moisture that was flowing from with in me. Our kisses got more intense, "Stop! This is going to get uncomfortable." I managed to say in between kisses.

Here I thought we might carry this on in the house and in my more comfortable bed. But I was mistaken when Ryan grabbed me by the arms and forced me in the back seat only to follow very quickly. After, he discarded his pants and removed my blouse.

I attacked him with my kissing, placing my tongue in his mouth and just kissing him with more aggression than before. He moved my body so that he would be closer to me. Once my skirt was around my waist and my panties moved to the side so there was room for his hard manliness, I kissed his neck when he pull away so he could look at me in my eyes.

He then inserted into my wet and ever-so-yearning. With every movement, it just made me climax more and drive harder to have all of him inside me. I just wanted him, and with every pump I drove harder. I clawed at his back and moaned every time his made his way deeper into me and I would get a little tighter.

He then surprised me and thrust into me so deep and rapidly that I could not contain my orgasm and released what I had pent up inside. But at that exact moment, so did he. He then fell onto me, and we were breathing so heavy that I could have passed out. After straightening up we headed into the house. Ryan needed a shower, and I wanted to talk to my brother.

Walking into Matt's room turned out to be a mistake. "So how was fucking in our driveway? That's one even I haven't done yet." I just look at him with shock and disbelief, the color draining from my face and the humiliation following. Here my brother had been spying on my husband and I having sex in our parents' driveway.

Unable to say anything, Matt then hugs me and laughs. "You were always the more daring of the two of us. I can't believe you just broke in our parents' driveway." I playfully slap him and join him laughing. I never thought that it would be me to be the first to have sex in our parents driveway. I was sure Matt had broken in the driveway a long time ago with all the girls he had. We sit on his bed; I tell him how my night went. But when I get to part about remembering Dad, he went silent.

I was not thinking that maybe bringing up old times with Dad might hurt him. I tell Matt how much I miss Pa and wish that I would have been more help. As the tears stream down my face I didn't realize the exhaustion from have sex and the memory of my father had drained me that I fell asleep in his arms.

CHAPTER 5

The visit with my mom and brother was the best thing I could have done since marring Ryan and having Elijah. I felt this surge of energy that I was on top of the world. I was ready to make my restaurant a success. Ryan stayed for the rest of the trip; I was all right with his decision but would have preferred that he head home so I could spend more time alone.

But we came to a compromise that he would not get in the way with my fun time with Matt. Yet after Matt met Montana, it seemed to become more of a threesome than a couple's thing.

With in a few weeks of being home, I started to receive calls from musicians to help choreograph their music videos. After asking where they got my name, I was a little easier at accepting their requests. It seems the party I attended with Matt turned to out to pay off. I guess Shelly was serious when she said she'd let other artist know someone who could help with their music videos and started offering my name out to other bands due to my dancing ability.

I accepted their offers and flew out to help choreograph their music videos. Ryan put up a huge protest at first. "Baby, besides owning the restaurant and being a mother and wife, this is the other thing in my life that makes me happy." I defend myself when Ryan decided that I will not be going anywhere.

After taking time off work and doing a month of videos for musicians, I finally decide it would be easier to buy a warehouse in Lethbridge so that I wont be away from home much and that Elijah can be closer to his father. I tell my clients that they have to come to Lethbridge if they want my help. To my surprise they actually came, and in turn I made major profit by basing my company at home instead of travelling.

Being that it has been two months and all I had done was focus on music videos, I finally realized that if I want my newly owned restaurant to take off, I need to put more attention to it. I start looking at the accounting of the restaurant and realized that there needed to be a cutback on food supply and staff. After making certain cutbacks I also put one of my college friends to use and make him a mystery customer for my staff, only to find out that I needed to be harder on them and that my standards were not being met.

As Elijah seemed to be growing, so was his independence from me. For the first time my son would rather be with his father. I look at the two of them as Ryan bathed our son. I see the resemblance in the color of their skin, the shape of their eyes, and their stubbornness. When Elijah tells daddy that he doesn't want to do some thing I have to laugh to myself.

After Ryan finished bathing Elijah, I felt I should discuss my concern. "Babe, I was talking to my brother and we had a good conversation. I have some thing I want to talk to you about. I really miss my family and want to move back home. It would be a good decision that we should move to Vancouver and truly start fresh."

Looking at Ryan I saw the shock on his face. I couldn't imagine why. He knows how much I love and miss my family, yet his face looked like I plan on running again. "Why? We have a great life here. A restaurant, your choreographing, a nice apartment, everything is going well," He says to me after putting Elijah in his crib.

"Look, I can run the restaurant from afar, I need not be in the same area. I miss my family, and I left home at twenty to get away from my father's death. But they need me. I know you like being near your sister, but what about my brother? I too would like to be around him." I plead to Ryan.

He kisses Elijah and cups my elbow as he escorts me out of our son's room.

"Babe, I have noticed that you are not as happy as you were when you went back home. But please let's just stay here a little longer, then we will move." With that he places a kiss on my forehead. If I didn't know him better I would have argued more.

But knowing that he has stated his piece and that if I argue more with him, I will end up not getting my way. I just close my eyes and accept the kiss of closure. I head to the computer to e-mail my brother that I will move back home but with some time. "Anyway, how is the wedding plans coming?" Ryan asks while getting himself ready for bed.

Having been so busy, I had totally forgotten that we were had to have a proper wedding ceremony. "They are going great. Everything is as scheduled." I was lying through my teeth, but it seemed to give him the satisfaction he wants. I sneak out of the living room to my small office to look over what I have arranged for our wedding. Since it is only three weeks away from that date we planned to wed. Noticing that I really have nothing planned for my second wedding, I decide that I should put more attention to this.

Being that Ryan is getting married for the first time, and I know his sister is looking forward to the wedding. I feel it is best if I let her make all the plans, not knowing how a Lebanese wedding should go. I call up Sherri and tell her where I want to be married, what time, and some of the particulars. She tells me that she will do her best at making everything right for Ryan.

After retraining my staff and letting them know the way things need to be done, I ask another friend whom I barely know to come to the restaurant. After dinner they tell me that they had a great experience and they wish to return frequently. My staff is happy they did so well on their performance report. I decide to allow them to have a party and bring one guest each.

After putting Elijah to bed and with just a few weeks prior to the wedding, I sit down and read the mail. Flipping through I notice a letter without a return address. It is neatly addressed to me. I open the envelope. Ryan is at work so I am not worried that he will be reading over my shoulder in case it is a letter from Shane apologizing.

> *Dear Daisy,*
>
> *I hope you are enjoying your newfound life. But I would not get too comfortable. As easy as it is to gain privilege, it is also easy to lose it. I believe that as much as you think things are going well. That you may find out that the biggest surprises are yet to come and will come at the most unapt time.*
>
> *I feel you have taken away much from my life, and just in case you are not too smart, be forewarned that I will take from your life just as much and if not more than you have of mine.*

I felt my chest close up and the breath from my body leave. Having to slow down my breathing I'm not sure whether Ryan knows anything about Runée's whereabouts. Placing the letter at the bottom of my filling cabinet. I grab a bottle of Red Wine and head for the veranda with my smokes in hand. I light up, wondering when this whole Runée Nightmare will end.

Staring off into space I not only not hear Ryan come home but don't hear him come up behind me and grab the smoke from my hand and break it yelling at me. "Daisy, what is going on that you have to smoke again?" He looks at me with such intensity that it sends shivers down my spine.

Why should I tell him? He would only think I was crazy and should relax. I look at him, a little hazy since I have had about four glasses of wine, and could use more since my glass is looking shallow. I start to laugh at him, not knowing why, probably the wine talking and my nerves slipping.

I then go into my cigarette pack and pull another one out, which Ryan takes out of my hand as well as the pack I have sitting beside my chair. "What? Why do you have to be like that?" I slur my words to him.

"I hate you, why do you have to come home and take my smokes away from me and disturb me? You have no right being my boss." I yell at him with a little more sobriety while getting up from my chair and grabbing my smokes back from him.

Ryan then gives me the look not to push him any further or else I will see the backside of his hand. "What the hell has you so upset that you are freaking out, drinking and smoking?"

"That stupid ex-girlfriend of yours. She sent me a threatening letter, and it makes me wish I were still in Mexico. Then Renée wouldn't be able to hurt me or bother me anymore."

This only enrages him more, where he grabs me by the arms and throws me over his shoulder and on to the couch. Hovering over me, he raises his voice and demands to know where the letter is. I tell him that I have to get up 'cause I put it in the filing cabinet.

"I'll get it, you don't move or smoke." Shortly he comes back with the letter, reads it, and then rips it up. "She is in jail, there is nothing she can do. Where is the strong determined woman I married and fell in love with?" Pulling me up from the couch he then takes me in his arms and kisses me. I kiss him back but am still mad and hurt by Ryan's reaction. He picks me up and carries me to our bedroom to make love, thinking that is the best medicine for my stress.

In the last few weeks before the wedding, I'm busy with music videos, spending up to 16 hours a day at the studio, and two hours at the restaurant. I continue bugging Ryan to move to Vancouver, but this only makes him madder.

While I was working in my office at the restaurant, Ryan comes in with a jewellery box. "Open it! It's an early wedding gift." Not sure what to expect, I open the box and see a key. I look up to him and give him a confused smile, only to have him come around my desk, step behind me, and blind fold me.

"Ryan what are you doing? I have work to do. I don't understand. What is the key for, I have a car." I got up and was led out of the building toward a car only. We start driving, and I have no clue where we're going, but I wait patiently for my surprise. We stop, and Ryan gets out to run around the car and help me out. He leads me through a fence and into a door.

Once inside he takes the blindfold off and I adjust to my surroundings. I see we're in a house, and it is decorated. It's beautiful with its traditional furniture and bold colors. After touring the four-bedroom house with a large living room, recreation room, and huge kitchen, I finally ask, "Is this ours?"

"Yes, I bought it, and my sister helped me along with your mom to decorate it for you. Do you like it? It also has state-of-the-art security system so you don't have to worry. A large backyard for Elijah and close to schools and work." I kiss him and hug him; granted it's not Vancouver, but I really do love it.

Looking around the furnishings again I could see where my mother's influence and tastes were put. Granted that Ryan had his sister help pick out the furniture, the place did look pretty good. With a few minor changes and some landscaping I could possibly fall in love with the place.

I seeing the backyard was fenced, maybe that meant we might be able to get a dog. The house was in a good neighborhood with other fancy houses, near the golf course, and true it was six blocks from the restaurant. I knew there was a elementary school nearby.

I still had this dread in my gut, that Runée was serious about her threat. I suppose I could live here a few years and still encourage Ryan to move to Vancouver. As much as this place was nice and in a good location, I just wanted to start my life in a securer community, with my ocean to view.

After moving into the new house and settling. A few days later I am surprised by my mom and brother who brought Montana along with them. I get them settled into their rooms and took them around the city. I show Matt the, studio and he is impressed. I have a band to work with so Matt helps with the choreographing.

Being that the wedding is in a few days, my mom and brother have come down not only to help with the house but with the final wedding details. As well as watch Elijah while were on our honeymoon in Paris.

As the day of the wedding approached, I felt very nervous since I left all the planning to Ryan's sister being that I was so busy with the restaurant, the music videos, and the move to our first house. The hair stylist arrived at the house and did my hair in a French twist with crystals clipped on throughout.

I go to put my wedding dress on, just as lovely as the first day I saw it when my mother and I had gone dress shopping at one of the most prestigious wedding shops in Vancouver. It was tight fitting around the chest with crystals, the long skirt of silk and elegant lace starting at the chest ribbon. It had a three-foot-long train of silk and embedded rhinestones.

My bouquet was of crimson red roses and baby's breath. There was lace in the bouquet with crystals and glitter spayed to make the flowers more magical. I looked at my wedding band, this ring of white and yellow gold, woven so beautifully together yet antiquelike.

How are we supposed to do the ring exchange if I couldn't get this ring off my hand? Granted the engagement ring Ryan gave me was beautiful, but it didn't exactly match my wedding ring due to its old-fashioned style. But they still complemented each other. Giving up on trying once again to remove the cursed ring, I go to the mirror to make sure I look perfect.

Hillary walks in looking beautiful in her baby yellow elegant long evening dress. Her hair is perfect, pulled up at the front and crystals throughout it as well as mine. "Don't stress, Daisy, you look beautiful. Any second thoughts?" She comes up to me laughing.

"Ha ha, very funny. Like I have much choice. But honestly I do love Ryan and do want to marry him. I just can't get this ring off." I show her my first wedding band.

My brother then knocks at the door to ask if we are ready. He's dressed in a black and white tuxedo with light silver pin strips running vertical. His hair slicked back and napkin in his breast pocket matching the pinstripes with a red rose boutonnière on the other side of the tuxedo. Being that a bride can never really feel ready, we agree. I ask Hillary to step outside so that I can have a moment alone with Matt.

"Matt, I really appreciate you walking me down the isle." Tears start to well up in my eyes and I continue, "Granted, it would be nice if Dad were here. Oh god how I miss him." I manage to get out before all my tears fall. Matt comes to my rescue and holds me while I cry.

When I married Mark I didn't think much about my dad, because my family wasn't there. And when I married Ryan the first time, well I never thought of anyone since I was in shock and numb to the pain.

"Don't cry, you'll ruin your makeup." He takes his napkin out from his breast pocket and helps to dab away any messed makeup. "Dad is here, we just can't see him. But I bet he's thinking how beautiful you are and proud of you he is." After hugging me he says, "Anyway we have a little boy who is so excited to see his mommy and daddy marry. So come on, sis, let's not keep the guests waiting."

My mother walks down the isle first with Elijah. Then Hillary walks down and steps aside to wait for me to join her. The music starts up, Matt and I stand at the beginning of the isle. There are candles and flowers along the pews, everyone stands up but all I see is Ryan, looking gorgeous. Just like my brother he is dressed in the same tuxedo, with his hair nicely brush and face clean shaven.

I smile, and both Matt and I walk down the isle. Once at the stage, the minister asks who gives the bride away, and my brother says, "I do."

I smile weakly and a tear falls. I am happy to have my brother give me away this time, unlike my wedding to Mark where I hadn't invited anyone in my family. Nor had he met any of them. Yet I still pine for my father to be doing it. Looking at me, Matt he kisses my cheek and wipes the tear away with his thumb. Turning to Ryan makes my eyes light up like the stars; I can't believe we are having a proper wedding.

* * *

Seeing Daisy as she walked up the isle with Matt was breathtaking. I could not imagine marrying anyone more beautiful. It was disappointing that my family wouldn't come to my marriage. They just didn't understand that the Arabic ways weren't the ways in this country, and that you were free to make your own decisions.

The minister said all the words he was supposed to say, but I didn't hear a word of it. Just to love her and be true to her. All I could think about was how Daisy was getting the wedding of her dreams to match with the perfect life I was going to provide her and our son.

With the final kiss sealing the vows, I grabbed her hand and we walked down the isle. Then later drove around the city for a while, with both Hillary and Matt in the limo; it didn't stop me from kissing my wife. I was like a little boy who had gotten the world.

* * *

Once we got to the banquet, Sherri had shown me how good of a decision it was to let her plan my wedding. I couldn't have done a better job. Along with the red rose and crystal theme, she had added swan ice sculptures, white twinkle lights, and candles on the tables. The meal was excellent and the wedding cake delicious. In the end we had so much fun, the dancing being the highlight and the night lasting till 3:00 a.m.

The honeymoon was so relaxing but at first we spent the first two days in our suite making endless love. Fearing Ryan was on a mission, I was finally able to get out of the room to do shopping and sightseeing. Spending as much time on the white sandy beach, I was so glad we had decided to go to Pairs.

After getting back from our vacation, I spend a bit more time with Matt and Montana, showing them my favorite clubs and having them help me with a music video I was contracted to do. Matt tells me how much he really is starting to fall in love with Montana, and thinks one day she would make a good wife.

A couple of months after the wedding and my family back home, I am starting to feel restless. All I do is go to the restaurant, work on music videos, and take care of Elijah and Ryan. Not that I mind doing it; I just feel like I haven't been able to enjoy time to myself. Sitting on the patio and looking out to the yard where Elijah is playing, I pick up the phone and call Hillary.

"Hey, what you doing?" I ask her while lighting a smoke.

"Nothing, just cleaning the house," she tells me with the music blaring in the background.

"Good, because were going out tonight. I'll pick you up at 9:00 p.m. Were going out all night." I finish the conversation off with a puff of my smoke.

After eating and getting Elijah ready for bed, I head to my room to get ready to go out. Since Ryan is working late, I have called his sister to come over and watch Elijah. As I am getting ready to go clubbing, Ryan sneaks up behind me, wraps his arms around me, and kisses me.

"What are you doing, Daisy?"

After putting the last earring in I said, "Me and Hillary are going clubbing. Girls night out." I give myself a once over, seeing in the full-length mirror Ryan coming up behind me.

Looking me sternly in the eyes through the mirror, he said, "No, your not. The clubbing days are over."

"Well just because I am a mom and wife, doesn't mean I can't go out and have some fun. Because you see that is all I do: work, take care of you and Elijah. So therefore I have no personal life. So whether you like it or not, I am going out." With that said I gave him a smile through the mirror and turn to head out of our room to the living room before picking up Hillary.

As I am leaving our room, Ryan grabs my wrist aggressively. "I see. Well you two will not be dancing with any men. Just each other, 'cause I will find out. And if I hear that you dance with another man, there will be hell to pay, and your clubbing days will be completely over." Then he pulls me into a passionate kiss so I don't fear from his anger.

Hillary and I head to a lounge to have a few drinks before heading out to the Rockhouse. Once at the club we grab some beers and hit the dance floor. Having a blast while dancing, I bump into a girl on the dance floor. Turning around to say sorry, I see that it is Mandy, Runée's best friend.

"You bitch! You ruined my friend's life. So what you and Ryan are over? Or are you cheating on him like your last husband? Because of you Daisy, Runée still has five more years left in prison and will never have the life she dreamed."

Hillary stops and joins my side, telling me to just leave. I look at Mandy with annoyance and turn to leave. I will not have this bitch ruin my night. Then I feel pressure on my right arm. Looking toward my arm, I see that Mandy isn't going to let me walk away from her.

Turning back around to confront Mandy, I receive a right fist to the left of my jaw. Shocked that she hit me, I pull my arm out of her grasp and punch back. One thing leads to another and we are both throwing punches.

The fight doesn't last too long; the bouncers are on us like glue. After we are pulled apart, I tell the bouncer that Mandy started it. Because Hillary is witness to the fight, she confirms my accusation. Mandy is thrown out of the club, and I am given a warning.

I furiously head to the washroom to tidy up. Looking at myself in the mirror, I see a swollen left cheek and eye as well as a cut on my face. "Why the hell did she have to come out tonight as well?" I said grabbing the paper towel Hillary got for me.

"I don't know why she had to get into a fight with you. Whatever the situation is, it is because of Runée." Hillary said, while helping me clean my face.

"Dame it! I hate them all. I wish Ryan had never met Runée. She is psychotic, and so are her friends! All I wanted to do was go out and have a good time. Forget about my life and enjoy being free." I yell while punching the washroom mirror. This frightens some of the other girls and shortly a bouncer comes into the washroom to see what all the fuss is about.

Hillary shakes her head and goes to get more paper towel for my newly cut hand. After wrapping the paper towel around my right hand, the club manager Bob walks in to see what the damage is. "Mrs. Gaston, this is totally unexpected from you."

"I know, I am so sorry, I will pay for the damages. I just got so mad at the whole fight that happened out on the dance floor." I put pressure on my hand to stop my knuckles from bleeding.

"Don't worry about it, Daisy. But if you don't mind I would like to talk to you privately and I have someone on staff that can look at your hand." Bob then left for his office.

After getting my hand looked at, I go see what Bob wanted to talk to me about. I join Hillary back on the dance floor after my meeting with Bob. "What did Bob want?" She asks.

"He had wanted to talk to me earlier this evening about a band one of his friends have. It seams they wanted my help in making a music video and weren't sure how to get in touch with me. Since I damaged the washroom, I cut them a deal." I look around the club, noticing it becoming very crowded, and I'm no longer in the mood to dance. I say, "We should go."

As we were crossing the road heading to my car, a car speeds up and tries to hit us. Hillary and I get out of the way quickly but stop to see who it was that was trying to kill us. The driver of the car stops and gets out of the car. It is Mandy. She must have been waiting for us to leave the bar. She walks up to me and tries to start up the fight she started in the bar. But I deck her with my right fist.

"Maybe you should get your hand checked out," Hillary offers while we are getting into the car as I'm moaning in pain.

"No. Granted it hurts, I just want to go somewhere to calm down." I drive us to a classy expensive lounge; this way no one who can't afford to be here won't be here. Like Mandy or any one else that might cause more stress.

Hillary and I talk about Runée, her loser friend Mandy. We also talk about the restaurant and the possibility to opening up another restaurant. "So how about coming home with me tonight? Seeing my hand is one thing, but I won't be able to hide my face. And I know I'm going to need support with Ryan, he's going to loose it."

I see that Sherri's car is gone, so I get very nervous that Ryan is home and I wont be able to put make up on to cover my face or get to bed before being seen. Asking Hillary to distract Ryan while I run up to the bathroom, maybe I'll be able to get cleaned up a bit.

I get rid of my coat and as I am heading upstairs. "So where did you two go?" Ryan asks.

"We went to a couple of lounges and the Rockhouse," Hillary tells Ryan while she joins him on the couch.

"Honey, aren't you going to join us in the living room?" Ryan asks me.

"I just have to use the washroom and want to check on Elijah. I'll join you guys in a minute." Feeling that I might be getting away with murder for tonight, I relax my shoulders and head up the stairs. In our bedroom, I take off some clothes, my boots but all in the dark.

The pain in my hand hurts a lot now. I'll have to play sick tomorrow, and then once Ryan goes to work, I can go to get my hand checked out. As I head for the washroom in our room, the bedroom light turns on.

My heart drops. Ryan comes up behind me and grabs my right wrist. Then he hugs me from behind and tells me how much he missed me. Ryan turns me around clockwise so he can hug me face on.

I turn my face away so that he can't see my left side. Ryan looks at me intensely trying to figure out what's going on. I see Hillary standing in my bedroom doorway just waiting for the trouble that's soon to come.

As if on cue Ryan takes his hand and turns my face so that I'm looking at him face on. I try to put up a fight, but that makes him turn my face harder. The look on his face goes from shock, to sympathy, and lastly to anger. "What happened?"

Hillary steps into the room, "Well when we were dancing, Daisy bumped into Mandy. One of Runée's friends, and they got into a fight."

I try to walk to Hillary's side for defense. But Ryan grabs my left wrist to stop me from leaving him. Then turning me to face him once again, he goes to grab my right wrist, so I'm trapped. "Is this true? You figured that since you haven't been out for a while, it would be fun to beat up another girl?"

71

Cringing in pain, "No, I never started it. I tried to walk away but she pulled me back and hit me first. Then we got into a fight."

Seeing my face and the look of pain on it. Ryan looks down to my hands and sees my right one bandaged. "And is this another fight wound?" he asks, taking my hand into his and looking over it. "Have you been to the hospital to have this checked out?"

"Not at first! I punched the mirror in the washroom. The medic at the club looked it over and cleaned it up. I'm fine." I pull my hands away from him and stepping over to Hillary.

"No it's not fine. Your hand is still bleeding, there probably is glass still left in there." Ryan walks up to me and pulls me with him out the bedroom and down the stairs. "Hillary, since you are part of this mess. Would you mind watching Elijah while Daisy and I go to the hospital? And what do you mean not at first?"

"Not a problem," Hillary says with a shaky voice. "By the way, Daisy, defended us when Mandy tried to hit us with her car then tried to fight your wife again." Hillary said in my defense.

Looking at Ryan, now wasn't the time to answer his last question. "Yah," I said as I was being aggressively dragged out of my house and forced into the car with him.

At the hospital the doctors remove the last few pieces of mirror out of my knuckles. The car ride home was quiet, which was fine with me. All night I wasn't feeling well, and now I really felt sick and just wanted to sleep. Ryan took this opportunity to accuse me of drinking too much and acting like I did with Mark. For this, there was no way he was going to allow me to go clubbing again.

"Its not like I go out and look for fights. You can't boss me around, were in Canada not Lebanon. I haven't been feeling well tonight, so I didn't drink that much. And don't accuse me of behaving like I did with Mark!" I yelled at him as I went into the washroom to get changed.

My stomach hurt so much; maybe I had had too much to drink. Probably getting into the fight didn't help my body. I stand there in front of the mirror looking at my bruised face. One minute I loved my husband, and then in the next I hated him. I just wish sometimes he were more accepting and not so controlling. If I ever told Matthew how it really was, Matt would not be happy with Ryan and would kick his ass.

CHAPTER 6

In February we go on another vacation in Spain once my face and hand healed, spending our time on the beaches. In shopping malls, museums, and attending the city's functions. But after our fourth day being away from Elijah, Sherri calls us to let us know that Elijah is being really fussy and won't eat or sleep. I decide that we should go home since I still am having sharp pains in my stomach, and my son misses me so much. Ryan solves our problem by having Elijah flown to us.

The rest of our vacation goes well. Ryan suggests I go to the doctors to see if I got food poising. But once Elijah arrives, my stomach doesn't hurt any more, so figuring it was anxiety, we enjoy our family time.

Once back home, Ryan and I work on the renovations at the restaurant. I work on another music video, which requires much of my time. I receive more letters from Runée, but deciding not to have them ruin my day, I throw them in my bottom desk drawer to read for another day.

I receive a call from the actor's society in Vancouver to come make an appearance on a talk show. Packing up Elijah, I head to Vancouver to attend the talk show while Ryan stays home to deal with the restaurant renovations.

The weather in Vancouver is terribly rainy for March, making it no fun for Elijah to play outside with Grandma. I attend the talk show, which goes smoothly, and at the end of the talk show one of the producers want to know if I have time to read lines for a play.

While I'm reading lines for the play I start feeling ill again. After my reading and as I'm about to leave, the people directing the play tell me they like the way I read, asking me if I would perform for them and help with the dancing.

Agreeing to help and perform without talking to Ryan first, I head back to Mom's to get some tender loving care. This flu I have is getting on my nerves, and I don't want Elijah to get it. Deciding to get my call to Ryan over with, I head to my room.

"Why is it your not coming home again?" Ryan demands to know after I have told him that I'm going to help with a play as well as perform in it. The fact that I didn't feel well slipped my mind.

"Look, after the Interview, I was asked to read for a play. Then the producer asked for some dance help and for me to perform." I tell him in between sneezes.

"Yah, well plays can last a year. I'm tired of you never being at home where you belong," Ryan snaps at me.

"They are taping the play, and I'm only needed for two weeks. I'm sick, and I don't want to travel while being sick. You'll be fine without me for a couple weeks."

"Fine! Since I don't have much say. After these two weeks both you and Elijah will be on the next plane home, sick or not." He grunts at me and takes a big pause before saying, "But this trip to Vancouver is not one so that you can party with your brother!"

With that all said, I perform in the play as well as direct the musical dance parts in the play. By the end of the two weeks, I'm feeling much better. Must have had a touch of the stomach flu, but I'm fine to fly back. Giving my mom a hug good-bye and telling her to pass my love onto Matt, since he is on a job, Elijah and I head home.

Dropping by the old apartment to see how the tenants are doing, I receive more mail addressed to me from Runée. I go to the grocery store only to bump into Mark's mom.

"Hi," I say as I bump carts into Marks mom, dreading the anger she is probably feeling toward me. "How is the family?"

"We're good. How about you?" his mom asks me.

"I'm good, just got back from visiting my mom and doing a talk show." I tell her and then ask, "So how is Mark?"

"He's good. Living in Edmonton as a cop now. He's been dating a teacher there too. They seem to be really happy," Marks mom tells me proudly.

"Well I'm glad to hear that everyone is doing well, and that Mark has moved on and is happy. I am really sorry with how thing happened. You have to know it was never meant to be. I didn't intentionally . . . ," I say with compassion.

"I understand! Granted at first we were all hurt, but then we found out what had happened. We've all moved on and hope that you are happy," his mom says with a friendly smile.

"At first I didn't have a choice in the direction of my life, but now I am happy and things are going well. I want you to know that I miss you. Is it possible if I could get Mark's number? I want to call and make things better," I ask my former mother-in-law.

After getting his number we hug, and I head home to relax. Since my stomach is still hurting and I'm throwing up at odd times, I head for the couch so that I don't wake Ryan. Still not getting any sleep or comfort and remembering the letters, I go retrieve them out of my purse.

One letter reads,

Dear Daisy,

I am thankful to you. If you hadn't come along. I wouldn't be spending my life in prison. With all these women who are just as crazy as you. I want you to know that when I get out I will reclaim what is mine.

Another letter reads,

So I thought I should fill you in on how I spend my time. Cleaning, doing crafts, educating myself. But everyday I think about how you ruined my life and took my man away from me. Just because you got yourself pregnant was cynical and selfish. I have made some friends here and they agree that you were in the wrong. So be warned that when we get out, we will make your life as unpleasant as ours is.

The last letter reads,

Today would have been my wedding to Ryan. I would have worn a long pink bridal gown with a five-foot train. My mom would have been so proud of me; I would be able to give her the grandchildren she so deserved. I want you to know Daisy that when I get out of prison. I will not only have Ryan back, but you will be in jail for attempting murder of me and I will be raising your precious son that started this. He won't have it as well as he does with you. Cause I will blame him for the rest of his life for the ruin of my life. So I will serve the rest of my time in jail, but if I were you I'd hold on to my child and enjoy every moment with Ryan. Because they will be your last.

Feeling a mixed amount of emotions, I grab a bottle of wine out of the wine cabinet and head for my studio to think. Once at the wear house I light up a smoke and pour a large glass of wine. All I can think of is how I want to kill her. Why I let her get under my skin I'll never know.

Putting the music on, I drink some wine while slowly dancing and crying, but the music turns more upbeat, and I dance more vigorously. Crying, angry, and in pain, I just dance to try and make the pain go away but end up hurling myself violently. Sitting down at the edge of the stage I cry and hold my stomach.

* * *

Waking up with Daisy not beside me in bed, I head down stairs to see what she is up to. But I don't find her, and fearing she's gone to do something stupid, I grab Elijah. She hasn't been herself since she got back from Vancouver, and she's been so sick. Heading to the studio in hopes that she is working on a video, my fears fade when I see her car parked outside.

Placing a sleepy child in his playpen, I go stand by a wall and watch Daisy. The music is blaring, a few lights are lit, and she is dancing on the stage. I watch her as she throws up and then sits down. She seems to be crying while smoking and drinking something. Not willing to let this go on any longer I walk over to her. Daisy is clearly surprised I'm here.

I grab the smoke out of her hand for I hate it when she smokes. I also remove the wine from her other hand and pull her into my arms. I let her cry a bit before asking her what's wrong only to have her pull away from me to throw up again.

* * *

After throwing up and having Ryan help me clean up, I address his question. "I keep receiving letters from Runée, and I am tired of being threatened. I'm very stressed with work and being sick all the time. I don't need her or her friends to harass me. Why couldn't we move to Vancouver where she wouldn't be able to find me! If I wasn't so sick, I'd go kill her!"

"Your not going to kill her, just ignore her. Smoking and drinking isn't going to help you get better from the flu. Were going home!" Ryan demands as he helps me to my feet and into the car.

Once at home and Elijah is back in bed, I pass out in our bed, only to wake up with a violent fever. Ryan comes in to check on me before heading to the restaurant.

But noticing I have an extremely high temperature and am delusional, Ryan has his sister come over to watch the baby while he takes me to the doctor. Once the doctor looks me over, he tells us to go directly to the hospital to have some tests run.

At the hospital the nurses take blood, my vitals, and hook me up to an IV. Within two hours a doctor comes into my room, having received the test results. He has me taken to have an ultrasound done; it seems I am pregnant but might be loosing the baby.

Still delusional and incoherent, I'm not able to understand everything that's being said to me. The next day I wake up with a lower temperature and less stomach pains. Trying to remember all that happened yesterday, I only remember the doctor saying that I'm pregnant and might loose the baby. Not knowing whether I lost my baby, I start panicking, which brings the nurses in to get me to clam down. They tell me to relax, or I will cause harm to the baby.

Later in the day the doctor comes to see me. He lets me know that I am three months pregnant, and the baby was having a reaction to the wine. Also getting the flu didn't help my baby, so I needed to get more fluids into my body. The doctor warned me that I was going to have to cut back on work and relax more. This pregnancy had a bad start, and if not careful, I would loose the baby at anytime. It was going to be a high-risk pregnancy, so no stress or else I would be spending my pregnancy in the hospital.

When I was fully recuperated and back to normal, the doctor let me leave the hospital. And Ryan wasn't going to let me leave the hospital unless I was fit to leave. As we are exiting the hospital, Ryan and I bump into Runée's sister Lilly. She glares at me and tells Ryan he made a big mistake. Ryan takes my arm leading me out of the hospital before Lilly causes me stress or I beat her up.

After a week of straight bed rest as ordered by Dr. Ryan, I was finally able to go to the studio now that my cramps had subsided and I felt well. Working on the video for the Rock House manager Bob's friends. Ryan drops by for a visit, and I feel it's a good time to tell him of an idea I have.

Eating with him on the edge of the stage, I tell him, "Baby, I was thinking in order for me to totally heal, I need to go and see Runée in person, or else she will always be able to hurt me. So if I go, then Runée will know I no longer fear her."

"Absolutely not! You are pregnant and at high risk. I forbid it, and you will not bring up her name again." He finishes his sandwich and gets up to leave.

"Yah, I would do it carefully so as not to hurt the baby. I need to get her out of my mind." I try to finish but am interrupted by his anger.

"Daisy, I said no! And not to mention her or the subject again!" Ryan then pulls me to him and kisses my forehead.

As if his threats were going to stop me. I had already made up my mind and felt he needed to know what I was about to do. It bothered me that he always felt he could treat me like a child. I was a grown woman with secrets he didn't know about, and if only knew about it, Ryan would go nuts and feel inferior.

A few days later, as planned, I leave a letter in the office for Ryan and fly out to Runée's prison. Once I get to the prison and directed to the visitors' area, I await for the surprised Runée.

She sits down with a look of shock on her face, "Why, Daisy, what a surprise. What did I do to deserve this privilege?" Runée asks like a Cheshire cat.

"I figure it is about time I visited my dear friend. I mean you write me a letter every month almost. So what kind of friend would I be if I didn't visit you?" I glare at her with a sly smile.

"So you figured that you would come and have me personally tell you what's bothering me?" Runée says.

"Actually I came more to let you know that I'm done with your letters, and I want you to know that it's over. Ryan is my husband and you have to come to terms with the fact that it was never meant to be for you guys." I put my hands together, feeling not too bad. That went pretty good.

She looks at me with one eye and leans back in her chair before trying to put me in my place. "Daisy, you remember that day when I went after you in my car. Well you see a week before that I had miscarried my child with Ryan. Just after he dumped me, I found out I was pregnant."

"When I told him about it, he called me a slut and said I was trying to trap him. He also denied that I was pregnant, so when I showed him the test results, Ryan said it wasn't his and that I was cheating on him. That was when I ran into you at the grocery store and I snapped because he accepted the child you two created by accident and married you." Runée was crying now.

"The fact that you were with someone first and he probably would have raised your child really made me pissed. Ryan didn't mistakenly get me pregnant. God wanted me to have his baby, but when I had heard you had gotten married to Ryan, that's when I started to loose the baby, and the accident topped it off!" she screamed at me through her tears.

I don't know why but I felt sorry for her and believed her. I started to feel some pain in my stomach but tried to hide it. "Wow, I never knew. Ryan has never mentioned it and I am truly sorry. At first I didn't want to marry Ryan, I was forced into it. But now I love him and I'm sorry you'll have to move on."

I got up to leave having said all I needed when she says, "If I were you I'd watch my son very closely. And congratulations on your pregnancy!"

Feeling the blood drain from my body from the shock that she knows and the intense pain, I leave immediately. I had to sit down in the lobby of the prison so that the pain in my stomach would subside. Pondering over the new information, I break down and cry. Why would Ryan deny a child when he clearly accepted ours? How cruel and heartless. I wouldn't be surprised if he deliberately wanted her to lose her child.

At the airport I call Ryan and let him know I'm on my way home. He freaks out at me and I tell him I'm not too happy with him. After hanging up on him and boarding the plane, I fall fast asleep.

Expecting to drive myself home, I'm shocked to see Ryan but not surprised at the same time. I had to pick up my car later because Ryan wanted to baby me since my pregnancy was high risk.

Once Elijah is in the car, Ryan starts in on me about how I could jeopardize our child, blaming me for being irresponsible and not wanting to be a mother.

That's where I snapped. Ryan was accusing me of being unfit and unworthy, when he's to talk. "You are so hypocritical, I found out your big secret!" I yell at him.

As Ryan goes to pull the car into our driveway, "What are you talking about? I have no secrets from you," he says.

"Ha, that's calling the kettle black. I know about your child Runée lost!" I yell at him. "I know how you ignored it and accused her of being a slut. But when you found out I had your child, we had to get married. We never were together intimately to have a child, but you and her were a couple. So if there was anyone you should have married, it should have been Runée. But you denied her!" Not wanting to hear from him I went into the house and locked my self in the office.

Ryan had brought Elijah in and had him settled. "If you don't unlock this door, I will break it down." With that said and my delayed reaction he started to slam into the door.

I finally opened the door, sending Ryan tumbling into the room. "I don't want to hear what you have to say. I was still married to Mark when she was pregnant. But why?"

Ryan sits down, "Fine! Yes, it's true, she came to me after we broke up and claimed she was pregnant. Even brought me a pregnancy test showing that she was pregnant, when I didn't believe her. Both Renaldo and Sherri told me that lots of girls would try to trap a guy by claiming they're pregnant. But she had proof, so being that we only slept together a few times and the fact that I used a condom meant the baby wasn't mine."

"Yet you give me an ultimatum, marry you or lose my child to you. When I just got divorced. And it only takes once to get pregnant. Look at us, mistakenly we slept together once, she was pregnant with your child while I was still married." Shaking my head I pace around the room,

"It was all a scam. When you found out the son I had was your biological child, you totally denied the child Runée was caring as your child." I couldn't believe it he had a child on the way and didn't care. But when he found out I had given birth to his son because of the DNA test that he had asked the doctor to be done that day. It was like the child Runée was carrying didn't matter.

Would he have suggested her to abort the child if she hadn't lost it? And if he had believed her? Yet she only lost it when we got into the accident even thou she thought she had lost it before then because of the blood loss she had after Ryan shunned her.

I remember him always telling me that if a girl he was involved with got pregnant, she would have to abort it. So maybe he couldn't go to the extremes to get her to terminate her pregnancy, therefore ignoring the proof and child that was rightfully his. But why then want the child I had? It was sickening, like a game. In the end 'cause he loved me and I had given birth to his baby after having to get a divorce, Did that mean he was free to marry me and claim our child?

So maybe I never had to marry him, and it was all a scam. If it was true that a woman getting pregnant would have to marry or die, then he should have married Runée 'cause she was single and pregnant with his child before he even found out that Elijah was his. I was married, and we thought the baby was Mark's until the DNA test was done. Thoughts were just flooding to mind. Who asked for the DNA test? Because if it had not been done, I'd still be married to Mark, and Runée wouldn't be in jail or have lost her baby.

Not wanting to be around Ryan I head out of the office to think, grabbing some water and making way for the den. "Don't follow me! I don't want to hear it. Just leave me alone."

The next day I'm having coffee, still not talking to Ryan. He comes up to me and hugs me. "I am sorry about what happened, but do know I love you." Still hugging me, he continues, "That is why I've decided to prevent more stress; we will sell the house and be moving to Vancouver so you can be closer to your family."

I hug him back. Granted I'm still made at him, confused, but now I was very happy about being close to my family. We have breakfast together to discuss all the details. Instead of selling the house, we'll rent it out like the apartment. At the restaurant we will promote Hillary to assistant manager if she will except. As for my music video clients, I will just buy a new warehouse studio. Excited, I go and call my mom to tell her the news.

It has been almost two years since that night Ryan and I had mistakenly slept together, changing our lives forever. So much has happened that I can't believe we've survived. I write a letter to Runée and put it in my desk to send it when I get back from Vancouver.

> Runée,
>
> First I want to say that I am sorry for all the pain that you have suffered. I have talked to Ryan about what happened. Although I haven't talked to him about how it makes me feel. But I want you to know that if I had known I would have found a way to help you. Whether by talking to him or what. I know I would not have married him. You see the only reason at first I married him was because I thought I had no choice, otherwise I'd lose my son. But now I see that because he loved me that it was a trick. He loved me so much he was afraid to lose me. Granted I do love Ryan and we are happy. We have been remarried and with that wedding I really did want to marry him. So I don't know what to say except, I am sorry for your lose and I don't think I could ever forgive Ryan for denying your child with him.

Before heading to Vancouver in May, Ryan and I work at the restaurant getting it ready for Hillary. I work on some dance moves with some new music, but not to crazy because I have put on some more weight and look more pregnant than I did when I was pregnant with Elijah. After writing the letter to Runée and having talked about her and Ryan, I was feeling much better.

We arrive in Vancouver and look at some property on the west side. There is one in particular that stands out to me; a white mansion with large Roman pillars, tennis court, and pool in the back yard. The land has been landscaped, with an eight-foot cast iron fencing around it and a beautiful gate at the entrance of the drive way. There is a three-car garage, a wraparound driveway in and out of the property with a large water fountain in the middle. Inside the mansion are six bedrooms, one set with an adjoining bathroom.

All bedrooms very large and modern. When you walk into the place, you walk into a large grand foyer that overlooks the sunken living room. A large executive kitchen is on your left. There is a den near the kitchen and a large dinning room. All the bedrooms are on the second floor, but underneath them is a theatre and the laundry room with an adjoining bathroom.

Loving the house, I don't look at any more. Ryan fears we can't afford it, but he doesn't know home much money I have. We spend a little time with Mom and for myself looking for a new studio. Debating on what furniture I want to take when we move, I go shopping for new furniture for the new house. After all the necessary things are taken care of in Vancouver we would head back to Lethbridge and take care of things there so that we could be moving to Vancouver.

Once back in Lethbridge, I can tell Ryan feels guilty about what he did, so as a way to apologize and keep my stress down, he's letting me have my way, and I'm enjoying it because I still haven't forgiven him for what he did to Runée. After we've packed all our possessions into the moving truck and Hillary is set with her new position, Elijah and I make the journey to Vancouver with Ryan following behind.

During my sixth-month check up, the doctor tells me that I am doing well and the baby is perfectly healthy. Since we have moved to Vancouver I have been asked to help with the play I preformed in earlier in the year. The house is decorated to my liking, and Elijah is enjoying spending time with his grandma. Ryan has been back and forth to Lethbridge to check up on the restaurant. But while we've been here, Ryan has worked at a restaurant in Vancouver as the manager.

Ryan has found time to watch me at my plays and notices how well my students and clients are doing. As I'm in the middle of my third trimester, we make a trip back to Lethbridge. I have business to do in the restaurant and will to check up on the property we have renting out. Elijah is at our old house with Sherri when Ryan and I are invited to attend a play by one my students I trained when we were living in Lethbridge.

After enjoying the play we attend the afterparty lunch and have a great time. But by late afternoon, I tell Ryan we need to go home. Something doesn't feel right.

"What is it, the baby? Are you starting to get pains again? I told you not to come with me on this business trip. This city is bad for you, it causes you too much stress," Ryan stresses to me as he helps me with my coat.

"No, it's not this town. I don't know what it is. But I have a feeling something's not right with Elijah," I reply as we hurry to the car. Ever since Elijah has been alive, we have had this strong connection. I have always known when he was going to get sick before the symptoms appeared. The connection I have with my son was strong. I remembering when I ran away to Mexico and was kidnapped when Ryan bought Elijah, and he wouldn't eat or sleep. We were deeply connected, which is odd that Ryan doesn't share the same connection after we both being felt the energy when I was pregnant with our son.

Getting back to my house, I arrived to what would be any mother's nightmare. There were police cruisers outside with their lights flashing. As Ryan was pulling up into the driveway, I opened the jeep door and jumped out of the moving vehicle. Running into my yard and house, with tears streaming down my face, I run into a police officer who catches me, seeing Sherri on the couch with an officer questioning her.

My vision goes blurry; I hear Sherrie, and all she is saying is, "I'm sorry, Daisy." Not comprehending what's going on, I run from the cop who is holding me to the backyard. Elijah has to be out there playing in his sand box. That's his favorite thing to do, "build mommy sand castles." I did not realize that I had collapsed on the deck crying.

I hear Ryan's voice faintly in the background, "Can some body please tell me what is going on? And where's my wife, she's pregnant and it's high risk."

Hillary comes to get me from the deck. I hadn't seen her when I came home. "What's going on? Where is Elijah?" I ask through my tears.

She is hugging me before responding, "He was kidnapped when Sherri was upstairs." I look up at her, not wanting to believe a word. But she just pulls me into another hug.

Coming back into the living room, I see Sherri. She is still crying. "Sherri, what happened? How is it Elijah was kidnapped?"

Sherri comes to me and hugs me. Then through her tears she goes to tell me what she has been telling the police. "We were playing in the backyard when I heard a loud noise in the house. I went in to check and see what it was. When I couldn't find what made the noise I went back into the yard, and Elijah wasn't where I left him. The back gate was opened, and there was a note left where Elijah was playing." With that revealed Sherri hugged me again.

Ryan is talking to Hillary in the corner quietly, and I can only speculate it has to do with me. There are some police collecting evidence while two are looking at a document, which I quickly go over and grab out of their hands. It is the letter that was left where my son was playing.

I hear one of the officers tell me to give it back because it is evidence, and they need to get it to the lab. The letter is directed to me, and goes to tell me that I will be suffering as they have been made to suffer. That my son is now their child, and I will never see him again. If I go and look for him, then he will die. I should just let him enjoy what life they will give him. He will not remember me any way. So I should just move on with the new child I am having.

The letter drops from my hands, the noise dies down, things go black, and Ryan screams, "Daisy!"

CHAPTER 7

I wake up hearing beeps, see wires on me, and the smell of hospital. Hillary is sleeping at my bedside. Looking around, I notice Ryan is nowhere in sight, thinking that maybe what happened was a bad dream, but then I wouldn't be in the hospital if it were a dream.

I start stressing out and try to remove all the things plugged into me. The nurses hear this and come into my room. Hillary wakes; they all try to comfort me. The doctor sees me only to tell me that I just about went into labor, but they stopped it. He warns me that I have to calm down or the nurses will be forced to give me something to calm down.

Managing to calm down, I am not sure whether I did dream this whole thing or if it's real. When I go to ask Hillary, she tells me that Elijah is fine, and I just had a bad spell. I remember going to a student's play and having a good time. Maybe Hillary's right, somebody put something into my drink at the afterparty lunch. Or maybe being in this town is bad for me, and I start tripping out about what Runée might do. But I had written her that nice letter, telling her that I forgave her.

A nurse comes in with a syringe; she tells me that I'm not calming down. How can I calm down when they wont let me see my son, who they tell me is perfectly fine? Once the nurse drugs me, she goes to tell me that I'm in a sterilized room to prevent infection and the baby getting sick. That is why Elijah isn't allowed to see me, but if I calm down and relax, then I will be able to go home as soon as the baby is out of danger.

Ryan comes to visit me, and I can see the black shadows under his eyes, his unshaven face, and weary body. I wonder what's causing him to look so drained. He goes to tell me that it is our health. I ask him when it will be all right for us to go back to Vancouver, since this town is causing me to panic. Ryan can only tell me that when the baby and I are out of danger, then we will be transported.

Being trapped in the hospital for a week and starting to feel well, I'm missing my son badly that I figure it can't hurt to use the public phone. When I'm in the hallway I overhear the nurses talking about a patient who is pregnant and has to be kept in the dark about her missing son so that she doesn't go into premature labour. Feeling my skin go white, I realize the nurses are talking about me. Grabbing what belongings I have in my hospital room, I make a break for it.

As I walk to my house in Lethbridge, I try to fathom the idea of Ryan and Hillary lying to me. Thinking back to what I heard the nurses saying, I hated that I'm pregnant and that my new baby is at risk. But it is also making me hate it because of the tight restrictions it is putting on my life. When I see my house, there is caution tape around it. Tears streaming down my face, I come to the reality that it wasn't a dream. The people I love were just trying to make it seem like a dream so I wouldn't stress. But what they didn't know or understand is that I needed to know the truth.

I go up to Elijah's room and hold a teddy while crying on the floor. I don't know how long I had been there, but I don't hear Ryan as he enters. "What are you doing here, you are suppose to be in the Hospital! You are putting our child at risk."

Looking up to him with rage, I get up holding my son's favorite teddy. "It seems all you care about is this child!" I point to my stomach. "But what about the son we have out there, with some kidnapper? Do you remember when you bought him from the Mexicans and he wouldn't eat or sleep? What do you think is happing while they have him," I smack him. "All I know is because you feel you need to protect me and our unborn baby, you might be killing our son that brought us together. And so help me god if he dies, then this marriage will be over!" And with that said I storm out of the house.

We stay at Ryan's sister's house since ours is a crime scene. After a few days of deliberating, I tell Ryan that I need to see Runée to find out where my son is. Of course Ryan forbids it and goes to tell me that she is not behind this. The police have already checked her. Being that Ryan doesn't realize my true powers and talents, I ignore what he has to say or what the police have to say for that matter.

While he's at the restaurant I leave to see Runée in jail. Talking with my brother on the flight makes me feel much better. Once at the prison, Runée is not surprised to see me.

"Why, Daisy, you look fabulous. What did I do to deserve this visit?" she goes to play me like her friend.

"Well seeing that you are doing well. What I have come for is the return of my son. It seems he's been taken, and you're behind it." I demand of her, not wanting to play games.

"Now why would I want your son? Being that I am in jail."

"Because Ryan deprived you of the child you too were to have. Because you hate me!" I yell at her.

"I received your letter, and I don't hate you anymore. But Ryan was under your spell, or else he wouldn't have done what he did."

"I had no part in what happened. It was his sick game, but Elijah is a child and innocent in all this. Please return my son," I beg of her.

"Both you and Ryan are unfit to be parents. Heck I'm surprised this hasn't caused you to loose the child you are carrying. I heard that you almost did, but yet you are here confronting me. Daisy you are stronger then I thought, but you will lose. Who ever has your boy will take better care of him then you could ever. As for the child you carry now, it didn't cause the death of mine, so I wouldn't worry about losing it, unless your inability to control your stress helps." With that said Runée gets up, bows with a grin on her face, and leaves me sitting on the other side of the table staring enraged at her.

I get up, and without thinking, go after her. I grab her by the collar of her shirt. "Where is my son you bitch?" I feel the familiar sharp pains in my abdomen. A guard comes to separate me from her.

As the guard pulls her away from my grasp, she yells, "Leave him alone, he will be fine. But if you keep it up, you'll lose the child you are carrying and therefore will understand the pain I have suffered here in jail." The guard pulls her out of the room but not before she can point to the floor and laugh.

Clutching my stomach, I look down at the floor and see blood. The pains get sharper, and I scream in pain. The guard calls to another guard to call 911.

I awake to Ryan's voice, in pain and hearing a whole bunch of commotion around me. I realize I'm in the hospital again, dreading that I have gone and done it, that I'm about to loose my baby. I hear the doctor and Ryan tell me to push. I push with every bit of strength I have left in my body.

Watching as I give my final push and a baby girl is pulled out, I see the nurse take the small baby away. Dreading that she's dead, the doctor tells an assistant that I'm haemorrhaging. Ryan kisses me and comforts me, but that's all I remember as I drift off into abyss.

I lie in my hospital bed for a while, sad that Runée has won. My son is missing and I have lost my second child. I feel empty and alone. Staring off into space, the doctor comes in to check my vital signs and make sure I'm healing.

"Doctor, what happened to my little girl? When did she die? Was it due to my blood loss?" I ask with little emotion.

The Doctor looks at me funny, then comes over to pat my hand. "Sweety, your daughter is fine, she weights six pounds and is perfectly healthy. In fact your husband is with her right now. You lost a lot of blood, so you had a blood transfusion and have been out for a few days. Some due to healing and the rest to the stress in your life."

"When can I see her?" I ask not believing that she didn't die. Hearing that she's healthy and we're both okay, I thanking my lucky stars. I try to make it out of the bed, but the doctor informs me he'd like it if I take it easy.

Ryan comes in to my room with our daughter in her little bassinet. He places her in my arms and kisses me. I can see he wants to yell at me for my actions but just lets it slide. "She looks just like you, Daisy. What do you want to name her?"

"You mean you haven't already named her?" I ask him surprised.

"After all you've been through, it was the least I could do," he says with some humour, knowing I was upset with him naming Elijah without my consent.

Not sure what to name her, I ask how he knew I was at the hospital in Toronto and when he got here.

"Well I got to my sister's after being at the restaurant realizing you weren't there. Guessing you were visiting Runée, I booked a flight to Toronto, and as I was leaving the phone rang. It was the hospital telling me you were here and might lose the baby if it wasn't delivered, and that you might die as well if they don't take the baby. I told them to do what they could, and I was on my way. I got to the hospital just as they were about to take her out. As you were coming to. I told you to push. They took the baby and then fixed you up right away," Ryan finished as a nurse was coming to collect my little girl.

As I held her, I noticed her tinny features and her fragile bones. The nurse took my little girl away in her bassinet, "Bye, Sonyia," I said to my little girl as that would be her name.

I ask Ryan if Elijah has been found, and he informs me that our son is still missing. I close my eyes and thought back to my meeting with Runée. She had mentioned that she knew I almost lost my child. With this information I was going to find my son. Ryan crawls into my little hospital bed. I look at his stressed face and let him fall asleep on my shoulders.

At least we didn't have to worry about me losing my baby. Now I would be able to go after the kidnappers, and I knew just who they were. Runée should have denied it, but maybe she was hoping what happened would. She was probably praying I'd lose my child. Obviously, thinking about what Ryan did to her and how much she said it hurt, she felt I deserved to walk in her shoes. What she didn't know what that I had resources and weapons unknown to both her and Ryan. Closing my eyes I joined Ryan in a peaceful sleep, for tomorrow the war was on, and I would win.

*   *   *

Daisy was still sleeping, and she was going to need all the sleep. Now that our daughter was born a little premature, both her and Sonyia wouldn't be allowed to leave. Knowing this was going to bother Daisy that she wasn't going to be able to search for our son, I felt it best to find out what was said that set her off, and finally put Runée out of our lives, whatever the means.

As the cab got closer to the prison, I couldn't help feeling of anxious, not only for what I was going to do, but after yesterday's events: getting a phone call for the hospital in Toronto to tell me my wife and child were in jeopardy, that I might lose one or the other, as well as the fact that I might have had to chose one.

If it wasn't for Daisy owning a privet jet, which I didn't know about. Thank god her pilot recognized me and saw that I was distressed because there was no flight leaving immediately. If it wasn't for him I might not have made it in time to make the decision. He had managed to tell me that she had hired him within the last year, about the time she became a big-time choreographer.

The stress of thinking about the fact that I just about lost my wife last night made my brow sweat, and I didn't hear the cab driver tell me we were outside the prison. Paying the cabby, I went inside and spoke with a guard in charge of visitors.

"My wife, Daisy Gaston, was here yesterday visiting Runée. Do you remember her?" I asked the guard as I signed registration.

"Yes, how is she doing?" the guard asks. "She gave us quite a scare."

"She and the baby are both fine. But I would like it if you would keep that to yourself." I mention with a harsher threatening tone. While looking at the sign-in sheet, I see that Runée hasn't had many guest, except for my wife and her sister Lilly.

I sit at the table in the visitors room, the same room Daisy was in yesterday and just about lost our second child. Waiting for Runée to come in, I finished viewing the tape of Daisy and Runée's meeting. Shaking my head, I couldn't forgive myself for my behaviour. What I did was wrong, and the fact that Daisy knows the truth and wont forgive me makes it hurt more. I should never have gone out with Runée; things would have turned out easier. I'm just lucky Daisy hadn't found out before we got married or else I don't know what would have happened.

"Oh baby you came to see me. I just knew that you wouldn't be able to stay away forever," Runée said happily as she came around the table to kiss me.

"Runée, enough with the pleasantries. Where is my son?" I demand from her as I squeeze her hand to get it off my shoulder.

She goes to sit down. "Oh he's fine. With some of our friends, can't wait to have Mommy and Daddy together."

I shaking my head at her delusion. "Runée, we are over. Have been for sometime. And my son is not your son."

Runée laughs at me. "Silly he's ours. Remember I told you that we were having a baby?"

I look across the table at this woman. She is acting so different from the conversation I had seen her have with Daisy. Runée is acting like we never broke up, and that Elijah is the son she was carrying. But she never found out the sex of the child she was carrying. Or did she? "Runée, stop with this act, I know this isn't you. I saw the tape of Daisy's visit."

She looks up to me strangely. "How is Daisy and Mark? Did they have more children?"

The blood boiling in my veins, I fly across the table to strangle her. I can't take this crazy woman and how she is trying to hurt my family. My vision goes blurry as I strangle her. I don't realize the guard hitting me to stop strangling her. As I'm being pulled out of the visitors room, I hear Runée yell at me how she loves me and to visit her soon.

When I get back to the hospital I check with the doctor on my wife and daughter. I also ask them if they are ready to be transported to another hospital, which the doctor thinks that they are. They'll just get doctors set up for Daisy and then arrange to have both mother and daughter flown out. Now to go see my lovely wife and ask her about the jet.

As I enter Daisy's room the phone was ringing. It was my sister calling to tell Daisy that she has some more music videos to work on. I get one of the numbers to call a client and tell them she isn't going to be working on any videos for a while. But all I'm able to get is the client's machine. Leaving a message, I head out to see how Sonyia's doing.

When I get back the artist calls my cell, removing myself from the hospital to talk. She asks why Daisy can't work on this music video. I fill her in on how our son is missing, how Daisy delivered our daughter early due to stress and needs to rest.

The artist gives me a contact number to a friend of hers who is in the FBI. She also gives her best wishes and tells me to tell Daisy that they still want her to work on the music video, so they will wait till Daisy is better and can work. I let the artist know that I'll be getting in touch with the secretary to have her inform some of the other bands that my wife is taking some much-needed time off. She agrees that Daisy needs some time to herself, and that the other bands shouldn't have a problem and will probably wait to finish their videos.

*　*　*

It has been a week. Most of my time in this hospital I have slept, taken care of my little girl, getting her strong. Every time I mention Elijah, Ryan distracts me from the topic. Ryan asks me at the end of the week if I feel like going home. I agree that going home would be good. I want to get looking for Elijah, and the sooner we get back to Lethbridge, then the sooner I can work on my case. But for some reason, whatever medicine they have me on is always making me drowsy.

The doctor feels that both Sonyia and I are well enough to fly home in my privet jet. As I settle in my seat, Ryan asks me how and why I have my own jet. I tell him that I don't want to talk about it. I'm just trying to buy my time till Ryan leaves me alone and I can find my son. The jet takes off while I drift off to sleep, and I wake up not in the Lethbridge airport.

"Where are we?" Groggily I ask while picking up Sonyia.

"I decided it would be better for you to come home to Vancouver," he says while helping us off the jet.

I try to fight him to get back on the jet while yelling at him, "We need to be in Lethbridge, that is where Elijah is. I have to find him, and you're not helping."

"No, you are going home with our daughter and taking care of her and yourself. You are still not well enough to tackle such a task, physically and mentally." Grabbing my arm he shoves me into a waiting limo.

While we drive to the house, Ryan informs me that work has been informed that I am taking time off. My mother also knows I will be home and awaiting her call.

Furious with Ryan, I ignore him the whole way home and feel trapped. My loving husband also lets me know how important it is for Sonyia and me to be safe.

Being in Vancouver will do that to us. I tell him that I disagree and that I don't want my mother's help. Ryan tells me that he's called to tell my mom I want to be alone, but I don't believe him when he looks away.

At the house I notice some boxes lying around that Elijah and I were using for a makeshift fortress. Seeing this brings tears to my eyes. I go up to the nursery not realizing that I hadn't put it together yet. But without thinking I walk into Elijah's room to put Sonyia in, and I collapse with my daughter in my arms while weeping.

Ryan brings what little we had from Toronto into the house and finds me in our son's room. He goes to lift me off the floor. "Get your hands off me. Take Sonyia! Find her somewhere to sleep. I need to be alone!" I yell at him with such rage.

He takes her, and I look around my little guy's room. I see his teddy bear he loves and sit down on his bed. I cry while hugging the little teddy. It's funny I can still smell Elijah on his bear.

Once I got myself under control, Ryan tells me that we can go shopping for our daughter's room, as well as buy some new furniture. He informs me that my mother knows not to come, and that he is going to pick up my prescription. While Ryan is out I grab a glass of wine and head to our room. Sonyia is in Elijah's playpen fast asleep, so taking a page out of Sonyias book, I down my wine and go to sleep, only to wake to my mother rocking my little girl the next morning.

"What are you doing here mom? I told Ryan that I didn't want any company." She smiles at me with knowing information.

"Ryan called me a couple days ago telling me all that's happened. Then he called me this morning, and I came over to keep you company."

"Why would I need company when Ryan is here? Does Matt know anything?" I ask her sceptically.

"Well that's the funny thing. Ryan left this morning to continue looking for your son. And your brother has been informed. He will be by shortly," Mom goes to tell me as all feeling leaves my body.

Very angry I get out of bed, shower, and pace about my house. Mom try's to get me to settle down. But I tell her that he shouldn't have left without me. My mom doesn't understand, but I know when my brother comes over he will understand.

All my brother suggests once he gets to my house is that we go clubbing and make music videos. I try to talk to him about a plan brewing in my mind. But he refuses to hear it, saying that there is a team working on the case. Finding out from my brother that a musician hooked Ryan up with a FBI agent makes me madder.

Annoyed that everyone seems to be keeping me in the dark and not asking for my help or input, I start pacing the room.

"Anyway sis, you look too ill to be fighting the good fight. Let your big bro help to get you better." And with that Matthew gives me the biggest hug.

So for the next few days, we go shopping for the baby. My mom and brother both spend the night at my house. I don't receive any calls from Ryan, which makes me nervous, but then I find out Ryan's talking to my mom or brother. What my family doesn't realize is at night I am grabbing a bottle of wine and locking myself in my room, to drink and cry myself to sleep. I know my son is getting sicker every day; I can feel that he's giving up and thinks I don't love him or am dead, being that he's so young.

Getting frustrated, having nothing to do at home, and not being allowed to search for my son, I go back to work making music videos. My mom visits and takes care of Sonyia. I work and work so much that I rarely come home, spending nights at the studio or with a client at a party. If I'm not working I'm clubbing with some of the musicians, but only the ones who are doing weed. I find that marijuana helps to relax me better than my wine or the pills the doctor had prescribed.

Ryan calls me from time to time, leaving messages informing me how the case is doing. How he went to visit Runée and she still wont budge but lets him know that our son is happy with her friends. Ryan tells me how they've questioned her friends and Elijah is not there.

With Ryan calling to keep me up to date, I just go out and get more high because the pain is too much for one to bare. I hate that he feels I am too weak to help in our son's case. The only reason he came after me in Mexico was because of his obsession with me.

Not knowing whether my mom told Ryan what I had been up to, he surprised me at home after being gone for a couple months. I'm sitting outside in the hot tub high and drinking wine. Ryan smacks the glass out of my hand and yells at me. I was in a state of "who cares?" Ryan grabs me out of the hot tub dragging me by my hair, back into the house to the living room.

"So wine's not enough. You have to get high!" He throws me to the couch and smacks me.

I hold my swelling face and look at him. "Well you see it's the only way to get through my miserable life. My husband is probably rekindling his old relationship while my son is forgetting who I am and possibly dying. And I am left in the dark to take care of a child I don't really want." I yell at him still in that "who cares?" attitude.

"You are suppose to be taking care of our daughter. But your mom is taking care of her while you take care of your needs," he shouts at me, then grabs my wrist and drags me to our room, throwing me on our bed.

"Stop hurting me! I hate you! I never had to marry you. You just tricked me because you were obsessed with me. This would never have happened. It's all your fault," I finish as I lose my voice, only to have my body tremble in frustration.

Ryan grabs me roughly, looks like he's going to hurt me, but then pulls me into him. And just pets my hair while he cries because his wife is a disgrace.

I don't remember much of the rest of the night, except that we manage to make love.

The next morning Ryan finishes playing with our daughter, telling me we need to talk. We sit down and talk. He demands I quit the pot or else I will lose our daughter and him. Ryan figures the case will be solved with his new plan.

The plan is for me to die, and he will go to Runée with this. Pretending that he has come back to her and wants to have the life she's always wanted.

I don't like the idea, but he won't listen to me, talking down to me and treating me less of a person. Ryan gets Mom to move into our house so that she can babysit me, make sure I behave and straighten out since he only came home for a quick trip to bring me back to reality.

I go for a walk on the pier to ponder. Matt follows me, thinking I might do something stupid. But I only sit on a bench and talk to myself. Ryan is treating me like a child, won't listen to me, comes home for his pleasure, then buggers off again. I don't even know what's going on with the restaurant since Hillary is also keeping quiet. My brother comes to sit down with me thinking I'm crazy for talking to myself when I clearly knew I was being followed.

"Have you truly lost it, Daisy?" Matt asks.

"No! I can't understand how the FBI would want my husband to pretend I'm dead to get information out of Runée." I shook my head. It didn't make sense.

"Yah. The FBI would never do that. Their a lot smarter, and I have looked into it. Their not involved in you're son's kidnapping," Matt goes to inform me.

I choke back my breath, widen my eyes. "What?"

Matt continues talking to me, but I don't hear him for I'm lost in my thoughts.

Fathoming the this news, I'm not sure if I want to hate my husband, kill him or go crazy. He lied to me, but why? What good is going to come out of this? My son has been missing for about three months and there has been no FBI involvement. Does he think he is qualified into finding missing children. Whatever happened to teamwork in a marriage? Without thinking I get up from the bench and walk to the car with my wheels turning.

Ryan comes home after being gone a week since his last visit, to check up on me and to let me know that his crazy plan is working. I laugh and drink more wine, he's not fooling me. Ryan looks at me oddly as Mom serves dinner and we start talking about Mexico. I don't know how we get on the topic, but when I mention how Ryan doesn't care about Elijah, I can see that I have threatened his pride because I can see it as he goes to chew his food. Feeling that he is superior to me due to my behaviour last time he saw me, Ryan goes to mention how he had to buy our son away from the Mexican trader. My mom goes into shock and demands to hear the whole story, with the parts I had left out to save her embarrassment.

Ryan says to her, "Well, Daisy, took off after Runée tried to kill her. She went to Mexico and got kidnapped. Then the black market only wanted her and not Elijah." As Ryan was telling the story I got dreadful looks from my mom. Not being able to handle the embarrassment and disappointment in her eyes, I get up from the table, grab the bottle of wine, and leave. I also don't want to look more like a stupid child in her eyes than Ryan has already made me to look.

In the kitchen I hear Ryan yell my name, but my mom tells him I'm a big girl and that she wants to hear this story. I head to the deck upstairs, sitting in a swinging chair sipping my wine and smoking my cigar.

Expecting my controlling husband to walk in, I am shocked that my mother has come to see me. Not wanting to hear what she has to say I look away. But she grabs my face so she can look into my eyes. Mom is crying, "I want you to know that I am disappointed in your behaviour for these last months as would your father be. Ryan told me the whole thing between you, Runée, and him, so I understand."

She kisses my forehead, sits down beside me on the swing, and grabs a sip of wine while putting her arm around me. "Look, I understand a lot of bad things have happened to you. And it seems like ever since you moved to Lethbridge you became weak and out of control. But, honey, I know you're strong, I don't know what Dad would say or do to help you get through this. I can see that your husband is controlling, tries hard to protect you." She pauses to catch her breath and take another sip of my win.

"But it isn't necessary, I know you aren't a weak person, and Ryan has made you dependent on him. Granted he means well, but before you left for Lethbridge your were strong minded, determined, and very smart. I remember a certain someone going against her mother's wishes once she turned seventeen—even after her father died—to become an FBI agent, something I hated when your father was, but then she quit and moved to Lethbridge after a few years of my nagging."

Listening to my mom, I couldn't help but smile. "Yah, you were pretty pissed. But it made me feel stronger and gave me revenge on daddy's enemies."

Mom laughed, "Yes well then Matt thought he needed to join the FBI in order to protect you." My mom paused before she added, "Look your dad is looking down on us all. And out of all of us he is most proud of you, but I don't think he'd like to see his little girl second best in her relationship when she needs to be equal or first. And don't get me started on your bad behaviour." And with that being said she patted my leg, kissed me, and left for bed. Mom never said much, but when she did, it always had strong impact, leaving me with a lot to think about.

Mom was right and wrong about one thing. When I moved to Lethbridge I still was strong and determined. I went to college and met my first husband. But my independence probably scared him and maybe I wanted him to have a little control. But once I met Ryan my better judgement left, I became weaker.

My father would have been ashamed of me to let a man control me and run my life. I laughed to myself. Dad would have had it out with both my husbands. Mark for being too weak and Ryan for being too aggressive.

Looking at the glass of wine in my hand, I could see that I was trying to solve all my problems with drinking and once with the pot I had given up. While my son was out there, I was letting Ryan be the hero when I could have found my son right away. Then smashing the glass of wine to the patio floor, I got up heading for my office.

Thinking back to the Mexico incident, sure things had gone the way they did. But if Ryan hadn't interfered, both Elijah and I would have gotten out of the place, and the men would have gone to jail for a long time because they were a case that was on file for a long time.

Maybe if Ryan hadn't interfered I wouldn't still be married to him. Heck if I didn't weaken I wouldn't have married Ryan and Runée's child wouldn't have died. But due to the rapid events in my life, I was no longer thinking clearly. I was drowning and couldn't seem to get back to the surface for air.

After being in my office, Ryan tries to see me, but I don't want to talk to him because I am disgusted of how he's treating me and what he's done to this family. I go to my sons' room and sleep there for the night.

I didn't hear Ryan get up or leave; I don't care because he is not going to have control over me anymore or wear the pants in the family. Later in the day I tell mom she can go back home, and that I'll be fine. But I also request that she take care of Sonyia for the last time.

She looks at me with pride on her face. "Sure thing, sweety. What do you have planned?"

I fill her in and then go get packed before heading out, as mom takes Sonyia to her house for the next couple days or weeks. Once packed I head over to my mothers to finalize the last few details so as not to cause a crimp in Ryan's plan.

"Mom because I was once FBI, I still have contacts and skills that will help me find my son, faster then Ryan." I tell her with conviction.

I quickly show Mom how it is that Ryan's little scheme won't get interrupted, and no one will know I'm in Lethbridge.

"Sweety, you look normal. How is it no one is going to recognize you?"

Looking at Mom, I smile as I remove the hat I'm wearing. Revealing no more long strawberry blonde hair. I show her my new look, my short black hair, and freckles on my face. "So?" I ask her.

Mom looks at me with wide eyes, "Wow! You're right, I hardly recognize you. But did you really have to cut off all your hair?"

"It was time for a change, a new beginning and I have decided that I need to get my life back in order. Become a stronger woman and get some respect from my husband or leave him," I told mom with integrity and pride.

The only one in on my plan was my mom. She had been informed to let Ryan know I was busy with work and taking no calls. Matt was also to believe this and be used as an excuse for Ryan calling. I give mom my privet cell number that only she will be able to call. I tell her that I should only be gone for a short time. Kissing both my daughter and my mom at the door before heading to my car, I hear my mom call out to me, "Take care, honey, make sure to use caution and if necessary wear protection, and I love you."

But as I pull up to the stop sign before turning onto the highway, Matt stops me, "Get out of the car."

Putting the car into park I get out to see what is up. I know he won't be able to see my hair because I am wearing the hat. "What's up, bro?"

"I know what your up to."

"I'm not up to anything. Just going shopping," I tell Matt with confidence.

"Yah I don't believe it because I too have the same connection as you. And well I saw that a little FBI bird is active again and no longer retired. I know I won't be able to stop you or help you since I have my own cases to work on. But I wanted you to have this." Matt hands me a gun, which is actually my gun that I left at the head office. "It has been reregistered in your name. Take care and be safe. You know if anything should arise, the team and I will have your back in a heartbeat." And with no lecture, just a brother's love, Matt hugged me tightly and got back into his car heading for my house.

Because Ryan has the jet with him, I decide to drive. With the long trip ahead of me. It gives me lots of time to go over every detail, and staying in hotels I can do my research on the laptop. With backup from the team, I was reinstated my passwords and accesses to anything I needed.

Once back in Lethbridge, I called up Hillary to have her meet Samantha for coffee a new girl I wanted to hire for the restaurant. Since I will be going as Sammy or Samantha with my new look. I watch her at my restaurant to see how things are going. Hillary seems to be handling herself well, but just then I see Ryan. He looks tired, I hear him ask Hillary if everything is going to be ready for the prime ministers party. She tells him everything is fine and that he should go get some sleep.

I sit at the coffee shop where my friend and I are to meet, pondering what Ryan is up too. Watching Hillary come into the shop looking for someone, I notice just how drained she looks. Hillary takes a seat, orders her drink, and waits. Getting up from my chair I go to join her. She looks up at me like she knows me but then asks, "Samantha?"

"Yes." Sitting down with my coffee, I figure that I will add to her stress. "Why is the prime minister having a banquet? Why are you so stressed? What is going on with Ryan? And why haven't you been the friend you need to be for me?"

Looking at the confusion on her face is funny as I started to laugh, but then she gets angry. "Who the hell do you think you are to ask me such personal questions? If you came here looking for a job, you can forget it. If I were you I would stay out of your future boss's life."

Hillary gets up and storms out of the coffee shop, but as she reaches the door she stops she turning around and walks back to the table and looks at me intensely. "Daisy? Is that you?"

I smile at her, "Had you going."

Hillary sits back down and then whispers to me, "Ryan said you were dead."

So it seemed Ryan hadn't included my best friend in his scheme by allowing her to think I was dead. I could see the pain and happiness on her face as she shed a few tears. I was not quite sure what Ryan was doing, and frankly, I was thinking it was becoming the end for us. "No, I'm not dead. But for some reason Ryan feels it will help him recover Elijah."

After wiping her tears away, she goes to say, "So then won't this ruin his plan. And what is going on?"

For once I agreed with her, "I don't know what's going on with him. But I do know what's going on with me. And if you didn't recognize me, then who else will?"

"Yah, but Ryan loves you, he'll know it's you," Hillary informs me as she sips her tea.

I laugh to myself, "Well you see I know about the banquet tomorrow. So therefore I have my ways. Plus Ryan did see me, just as you did."

Hillary thought back to today and smiled. "I vaguely remember seeing you at the restaurant. Oh, man. You look so different. Is it permanent?"

Laughing, "The cut yes, but the color I'll see how it sits with me. And the freckles, no, props."

"So then what do you want from me?" she asks

That's what I was hoping she'd ask. I tell her how she is to keep my appearance, whereabouts, and anything pertaining to myself a secret. I also ask that she look into what ever it is that is bothering Ryan and what he's been doing. Hillary agrees to keep everything I've asked of her as hush. We hug before I go to rent a hotel room at a lesser known hotel in town.

The next morning I get Hillary to allow me into the restaurant with out anyone seeing me, including Ryan. I make copies of the money in the safe, the paper work, the bills. Noticing that Ryan has been spending much time in Toronto as he said he would. I also notice he's neglecting the business, which shows in all the information I have gathered.

Going to my old house pretending to be FBI, I ask the people renting my house if I can look around for any evidence. Abiding, they allow me in. Visions of the day I found out Elijah was kidnapped four months ago come floating to mind. Blocking any reaction on my face I get straight to business. Looking around, I ask if anyone has gone outside into the yard or in the nursery.

The missus says no, so I head to those areas to gather evidence. I collect footprints, take photos, and notice some hair on the latch to the gate. I am surprised that there is still evidence to collect.

With all the evidence I do collect I head back to my hotel to process it all. Spending a good four hours going over any conversation I've had to anyone that could have lead me to any hints. I request Hillary's help in going to the hospital to collect a hair sample from Runées sister, Lilly,

She had said something the day I left the hospital to make me suspicious of her. I make a few calls and then courier the evidence via my jet, having my brother pick it up and analyze it. Only to wait for the results from him.

Since I have some time on my hands, I go to my restaurant to "secret shop." As I'm there my privet cell rings, it is Mom letting me know Ryan had called to check up on me. He seems to be content with her excuse. I find it funny that after he left from Vancouver it only took him five days before calling to check up on me. Once I saw all I need to see, I go to the hotel and call Hillary to request she take the day off and join me for some R & R.

We go to the malls in Calgary and do some major shopping, spending lots of my money. Afterward we attend a hockey game then hit a local Irish pub to celebrate the team's victory. While at the game Ryan calls my cell, and I had to take the call outside so that he doesn't hear the game.

"Why are you not answering the phone at home?" he demands to know.

"You know I have a life too. And that's what I have been doing. Isn't that what you wanted for me to forget about our son and get on with life?" I say harshly to him.

"Daisy, we are not getting into this again. Your mom tells me you've been busy at the studio. I just hope you haven't drifted back into your old ways 'cause it will make this all hard for me." Ryan tells me with strain in his voice.

Hearing the tiredness in his voice, I decide to push him. "Look, I'm busy at work and you are probably still trying to win Runée over or already have, and things are going swell."

"Look, things are running smoothly, she's coming along."

"Glad to hear it. Have to go." And with that I hang up on him, turn off my cell, preventing any tears from falling since I just saw him in Lethbridge. I know he's lied, and what exactly is going on now, I will find out later.

On the way back into town, I get a call from my sources telling me that the DNA from Runées sister Lilly is the same that I collected off the gate, but they don't have anything to match the other DNA to, but it is female, most likely it was a friend of Runée and Lilly's.

Hillary tells the chefs at the restaurant that there will be an important food critic in tonight and to cook like they never had before. The chefs were also told not to talk to Ryan about it since he had too much on his plate. As I am eating one of the plates brought to me, I see Ryan come into the restaurant looking dashing and frazzled.

My husband goes to talk to Hillary, telling her that he will be heading to Toronto. She asks him why he's all dressed up. Ryan responds by saying his family is throwing a party for him. Having some family friends over and girls. I try hard not to overhear the conversation, let alone look at how nicely dressed he is, while wondering what he's really up to.

Ryan does catch me looking at him, smiles, then looks more curiously at me. Hillary catches on and distracts him. I finish eating all the dishes I needed to sample;

my conclusion is that my chefs need to pick it up a notch. After writing all my notes down, I head for the door.

I have my hand on the door handle and am about to open the door when a man puts his hand on my hand to open the door. I let the man open the door while I hold my breath and try not to look at him. Once outside I look up to him, seeing Ryan. Smiling meekly at him, I briefly thank him and leave. While he was looking at me I feel his eyes penetrating me, trying to figure out if he knows me.

Once in my car I calm down, but then my regular cell rings, and it is Ryan. Hesitating for a moment before picking up, I calm my heart down and answer, "Hi, baby."

"What are you up to?" He asks

"Just was putting Sonyia down for a nap," I said as I check the time to make sure my excuse would work. "What's up?"

"Nothing. Just was thinking about you. I saw someone who reminded me of you, and how much I love you."

My body tensed, he almost recognized me. Realizing that I wouldn't be able to get much work down, I had to work quickly. Not only was he not trying to find our son, but was looking at other women. Maybe even having an affair on me, but then why call when you remember your wife? "Well that's good. How is Runée? Is she talking yet?"

"Well she believes you're dead and thinks were going to be married when she gets out of prison. And she says our son misses her but is thriving," Ryan mentions to me quietly.

I lean back into the seat of my car, close my eyes. Hearing that Elijah is doing well was good, but he was almost two years old; he could very easily forget me. With sadness of being away from my son, the tears started escaping and I manage to say, "Well I have to go." On that note I turned my phone off.

Once I collect myself and got back on track, I drove to Lilly's house. Noticing she's not home and most likely pulling night shift at the hospital, I break in and do some searching. I notice at the bottom of her closet a bag with black gloves and a shirt. Hoping these things will lead to my son, I photograph them and collect them. I rifle through her lingerie drawer and see at the back of the drawer a letter.

Opening the letter I can't help but notice it is a letter from her sister Runée.

Lilly,

You must do this for me. I know that Ryan is mad to lose his son, but in the end he will thank me. I know that his marriage isn't doing so well. Daisy's going off the deep end, and Ryan is been visiting me. No one will know, Ryan will want to protect Daisy from losing the baby and will move her from the house. Probably rent it out and all evidence will be gone. Please keep Elijah quiet, it will help everything. I'd be a better mom to that little boy.

Shocked with that letter, I photograph it and hook up my special fax to send it once I have put finger print dust on it. I then snoop through her night table and find a card from Runée.

> *Thanks sis,*
> *Everything couldn't have gone better, I love that Daisy killed herself because she lost her precious son. Well now both Ryan and Elijah will be mine when I get out of here. I owe you and Mandy big.*

Holding the card in my hand, I knelt down and cried. This proves that she and Mandy did take my son. So where was he because there was no evidence that he was living here? After spending thirty minutes collecting any possible evidence, I leave Lilly's place as if it was untouched. Sure she was involved, but if anyone knew where my son was, it was Mandy.

I sent the items to my colleagues via my privet jet. I told the pilot that my brother, Matthew, needed these document and evidence. Granted I was still going by a different name, but my pilot did as I requested. And it wasn't a complete lie that Matt was meeting the pilot to pick up the package.

Hillary and I were at a coffee shop talking about a guy she was interested in when my privet cell rang. It was Matt calling to confirm that they had run the DNA, the letters and the footprints to Mandy's criminal information. The evidence proved that Mandy was involved in the kidnapping, and Elijah was the kidnapped. There was skin and hair samples in the gloves I had found, and both belong to Lilly and Mandy.

I couldn't help my excitement; I had found out who had kidnapped my son. I jumped up for joy in the restaurant and cried happy tears. Being so excited my other cell phone rang and dropped to the floor opening, Hillary picked it up, and before she could talk to whoever was on the phone, I hugged her.

I was crying and hugging my best friend, and she asked what was so exciting. "I know who kidnapped my son. And I know he's alive because of the letters I've read and evidence I collected." I was so excited that I didn't care at that moment who heard me while hanging up my regular cell without talking to them, I did notice it was my secretary calling to probably book another client.

Hillary was so excited for me; we just hugged for a while. She wanted to know if we'd be telling Ryan. I told her that I wasn't going to until I found my son, and even then maybe I'd wait. Finishing up with coffee I decided I was going to get my son back from Mandy or whoever was watching him.

CHAPTER 8

Heading back to the hotel I gathered up all my FBI equipment I brought with me and checked out of my room. Then I went to the trailer park where Mandy was living and waited outside. I could see she was home and by the looks of her yard, she had children. Knocking on her door, a little girl answered, presumably her daughter. I stepped inside and could see on the walls pictures of Mandy, her boyfriend, and two children. She couldn't be hiding Elijah here but had to know where he was just from reading the thank-you card Runée had sent her sister. It meant that Mandy had more to do with the kidnapping than Lilly. And with Lilly having a successful career, it didn't surprise me.

Mandy came to greet me from the washroom, "Hello. Do I know you?" she asked with hesitation.

I smiled at her. *Oh we go way back,* I thought to myself. Since at one point she tried to kill me and Hillary with her car. But I said, "I'm Samantha, and I'm investigating the kidnapping of Elijah Gaston, and you are our number 1 suspect." Mandy's daughter walked back into the entrance while I saw Mandy's face go pale.

She then asked that we step outside, telling her daughter to go see what Daddy and Mike, her little, brother were doing. Once we got outside, Mandy was about to talk, but I was too quick for her. I hit her in the face, twisted her arm behind her back, and cuffed her arms. Trying to struggle free from me, I pulled my gun on her and told her to walk. Quieting down, she did as was instructed and walked to my car. I opened the door for her to get in. Once inside, I tied her feet, cuffed her to the dash, and got into the drivers seat.

Using my left hand to point the gun at her, I drove with my right hand. She was scared and yelling at me, but at the stop sign I hit her with my fist to shut her up. I started to drive north out of town. She was asking who I was, what I wanted, and if I was going to kill her.

"Mandy, we go way back you and I!" I yelled at her.

She stopped yelling to look at me, then said, "Daisy?"

"Yes! Where is my son? Where do you and Lilly have him hidden?" I threatened while waving my gun at her. "If you tell me everything, I may let you go without having to kill you. But right now you're looking at jail time. So who has my son? And you better talk." And on that note I cocked the gun.

I could see the stress, pain, and fear all in her face. "I thought you were dead?"

"No," I said with annoyance.

"Runée thought if we kidnapped Elijah that you would go nuts and kill yourself. So when Ryan came back into town declaring that you had killed yourself with a drug overdose, we thought our plan worked," Mandy said quietly

"Well Ryan was right on reading how psychotic Runée is. So where is my son?" I screamed as I continued to drive us farther north.

Mandy stuttered and leaned farther away from me when I screamed. "After we kidnapped him, I had to drive him to my sister's because we knew the cops would look at us as suspects. So when they came and saw that we weren't guilty, Runée was happy that her plan worked. And it was best to keep Elijah at my sisters."

"So he's alive? And if so, where does your sister live?" I asked while uncocking my gun.

"She lives in Edmonton. And he is alive, but probably not healthy."

That diverting my attention from my driving, and I looked at her with anger. "What do you mean not healthy?"

"My sister isn't the best person to take care of a child. She really didn't want to have to take care of Elijah, but I told her we'd pay her, and it wouldn't be for long," Mandy told me while making herself comfortable.

Turning the car in the direction we needed to go to get to Edmonton, I looked at her and said, "I hope you don't have to pee because it is going to be a long trip." After that we didn't talk, I didn't want to become more enraged than I already was. I just wanted to get to my son as fast as I could.

I was speeding when Mandy said, "You know if you speed, the cops will pull you over and then we won't get your son. And if we die, then you will never get to see him again." She made a good point, so I slowed down. "How is it you figured out we took your kid, and Ryan has been working on the case for months and hasn't figured it out?"

I didn't like that question, and I wasn't going to answer her right away. Thinking on the fact that it had taken me less than a week and Ryan was still working on the case not only made me mad but guilty. I had become weak and a negligent mother. Here my son was kidnapped, and I could have found him if I had only relaxed and used my mind.

Maybe I was afraid to rejoin the force even though I had never quit, but I could still have had my brother work on the case. I had the training, the brains, the equipment, and yet I became depressed, an alcoholic and a drug user.

The drive was not as long as I thought it would have been, considering I was focussed. About twenty minutes outside of Edmonton, Mandy woke and asked, "Would it be possible to call my boyfriend and let him know I'm okay?"

By now the cops would have been called, I did kidnap Mandy and her daughter probably saw but the cops wouldn't recognize me by my disguise or name. Kids never did what they were asked.

*   *   *

Here I was in Toronto and still getting nowhere. Runée was supposed to be getting out earlier on good behaviour. As I was heading for the hotel, I received a phone call from one of the cops that were working on the case in Lethbridge. He was informing me that Mandy was kidnapped by a lady named Samantha. It seemed she had gone to Mandy's house to ask questions about a kidnapping.

I asked the sergeant who told him this, and he told me that he heard the call, went to the location to check it out, and when he got there the daughter was filling out a police report. The little girl had seen the woman hit her mom and then cuff her. She then pushed her into the car with a gun, and they drove off. The woman was driving a Mercedes with a BC license plate, belonging to a car rental outfit out of Vancouver.

Once I heard Vancouver my heart dropped. Daisy was all I could think of. It couldn't be true but then it might explain why I hadn't been able to get a hold of her at home. She was rarely on her cell, and I could only reach her mom, who always had an excuse for her. Here it was I thought Daisy had gotten back into the drugs, but it seems she was trying to play hero.

I told the cop that I figured this Samantha woman was my wife Daisy. The sergeant who was working with me on the case was confused and thought my wife was in Vancouver. He asked me how soon I could get back to Lethbridge, and I told him as soon as the jet could fly.

When I'm airborne and finally able to make a call, I call my house in Vancouver, then I call Daisy's cell. All no answers, so then I call her mom. "Mom do you know where Daisy is?" I ask.

"She's out with Matt."

Trying to restrain myself from getting mad, I ask her again, "Do you know really where she is? Because I just got a call from the sergeant who is helping me with the case. And a woman that sort of matches Daisy's description has kidnapped a lady at gunpoint."

I can hear Daisy's mom go quiet and stop breathing. "It might be her and it might not be."

Shocked to hear that my wife was out there trying to find our son and not taking care of our daughter made me mad and scared. When I saw her last she was frail and emotional. I ask my mother-in-law what Daisy's up to. She informed me that Daisy went to Lethbridge the day after I left to do her own investigation. She had disguised herself so no one would recognize her and drove a rental car.

"Daisy could be in trouble, she has a gun. She could get killed, and so could Elijah," I said harshly

My mother-in-law laughed then said, "Ryan you worry too much. Daisy is stronger than you. She won't get killed. Trust me."

Hearing her say that bothered me and angered me at the same time. Did she not see how my wife was self-destructive? "What makes you say that?" I shouted

"She is her father's child. And she has secrets you don't know about, and when or if you find out, you won't want her for a wife." And with that she hung up on me. Why was it people in that family were always hanging up on me?

I got to Lethbridge in record time and viewed the sketches the police had drawn up of the kidnapper. It was that lady I saw in my restaurant the other day, and by what my mother-in-law had said about Daisy dyeing her hair to change her look as well as some other features.

Furiously I called Hillary to get what information she had. Bringing her to the police station, the sergeants were able to have it confirmed that Samantha was my wife and that she was investigating the murder.

Hillary said that the evidence proved Mandy and Lilly had collaborated to kidnap Elijah. Wondering how it was Daisy was able to get this evidence and the proof, the only answer I got out of her was that Daisy had connections.

The police found out that Mandy has a sister in Edmonton and some people saw a car matching the description heading in that direction. Getting into the police chopper, we head to Edmonton. The sergeant asked if I could talk my wife out of kidnapping Mandy and releasing her instead of going into this woman's house.

I call Daisy again but only get her machine. I call Matt, her brother, to find out what he knows. I find out that big brother Matthew knows everything, how it was my son was kidnapped by both Lilly and Mandy and that a recent thank-you card sent to Lilly. I tell Matt that Daisy is going to get hurt and is too fragile to be dealing with this. Matt goes to tell me that Daisy is a lot stronger then I give her credit for, and she has her gun.

What? My wife has a gun? She never had a gun. What was Matt talking about? Maybe she bought it on the black market to help her kidnap Mandy. "Look, Matt, Daisy was in a situation over a year ago in Mexico. And she wasn't strong enough to get out of that. So I hate to say it, but you don't know your sister as well as you think."

Matt laughs at me and says, "Ryan you don't know your wife. She is very strong, she could kick your ass if she wanted. I know all about what happened in Mexico, she told me, and she also told me how she was planning on escaping and bringing the whole cartel down."

Pausing Matt then went on to say, "After she rescues her son, whom you never found. Maybe then she'll tell you her little secret." And with that he hung up.

Oh this family was making me mad. All of them hanging up on me, my wife not answering her phone and both mother and brother saying Daisy had a secret. Very frustrated, angry, and concerned for my wife, I call her cell again.

*   *   *

I talk with Mandy about why they kidnapped my boy. She says that it was mostly Runée's idea. And since I had killed the child she was carrying, it was only right to make me suffer. After hearing this I then explained what really happened, how we got into the car accident that led to Runée truly losing her child whom she thought she had miscarried previously.

Mandy seemed to understand what I was saying. Turning the scenario around, I ask her if she was in my place, what would she do? Mandy tells me that she would do exactly as I have done if not worse. The car ride got quiet for a while, then Mandy volunteers information on the kidnapping. We talk about how the kidnapping was done.

I ask Mandy how things are with her family. She fills me in on how her kids are great, but the father (her boyfriend) isn't always the nicest to them. I mention how her boyfriend seems like an ass and she could do better. This makes Mandy worried, and she asks to use my cell to call her mom to collect the kids. Not worrying that she'll call the police since they probably already know that I kidnapped Mandy, I hand her my cell.

Mandy calls her mom to get her to collect her children. You could tell Mandy's mom was concerned, but Mandy reassured her mom that I was her friend, and we were just discussing a problem.

Some months ago we weren't friends; she was trying to kick my ass and kill me with her car. I thought her using the term "friends," was kind of funny. But if that what it was going to take to put her mom at ease, I was willing to go along with it. Heck I had stopped pointing the gun at her.

After Mandy gets off the phone with her mom, she informs me how her sister Michelle has no children and can be crazy, but in general she is a good person. I start to feel scared for Elijah now and look at Mandy with fear and anger in my eyes.

With out asking to use the cell again, Mandy calls her sister. I can hear the conversation clearly because I put the call on speaker, a new feature I had bought when I decided to go on this mission. As I hear a kid crying in the background and Michelle yelling at my son, I want to scream but Mandy puts her finger to my lips to keep me quiet.

My son is alive and I will be able to see him, to hug him and bring him home. Just hearing his voice and cries breaks my heart. All this wasted time made me so mad, all that mattered now was getting him back and never letting him out of my sight.

While I was being hushed, Michelle told Mandy that she couldn't visit for a while because Elijah was being bad as well as he had a cold. Michelle then screamed at Elijah and told Mandy that she had to go. Once Mandy was off the phone, I cried in frustration and gave Mandy a dreadful look.

Mandy received my glare and shifted her weight farther away from me to the passenger door. I increased the speed of the car so that the last twenty minutes of the trip went by very faster and I could hold my little boy. "My sister isn't going to just hand over your son," Mandy says.

"Oh I think she will," I say harshly.

Because Mandy never turned off my cell, the phone rings again. I pick it up and notice it is Ryan calling. Not wanting to answer it, I put the phone down, but Mandy answers it since I have been ignoring the calls.

"Hello," she says. "No she's driving right now. We are almost there. I'll try to get her to wait." As Mandy's listening to what Ryan is saying,. I grab the phone out of her hand, hang it up, and turn it off.

"What was that all about? He clearly cares about you," Mandy says trying to discipline me.

I look at her. "No he won't be protecting me anymore. Anyway it only took me less than two weeks to find Elijah. He's had five months to find my son," I yelled, focusing on my speed and trying to get to Michelle's house before the cops scare her off.

Parked outside Michelle's house, I ask Mandy if I can trust her. She tells me that she doesn't want to hurt me anymore, just help. She feels Runée and her have done enough. This she says with sincerity in her eyes. I uncuff her, untie her feet, letting her know I will still have the gun and will keep it pointed at her back.

Grabbing my cell, I must have accidentally turned it on because on cue it rang. Grumbling to myself I answer it.

It is Ryan, and I answer for some reason. "Look the police and I will be at Michelle house shortly. We've just landed in Edmonton."

"Ryan. I don't care what you say. I'm here and I'm getting my son. So if you don't mind, stay out of it!" I said with hostility.

Ryan grunted before saying, "Michelle is unstable and you aren't thinking clearly. Daisy, just wait for the police and FBI to come."

"My god if I never did my own investigation, Elijah would still be missing. You have had five months to find our son. And your success is 0 for 1, so therefore your part in the case in no longer needed. The FBI!" I yelled at him and hung up again.

After knocking at the door and being greeted by Michelle, I couldn't help but want to find my son. Standing in the front entrance I couldn't help but inhale the mouldy smell and see clothes sprawled all over the floor. Piled up dishes, toys were also spread throughout the house.

Michelle smelled like she hadn't taken a bath in weeks, her hair and clothes were messy. Besides her being short, she was butch, with strong arms. Michelle wants to know what we are doing here at the house, when she clearly told Mandy that she wasn't expecting visitors or wanting any.

Mandy told her I was her friend and wanted to see the little boy. My heart starts to pound; I was trying not to go mental, waiting to see which room Elijah was in.

Michelle explains that Elijah is sick and resting in his room. She tells us to come back tomorrow. I go to make a move forward but Mandy stops me and asks if we could see a picture since we are just in town for the day. As Michelle goes to the living room to get a picture, I whisper to Mandy that I can't take it. "I'm getting my son."

I look to a room on my right and my gut feeling tells me that is the room Elijah's in. Michelle comes back but she is not caring a photograph. She must have figured out who I was because in her hand she was holding a shotgun.

Pointing the gun at me, she says, "At first I was surprised that you'd show up. But with the media attention, my mom calling earlier to tell me my sister had been kidnapped. Granted I'm not surprised you have her at gunpoint. But you are not leaving with that child."

We hear the police sirens and the shouts of some officers outside the house, telling us to come out with our hands up. Michelle stops pointing the gun at me, but points it at the room I was suspected Elijah to be in. I scream, "No!" thrusting Mandy to the floor as I point my gun at Michelle. But I'm too late because without emotion Michelle starts shooting into the room.

I could only pray Elijah was on the floor hiding or not in harm's way. She laughs at me saying, "Now the kid's dead." Still pointing my gun at her, I threaten to kill her sister. This only makes Michelle laugh more while she brings her gun back around to face Mandy who is now behind me after getting up from the floor. "She's a traitor, she's weak. Like you were," Michelle says while inserting more ammunition.

With out thinking clearly, my anger gets the better of me. After having everyone calling me weak and my husband failing to find our son. I just start shooting at her. She backs up and tries to get out of the way. Michelle then starts shooting back at me. The sound is so loud as the bullets wiz by my ears.

One of the bullets hit Mandy in the leg, and I feel her go down. I continue to shoot at Michelle. "I don't care if the police or FBI are out there. I will kill you and myself before they take me," Michelle says in between shots at me.

I'm using the kitchen door way as a shield, when I hear the word Mommy coming out of Elijah's room. Michelle points her gun at his room again shooting at the door. Aiming to wound her, I shoot her in the thigh and come at her face-to-face pointing my gun at her, "Slide the gun Michelle!" I yell.

With her dropped to the floor and gun lying beside her, I kick her shotgun out of the way and she grabs onto my left thigh biting into. With my right hand still holding the gun, I club her with it. Michelle passes out and in the background, and I can hear Mandy crying in pain.

Hearing Elijah crying, I go to his room. Seeing my son in dirty clothes and filthy made my heart cry. Running to my son, I scooped him up into my arms. Elijah cries while saying, "Mommy." Looking him up and down I notice some bruising and that he is underweight but will survive.

As we are heading to the door, Mandy is waiting there for us because there are police with guns pointed ready for us. Michelle comes to and knocks me over sending both my son and gun out of my hands. I yell at Elijah to run for the door as Michelle grabs my hair and puts me into a headlock while pointing a handgun on me.

I watch as Mandy grabs Elijah by the arm and picks up my gun. The blood drains from my face; here I thought Mandy was on my side. Trying to struggle out of Michelle's grasp, I see Mandy put my gun to my son's head.

Feeling less pressure on my back, I scream at Mandy that I thought I could trust her. While Michelle feels like she won't have to kill the kid, she becomes more relaxed.

But Mandy quickly turns the gun at Michelle and I, shooting. She hits her sister in the chest, and as she released her grip on me, I fall to the floor and quickly make my way to Elijah. Once I have Elijah in my arms, the police bust into the house using the front door, back door, and windows.

One cop looks at Michelle, then checks her pulse and says she's dead. They come toward Mandy, Elijah, and I but when they see she is still holding my gun, they point theirs and tell her to drop the weapon. She looks at me and I reassure her that it will be all right, and I go to take the gun out of her hand.

Mandy is escorted out in cuffs; Michelle in a body bag. I hug Elijah before heading outside. With Elijah safely in my arms and the evening sun shining on us, I feel a warmth of pride. I did it, rescued my son. It took me less then two weeks, and I just wanted to take him home.

Ryan comes running from a cop car and hugs both Elijah and I while crying. Both my son and I are taken to the hospital to be checked out. The doctor tells us that even though we are both underweight, we will be all right to go home. My son has grown so much in the last five months that I cry because Ryan and my weakness deprived me of so much of my son's youth. Besides him being skinny, his hair color dyed black, he would survive.

Once released from the hospital in Edmonton, we all stay at one of Renaldo's brothers house. I don't talk to Ryan because I am still confused and angry. Ryan doesn't seem bothered that I am not talking to him but takes it as opportunity to yell at me.

"Why did you dye and cut your beautiful strawberry blonde hair?"

I glare at him before saying, "My husband told everyone I was dead. So instead of ruining his plan, I figured I'd stay dead. Anyway, sacrifices had to be made."

"There was no need for you to involve yourself. You could have killed yourself and left our children orphans!" he yelled at me.

"What does it matter to you? You had five months and never found our son," I scream at him while slapping him across the face.

I could see the shock on his face as well as the fact that he could see the hurt and pain on my face. Instead of getting into it any further, Ryan asked, "How is it you knew just where to look for the evidence? Who are these connections I keep hearing about?"

I look at him unimpressed and ask him, "Why didn't you involve the FBI like you said you had?" without answering his question.

"Yes I did. They were helping me," Ryan defended

"No, Ryan, the FBI were never called, or else Elijah would have been found. You only had the cops helping! I honestly think something was rekindled with you and Runée." I told Ryan as I could see the question running through his brain.

"Well how is it you know so much? And why do you own a gun?" Ryan asked.

Giving Ryan a devious smile I say, "Matt is FBI, and the last time you were home telling me the FBI were involved, Matt looked into it, and the FBI were not involved.

If you tell anyone he's FBI, I'll have to kill you." I turn away from Ryan before I can see the look on his face, and he could see that I wasn't being completely honest with him. But I could feel the heat coming from him, and I knew if he knew I was FBI, that would be cause for more problems than I was willing to deal with, including the fact that I wanted to be mad at him, and not have him mad at me.

Elijah, Ryan and I flew back to Vancouver. The next couple of years went by with a rough start. I ignored Ryan for a long time, and we'd get into big fights, but in the end I decided to forgive Ryan for his behavior.

He didn't ask me any questions pertaining to my brother's involvement in the case or being part of the FBI.

Mandy got off her charges lightly with my helping to defend her. She broke up with her boyfriend and cut off all ties to Runée while moving to a new city.

We did attend Hillary's wedding and work with more celebrity functions at the restaurant. Ryan still spent his time going back and forth between the restaurant in Lethbridge and the new ones I had bought in Vancouver. I was spending most of my time making music videos with my clients and with my two children.

Elijah took to his sister quickly and the two became very close for children who had been separated for five months. Even though Elijah didn't seem to be traumatized by his experience, I still monitored him for a long time.

PART 3

CHAPTER 9

As we rung in the New Year with Elijah being five years old, and Sonyia three and a half, I had new hopes that this year will be better then the last few years. Starting the year off being pregnant with Sonyia and everything starting out well, then only to have my son kidnapped and almost losing my daughter. Knowing what I knew about my husband and how he denied paternity to his child with Runée only to have her go psycho. Spending most of those years under great stress and neglecting my little girl made me feel sick.

But this year was going to be better I was going to spend as much time with my two little children, being a proper mom. As well as being a more determined wife and not take any more abuse from Ryan.

My brother and Monatana were going be married by the end of this year and wanted my help with the wedding plans. I was so excited to be getting a sister; she was a great person who knew all of Matthew's secrets and kept them secret.

Throwing a house party for all our friends and family was great fun. The children stayed up as late as their little bodies allowed. Ryan and I spend most of the night celebrating in our own little way and it was erotic.

Just before Elijah's sixth birthday, Ryan received a phone call from his family telling him that their mother wasn't feeling well. And maybe he should come visit for a little while in case she passed away.

* * *

After my son's sixth birthday, I land back in Lebanon. I was looking forward to seeing my mom, but my older brother Frank nags on me again for marrying a Canadian girl and not one from my country. Frank tells me how much I have disgraced my family, caused mama pain, and if I bring my wife around the family then I will pay severely.

Mama is very sick, and we have long talks about Daisy. Frank is wrong about mama not wanting to hear about my wife. She is happy to hear all I have to say about my wife and children. Mama tells me she wanted to visit, but Frank and Dad wouldn't let me. I show her pictures, and she cries because she fears she will never get to meet my new family.

I call Daisy to let her know that mama's condition is worsening and that I'd have to stay in the country a little longer. Daisy only goes to argue with me and tell me that she will be on the next flight. I start yelling at her in Lebanese, hoping this will scare her. I'm shocked when she retorts back in Lebanese and hangs up.

With the frequent amount of times Daisy has hang up the phone on me so that she could win arguments, it didn't make me mad anymore. The part that makes me mad is the fact that she thinks she can come to Lebanon without researching and knowing how much my father and brother hate the idea that I am married to a Canadian who has a mind of her own. In my country you marry a woman who listens to you, stays at home to raise the children, and is obedient.

I had to find a way to cut her off at the airport before she got into the country and something bad happened to her or the children.

*   *   *

Talking to Ryan made me sad. His mom was dying and their wasn't anything I could do for him. I knew I needed to be there for him and if I could meet his mom before she died, then I would at least be able to make her and her family understand that Ryan and I loved each other, so it shouldn't matter that I wasn't Arabic.

My mom is taking care of the children as I fly out in the privet jet to Lebanon. As I land and collect my suitcases I make my way to hail a cab but run right into Ryan.

"Baby, what are you doing here?" I ask him surprised that he is at the airport since I was going to surprise his family.

"I came to stop you from going any farther into my country," Ryan says as he kisses me and gathers my suitcase from me. "I am happy to see you, granted I told you not to come."

I smile at him then reply with "Remember I told you that you would not be telling me what I can and cannot do!"

"Yes, and I respect that, but trust me when I tell you it is not safe for you to be in this country," Ryan responds hastily. We head for a car and the driver takes us to a hotel on the United States Embassy side.

"Why can't we stay in one of the hotel in Lebanon? Why do we have to stay on the embassy's side?" I ask frustrated since I had just flown many hours to get here.

"Because you are too beautiful to be covered with a robe and veil. If other men saw you, they would want to claim you as their own or else beat you because they see you as a powerful woman. In my country the only powerful woman are the president's wife, and even she covers her beauty," Ryan said with determination of me not crossing the American Embassy wall.

Once in the hotel room, I sit on the bed and tell Ryan that it would be a shame for me to leave so soon when I just got here. I'd like to see the sights and shop. As I'm putting my suitcase down on the bed. Ryan comes up behind me turning me around placing his hands on my face and gently squeezes it before laying a kiss on me.

Returning the kiss, I open my mouth and take in his tongue. As we are kissing he leans against me. I lay back on the bed while I feel Ryan's erection in his pants. Removing our clothes slowly, he kisses my neck then works down to my chest and nibbles on one of my breasts. I run my hands through his hair and moan with pleasure. Completely naked we roll around on the bed, the sweat rolling off our bodies and down our faces. With intense kissing of love and passion, Ryan slowly inserts his penis into my every desire. As he thrusts deep within me, I arch my back exerting myself in my orgasm. Once his explosion is released Ryan collapses in my arms, laying a few kisses on me. I close my eyes in peace only to drift off into a deep sleep.

The next morning I am escorted to my jet. Ryan doesn't want to take any chances with me not returning home, especially after he insists how important it is that I can't stay in his country. He tells me that he won't be too long, and once his mother passes away he will return.

A week later from my visit to Ryan's homeland, he calls to talk to Elijah about leaving so soon after his birthday and that he will be away a little longer, so Elijah is to be the man of the house. When I finally get to talk to Ryan, I find out his mother has died, and the burial process is a long one. But once the will is read he will be back home. He does inform me that he will also have to stand trial from his father for getting a already married woman pregnant and then marrying her when she is not part of their culture.

I try to tell him something but he cuts me off to tell me to be strong, that he loves me and to take care of the children. Starting to cry, I want to know what is going on and why he is talking like this. Before the conversation ends, Ryan once again pledges his love to the kids and me. I am left with an odd feeling in my gut when the call ends.

I hate myself for not getting to tell him that we are going to be having another child. I know if I had he would be coming home instead of staying in his home country to clear up matters.

After not hearing from Ryan for a month, and with calling his sister to see if she has heard anything from him. I finally get a call from Sherri, but it isn't the call I was waiting for.

"Daisy, I hate to be the one to tell you this. But they executed Ryan for his sins against our mother and father, his country, and god," Sherri says.

I start crying, "No, no, I don't believe you."

Sherri starts to cry. "We are going to hold a funeral here in Lethbridge for him. You need to be here, and so do the kids."

My body is shaking, the tears are streaming down my face, and feeling nauseous I ask, "Has the body been brought back to us?"

Sherri tells me that he was buried beside their mother, and that we will only be having a service for his friends and family. After the call ends I go to throw up and bawl my eyes out. Not shortly after the call my mother comes bursting into my house; it seems Sherri told her and wanted her to be with me since I was four months pregnant now.

I feel totally withdrawn, hurt and abandoned because my husband was ripped away from my life and my family. It was bad enough that Elijah lost almost a year of his parents and both him and his sister were going to be raised without a father. And the new baby was never going to know its father, unless with all this stress I lost the baby.

I spend a month in Lethbridge after the funeral living in our old apartment since it was the only thing vacant that we still owned. But the funeral was really hard on me. Ryan's sister tried to comfort me; she finally explained her country's laws and rules. That is why he was killed for his sins. Sherri never went back to the country; she'd have her mother come visit her in Canada. Both she and Renaldo never wanted to go back because it was too dangerous for the women.

Because the stress of Ryan's death, the doctors told me I needed to take it easy and try to find things to keep my mind off his death or else I would lose the twins I was carrying. Since this would be the last gift from Ryan, I didn't want to lose the babies so I decided to stay in Lethbridge for my pregnancy. Working on the restaurants and some music videos, along with Hillary keeping my mind off things, I was able to get through the last five months without losing my twins.

After ten years of running five restaurants, three hotels, a couple malls, helping to produce and direct music videos, plays and raising my four, children I was feeling the need for a vacation. So when the opportunity to go on *Ghillagins*, a famous talk show, came up, I didn't pass on the opportunity.

I left Elijah, Sonyia and the twins, Angela and Alex, with my mom while I went to Las Anglos for the talk show. Feeling strong, determined, and successful, I walk onto the stage as everyone applauds my entrance.

Susan the talk show host opens the show with a brief detail of my life's history. Explaining how my husband had died ten years ago and that I'm a single mom raising four children. But I am a successful business woman who owns five restaurants, three hotels, and works as a music director and producer.

"What has it been like raising four children without their father and run so many successful business, not to mention finding time to direct music videos and plays?" Susan asks.

"Well at first it was hard, but I wasn't about to let my children down. I mean they are also part of my late husband. I had already suffered the kidnapping of my son four years before my husband died. And with that I had neglected my daughter, so I decided that I would get through my <u>loss</u> quickly so as to not affect my children. But with time, I have found ways to work my businesses and take care of my children, not to mention receiving help from Mom," I say with a smile.

"Wow, that's impressive. I'm sorry to hear about your son being kidnapped and then losing your husband, but I'm glad to see you've moved on," Susan says.

I look at her oddly, then the audience, before saying, "I don't understand what you mean. If by meaning I've moved on with my life, then yes, I had to for my family."

Susan laughs then explains, "Well I see you are wearing a wedding ring. When did you get remarried, and who is the luck guy?"

I laugh and shake my head. "No I'm not married, and nor have I ever remarried. This is the first ring my husband put on my finger. After he died I took the wedding band set that he had given me for our second wedding. When I tried to take this wedding band off, just like any other time I tried to remove the ring, it would not budge."

Susan looked at me shocked, then asked, "Why not get it cut off?"

I looked down at the ring, played with it. I remembered that dreadful day at the courthouse when I was forced to marry him, how mad I was at him, and how I tried to take the ring off the, but even then it wouldn't come off. Even the Mexican crime lords tried to take the ring off and they had no luck. "For some reason the idea of cutting the ring off just doesn't seem right. It is like by having this ring on, Ryan lives," I said with a little smile.

"Well then have you dated, and is there any interesting man in your life?" Susan asked.

I chuckled then replied, "It's not that I haven't met any interesting men, I have. I've dated a few and it never worked out because I never allowed it to. I didn't think it was right for my children to have another man be their father. I mean Ryan died when they were young and it's not fair to his memory to have another man fill the place of their dad, especially with the twins."

We finished the talk show, and I went out with a few friends of the music world I had gotten to know. Afterwards I went back to my hotel room with a bottle of wine. I don't know what it was but with talking about losing Ryan, it got me to thinking about how I had survived these last ten years. Granted it was hard, the fragile pregnancy, having to raise four young children alone, trying to get my life in order and trying not to have a melt down.

Even though I took the second wedding set off after five years of Ryan being dead because I thought I was ready to date, being back in the game was a lot harder with children. Some of the men understood, but others found it awkward. The twins were confused, Sonyia was fussy with all the different men, and Elijah was too understanding. I knew I wasn't going to be able to have another man in my life at least until the children were all grown up.

I would tell Sonyia stories of her father because she idolized him, but sometimes it hurt to think of the past, because Ryan was taken away from us unjustly.

The twins were still not able to understand their father being gone since the only man they got to love was their uncle Matthew.

As I drank from the bottle a large gulp of wine, I wondered how messed up my children might be that I never did remarry. Being ten years later, they had to be strong enough to handle another man. Yet the thought of having another man in my bed and life made me sick. I felt unfaithful to Ryan; in my heart it was like I needed some closure. If only going to his country wasn't so dangerous, granted a lot had changed, but the rich still treated women like slaves and doormats.

With Elijah being sixteen, he was into many school sports and activities on his way to graduating with honours. He also helped his fourteen-year-old sister with her homework when ever I was out of town. The twins were a handful being nine years old, and trying to keep them out of my hair was hard, but I wouldn't have survived without my moms help.

It wasn't like I lived like a monk; I went to all the hottest parties, events, and award shows. I did also go on occasional dates but I wouldn't let the men get to close to me. Some of my dating partners became friends and the other men thought I was too loyal to a dead man.

After finishing the bottle of wine, I went to the balcony and had a smoke. As I was smoking I remembered when Ryan would take the smokes away from me and break them. I knew it was wrong to smoke, but after losing him and with the possibility of losing the twins, I picked up smoking again. It was a way to calm my nerves and I wasn't about to go down the same road I did when Elijah was kidnapped.

How I missed Ryan. Tears started streaming down my face. I was starting to forget how he used to touch me, kiss me, hold me, and smell me. Maybe Susan was right. I should cut the ring off and date. I did need a man in my life that I could tell all my problems to, someone to comfort me, and another adult who would love me.

When I got home from LA, I sat Elijah down at the kitchen table to have a grown-up chat. "Babe, I was wondering if it would be all right if when I dated that maybe I might be able to consider a long-term relationship with a man. And maybe even lead to marriage. Do you think you kids would be all right with this?" I ask my son. I knew it was silly of me to ask him and later the other children, but I didn't want them to feel uncomfortable with a stranger.

Elijah came over and hugged me. "It's funny you should ask, Mom. Us kids are working on a way for you to date a teacher of ours. We want you to be happy, and if it means getting married to another man, then we are fine with it. Mom, we hear you at night sometimes crying 'cause you are lonely. I know you miss Dad, and I miss him too. But none of us really knew him, and so it isn't like another man would replace him. But they could always be our friend, plus Alex and Angela could use some male influence."

I cried because I could not believe my son was telling me this. "And when was I supposed to go out on this date with this teacher that my children are trying to set me up with?" I said with a chuckle, wiping the tears out of my eyes.

So four days later I went out with Elijah and Sonyia's Math teacher and my kids did pick a nice guy because I had a good time. I wasn't able to remove my wedding band, but Jason didn't seem to mind that I was wearing it and understood that it would not come off.

After winding down from my evening, I turned on my computer and brought up some of the files to check the accounting of my restaurants. While they were uploading to my computer, I decided to check my e-mail. I got a letter from a foreign user, a little leery at first to read the e-mail, but something inside my gut made me open the email.

*   *   *

The last ten years had gone by easier than the prior year when I saw in the papers that that Daisy was happy and moving on with her life. I was able to see article's in some papers that were lying around the house, but other then that I hadn't heard much about her.

After Mama's funeral I had to attend a meeting with my father and older brother. They wanted to discuss my involvement with my wife and how I had shamed my family. For my punishment I was sent to prison for five years; my family was told I was dead. After I was released from prison, my brother Frank had me tagged with a tracking device like a criminal. They gave me a new identity and told me that if I contacted my wife, and old family I would be shot for sure.

Accepting my new life was hard, but seven years later after coming back for my mother, I saw the first article of Daisy and saw that she was happy. She was posing for an entertainment award with a man on her arm. I was mad at first that she had another man in her life but soon learned to accept it.

Shortly after being released from prison I had an arranged marriage to a young Lebanese girl named Emily. She spoke no English, was very pretty, and behaved like a proper wife should behave in our country.

It was hard at first in my new marriage to have to tell her what to do and how to behave. But soon I fell into my old habits, the ones Daisy had broken. I didn't talk to Emily much, and when I did I made sure to remind her that I was already married to a beautiful woman and she meant nothing to me. So this marriage was false. Emily wanted to have a baby because she thought that would make me happy, but there was no way I was going to get her pregnant or accept any child we'd have. One day I would find a way to get back to my wife and family.

Because I already had a wedding ring on my ring finger I did not have to put a ring on. And I didn't want to anyway. It didn't help that the ring I wore wouldn't come off my finger and the only way to get it off was to cut it off or have Daisy remove it.

I remember when Daisy would try to remove her ring at first and would get so mad. I told her it would never come off just like my grandmother told me. If you are meant to be, the rings would bond you until one passed away.

So in other words Daisy and I were soul mates. Emily would never understand true love. When I saw a picture of Daisy in the *New York Post* a year after seeing her with that man she had four children. Two of them I had not heard of. I kind of recognized Elijah because he was looking more and more like me, and I could only imagine that hurting Daisy to have to see him every day.

Sonyia was looking so much like her mother, but the other two, a little boy and a little girl, I was assuming they must be twins. Just seeing their picture made me mad; I felt betrayed that Daisy hadn't mourned my supposed death long enough. Clipping the picture out, I added it to the others I had managed to gather over the years.

One day at work, the crew had the TV on and it was a program in English. I asked them why they were watching a talk show when they didn't understand the language. They told me because the woman on the TV was so beautiful.

I looked at the program on the TV and was shocked to see Daisy on a talk show. Turning up the volume I watched the program to find out she hadn't remarried, and that the two little children I had seen in the paper were mine. I had twins, and their names were Alex, after my grandfather, and Angela, after my mother. The crew didn't understand why I was crying. I told them that the woman's story is sad. It also saddened me that my wife hadn't moved on with her life, where as I had been made to move on with my life.

When the talk show host thinks Daisy has remarried because she is wearing the first wedding ring I put on her ring, I laughed. Starting to play with my ring, I can still feel her love and loyalty to me.

While I work I ponder all the information I heard on the talk show. I could see she was happy but at the same time I could see the pain in her eyes. It wasn't going to be long before she did go and find another man to replace me. After work I decided to find a way to contact her, now that my ankle monitor had been removed and I didn't care if my brother did kill me this time. Living with the pain of not being with her was slowly killing me already.

And if he should try to harm her, I would kill him. But then thinking back to how both mother and brother of Daisy's family had said she was capable of handling herself and that there were things I didn't know about her. Made me just wonder what it was. I didn't really know. And maybe Matt will use his FBI intelligence to find out that I was truly dead.

After typing the e-mail, I remembered how quickly she was able to find Elijah when she finally got strong enough to find him. Granted I had stopped her and not let her try and find her son, which was wrong of me. I gathered my belongings and made my way for home. I knew I wasn't going to be able to sleep in anticipation to a reply to my letter.

> Dear Ms. Gaston,
>
>   You do not know me. But I know of your deceased husband. This is not a prank letter or one to cause you more pain. The reason I know of your husband is because I worked with him. I have worked with him for the last five years since he got out of prison. I am not lying, and there is no way for me to prove to you that Ryan Gaston is alive except that the two of you are bonded by a magical ring. A

wedding band that cannot be removed by any one else, only by the one who placed it on your finger.

It is too dangerous for your husband that I send proof that he is alive. You must take my word and know that he still loves you and misses you terribly. He wants so badly to escape the hell he is living in but isn't sure how to get out. Maybe if you were able to contact the people who helped you find your son, then maybe you'll find your husband.

xoxo

I reread the e-mail twenty-five times, not believing what I was seeing. I called up my contacts immediately to find out where this e-mail originated. They told me it could still be a prank, just very well written and researched. Being in the media and all, I had received quiet a bit of prank e-mails. It all ended up being people trying to get money out of me some how. So like my colleague had said, I replied to the e-mail.

My reply was vague, stating that I needed more evidence in some form that only Ryan and I would know and no one else since they weren't able to send actual proof for fear of jeopardizing Ryan any further.

The next e-mail explained how Ryan and I were drugged and Elijah was the result. How both Elijah and Sonyia were born premature. The Doctors had also given Ryan a choice of who to save when it came down to me delivering Sonyia.

Reading this new information I knew it had to be someone who wasn't lying to me. My college had found the address of the server the email was sent from. It was a chocolate factory in Lebanon where there was a high rate of low-paid employees.

Over the next few days Matt got back to me with information on Ryan's execution order. But there was no order of a man being executed. It seems they don't execute men in Lebanon, just women who tempt men. Any man who has done wrong is sentenced to jail. Matthew did find out that there was a man who had spent five years in prison on adultery.

Upon hearing that a man had gone to jail for five years, made my heart sputtered. Maybe this e-mailer was right, that Ryan was alive. After hanging up the phone with my brother, I called Sherri and demand to know all there is to know about her country. She wanted to know why, and I told her because I was going to her country, and there is no changing my mind. As she tried to argue and protest, I hung up so that she knew I meant business.

A few hours later, Sherri called me back saying that she talked to Renaldo and he said it would be okay. After hearing how to behave as a woman of low social status and how to dress, I felt more determined then ever.

Both Renaldo and Sherri agreed that I should go to Lebanon as a poor widowed maiden looking for work in the rich parts of their country. If I remove all my jewellery, look messy and sad, I would fit in. Renaldo then gets on the phone after Sherri tells me how to dress and behave around the men. Renaldo wants to tell me to not be independent or defiant; I need to obey and not look the men in the eyes. They also warn me not to speak any English, or else I won't be believed and may be hung for being an impostor.

As I sit on the balcony having a smoke, Elijah walks in to talk about his last soccer game of the season and if we are attending. He notices the anxiety in my face and asks what's wrong.

I look at him before saying, "I'm going to be going away for a couple weeks or so. I have reason to believe that your father might still be alive. And if not, I may never get peace with his death if I don't go and investigate for myself. Before you or your siblings get excited, I want to look first. So please don't tell them."

Elijah hugs me and gets excited. "That would be so cool. But why do you now think he might be alive?"

"I received a convincing e-mail, and for some reason I still feel it in my heart that your father is alive," I tell my son.

Elijah looks off into the sky. He's gone through it with me, all the phoney e-mails, people trying to extort money out of me or hurt me. After looking to the stars, he then looks at me and says, "Well if you feel that Dad is still alive, then so do I."

I smile at my son. How did he get so wise and mature? "Granma will be watching you kids and Uncle Matt will be involved in my investigation as well."

As I watched my son walk back into the house, I couldn't help but admire his strength and courage. To have taken on so much responsibility at such a young age but still come out with good grades, an excellent attitude, and maturity to handle all his mom's stress. Looking at him I also saw how much he was starting to look like his father. And sometimes looking at him made me sad because it would make me miss Ryan so much.

The kids and I went to watch Elijah's soccer game before I left for Lebanon. He scored five goals. I smile as I watch my son play on the field with his team; Ryan would be so proud of his son. After the game the five of us go to a dance concert I had been working on with a bunch of misfit kids who had musical talent. Their concert was very good, and the audience really seamed to enjoy themselves.

After saying good-bye to the children and my mom, I head for my jet to fly to Lebanon. Once arriving in Lebanon my skin starts to crawl with fear of what I will find and if I will survive in this old-school country.

I'm staying in a hotel on the American Embassy side. The same one Ryan and I had made love in the last time I came to this country, where he cut me off from leaving the safety of the embassy.

I arrange to have an interpreter and culture expert help me out with all the particular details. As my interpreter, John, helps me to understand the way of the country better, I am able to move about in the embassy as I would in Canada or the United States.

Since this part of the country has not moved up with other parts of Lebanon, with civilization like the rest of the world. Women must cover their bodies from head to toe and only reveal their eyes. Women are not to be heard or seen. Being that this part of Lebanon is away from the ocean and not in the mountains, they are able to get away with being nomadic, and therefore less tourists come to visit.

While I look over the map of Lebanon, I ask questions. One being where the Gaston estate was since I plan to get hired there. Once I feel comfortable with the map of the country, John thinks it will be safe for me to leave the safety of the embassy to go sightseeing. He will guide me through the city to see how well I adjust to my new act and if I will be able to pass as a poor widowed maid.

I am dressed from head to toe in a black robe, with just my eyes visible, and we head to the city. We sightsee a little, but the heat is so unbearable that I want to head back to the embassy to take a cold shower.

After showering John wants to know if I feel like going back into the city alone. Besides the heat I feel that I can manage a trip to the city by myself. So the next day I go back into the city away from the safety of the embassy. While walking and being in shops I see the women are treated very poorly and with cruelty.

Once again back at my hotel room and showered, I sit down at my desk to combine all the information. Doing up a report, I make sure to mention that Ryan's mom did die when Ryan mentioned she did. The Gaston family is very wealthy, and Marshall, Ryan's second oldest brother, is running the estate and fields. I add to my report that Ryan's family is hiring and that my intentions are to pose as a cleaning lady while I snoop the estate. After completing my report I send it in to headquarters, I take another shower due to the extreme heat and not being accustom to their high temperatures makes me worried how long I will last employed.

Now getting myself ready for the task I have to achieve tomorrow. Getting hired!

CHAPTER 10

After two weeks of being in Ryan's country, I ready myself for my adventure of torture. Dressing in full headgear, removing all jewellery except my cursed wedding ring and only having my eyes visible, I leave the safety of my hotel room wearing a plastic finger cover over my ring finger so that my in-laws don't think I'm a thief and hire me as a maid.

I get hired on the spot at Ryan's family's estate, which is high on a mountain over looking the vast amount of land they own. The house is larger than my mansion back home, but it is very beautiful with lots of antiques and priceless artefacts.

As I start my job at the mansion, I'm allowed to stay in the maid's quarters. But Saturday is the only day I'm allowed off. When I have days off, I'm not allowed in the house but I am allowed the leave the grounds. With in the first few days of working there, I notice that the men of the house are rude and arrogant. They treat the other women working here very badly, except for a young maiden who is the cook. As I'm cleaning, I'm also noticing how the other staff move about the estate. I see that this young cook is trying to practice English when she's not around the men.

I work very hard at the estate, and look around but no trace of Ryan's ashes. I gander at all the family photos on the tables. I see many of Sherri's and her other brothers, but none of Ryan alone. There are a few pictures of Ryan in them. After five days working there in the bloody heat and being that Saturday is tomorrow and I want to go to the Hotel for a rest, I decide to check Ryan's old room, Sherri told me the layout of the estate before I left. Since I knew a little of the written language, I was able to pick up some words but still felt scared. I searched Ryan's room, and found no trace besides a few clothes.

I decided that I would sneak into Ryan's mothers' room. When I was hired and taken on the tour of the mansion, I was told not to go into this room that it was forbidden. Wandering through his mothers' room, I noticed more pictures of Ryan. I went through her lingerie drawer and saw a few pictures Ryan had sent her of Elijah and Sonyia. I smiled to myself that she had kept these pictures safe. After closing the dresser draw, I felt a cold chill up my spine and felt a shadow standing over me. I turn around only to be confronted by Ryan's oldest brother Frank.

Since his father had been ill he'd been the one taking care of matters, and out of all the men in this house he was the worst as I had observed with the other staff.

I tried to flee the room and tell him in Lebanese that I'm sorry but he hits me across the face knocking me to the ground. I go to get up and before getting back on my feet. He hits me again, and I see darkness.

I slowly open my eyes. Looking around I notice it is dimly lit, smells musky, and that I must be in one of the shacks on the property. I had heard stories about the shacks on the outskirts of the property; they were used for bad servants if they weren't going to kill them. I notice the pretty young cook ringing a cloth then placing it on my back, which is I felt was extremely tender and painful.

As I am lying on my stomach, I try to sit up, but the pain is too much that I lay back down. My face vial comes off revealing my golden blonde hair and tanned face. The maiden stops what she is doing. Shocked she starts to speak to me in English asking if I'm an angel. I tell her no. She then looks at my wedding band and touches it.

I also notice my wedding band is in plain sight, somewhere during the beating or this girl cleaning me, my plastic finger cover must have fallen off. As I play with my ring, I look at her and say, "It was the ring my dead husband gave me on our wedding day. I came to find out if he is still alive in this country or retrieve his ashes."

The maiden looks down at her own wedding ring, playing with it. "My name is Emily, and my husband refuses to commit to our marriage. He claims he is already married and will leave me."

After asking her if she is happy and finding out she's not, I ask Emily more questions but am interrupted by the dinner bell. Since she is married, she isn't allowed to live at the estate. Once she hurried out of the shack I gather my clothes and make myself presentable to serve my last supper.

I wasn't sure why I was going to be a servant one more time when I myself was just as rich and deserving as this family. Since I'm living at Ryan's family's estate as a maid, I have to serve dinner with the other girls. But as I'm about to leave the shack, it strikes me, I haven't seen any proof that Ryan is alive, and neither that he is dead. I haven't seen him visiting in the house, so maybe it was just a trap. But the e-mails felt so real and made me feel that there was still hope.

No I wasn't going to serve a last supper. I was going home or at least back to the hotel. As I was about to open the door of the shack I was startled when it opened and the head servant came in. She told me in Lebanese to get back into the house as it was time to serve the masters.

Wanting to flee, I decided it would be best to sneak away at night. While we were walking back to the mansion, the older servant was telling me how much I deserved my lashings. If I hadn't gone snooping around I wouldn't have gotten beaten.

Since losing my plastic rubber finger I had to keep my left hand hidden. As I served supper, my face hurts so much, my back stings worse than a sunburn. I served supper with out having shown my left hand. But while I was clearing the plates from Ryan's oldest brother Frank, he grabbed my hand and pulls the sleeve away from my finger. Dreading what was about to come, Frank started yelling at me in Lebanese, asking me where I stole the ring from. Since I knew it was Ryan's grandmothers ring, Frank immediately remembers me being in Ryan and his mother's room. He tries to pull the ring off, and it digs into my knuckle, not coming off due to the magic of it.

Frank calls me a thief and keeps pulling on the ring. It hurts too much that I deck him and pull my hand back. Then Marshall tries to attack me. I deck him too, and my veil falls down. I hurry outside and off the property, running for my life back to the hotel. As I run my back hurts so much that I want to stop, but for fear of losing my life and never seeing my children, I run faster.

I manage to make it back to the embassy before the police can catch me because surely Frank has called the police and told them that I stole their grandmothers wedding ring. I also get back to my hotel before the men can get me for not having my face covered and realizing that I am Canadian.

Once back in my hotel room, I called John over so that he could help me clean my wound. As he's cleaning my wound I ask him where the cemetery is so that I can visit my deceased husband's mom and his grave.

John explains the route I need to take and shows me a map so I don't get lost. He also recommends I go as an American with a guide so that I don't get kidnapped, and probably by now the police will be looking for a woman who has stolen property from the Gaston family.

While I rest in bed before my last day here in this godforsaken country, I call my children to let them know I'm coming home.

Elijah picks up. "Mom are you okay? My back hurts and so does my face. What happened?

I place my hand on my back and then face where Frank hurt me. Yah, I had never thought how Elijah would feel with our closeness in emotions and injuries. We shared pain: if I was hurting, so was he, and that was what helped me to know he was alive when he was kidnapped. So here I was in pain from a stern lashing, and so was Elijah. Another curse.

"Yes, I'm all right, let's just say that Uncle Frank is a monster, and I felt the brunt of it. So that is why your back and face hurts. But I hate to tell you this, I wasn't able to find your father," I tell him.

Elijah breaths slowly. "Sorry to hear, Mom, I know how much you wanted him back."

I start to cry, "Well I didn't find his ashes either. So I don't know if he is dead or alive, and I can't figure out why this dam wedding ring won't come off."

"Don't cry, Mom, you still have the teacher we set you up with. And you have us if Dad is gone, maybe the ring means you are soul mates and are eternally committed."

I had never thought of it like that, that maybe we would be together in heaven. *Well am I was I supposed to remarry or be with another man?* I thought to myself. "I think when I get back that I'm going spend some alone time and straighten out my life. Maybe finally grieve for your father's death, but I thank you kids for looking out for me and setting me up with the teacher," I finish off laughing. "Anyway I wanted to let you know that I will be flying out of here this afternoon and should be home nine hours after that."

"I will tell Uncle Matt and Grandma," Elijah said before we hung up.

"Why are you late?" I ask my wife Emily since she hasn't gotten dinner ready.

Emily paces around the kitchen and starts to prepare a meal. While she's doing so she says nervously, "One of our new maids at the estate was beaten today for going into one of the forbidden rooms."

Not thinking much about it since my brother has made it a strict rule that no one enters my old room or my mother's, I say, "Well it serves her right."

Emily doesn't like my response and I can see that I still scare her, just as I used to with Daisy. But I hate that she won't put up a fight like my former wife. "No! Because she has the face of an angel. She's not like us, and she speaks English very well."

Shocked to hear Emily raise her voice, I glare at her after hearing her use English to say the word "angel." "Is that so!" Knowing very well she was trying to learn English because it was the language I used when I was away from the family compound.

"Yes, she has beautiful golden hair and green eyes, with tanned skin. She didn't look like any other women in this country that work for a living!" Emily exclaimed with delight. "It was weird because she also wore a beautifully braided woven white-and-yellow gold wedding ring that belonged to her deceased husband."

I look up from my paper. Was Emily telling me what I was hearing? That Daisy had come to find me? My heart started to beat fast. Was it possible that Daisy was the maid that my brother had hired and she had been snooping around to find me. "Where is she staying? What is her name? Does her ring look like this?" I demand while showering her my wedding ring

Emily told me that the maid didn't give a name, but she was working at the estate and living there, and the rings did indeed look the same. After eating the supper, I needed to go for a walk and plan how I was going to get back to my wife and get her out of the estate.

Once arriving at my family's home I asked my brother Frank what all the fuss was about that the police were here. He said, "The new maid I hired is the same person who stole our grandmothers ring twenty years ago. And I caught her trying to steal again. She was in our mother's room snooping, probably looking for more jewellery."

"Where is she?" I ask my brother, knowing damn well that Mom had given me my grandparent's rings. Mother had told me that if I found true love, then the rings would prove the love by never coming off until death.

I look at Frank who has a swollen eye, and he tells me, "She took off after I tried to detain her, but not before hitting me and Marshall."

I look over to Marshall, and he too has a swollen face. After talking with my brothers, I go talk to the maids about the new maid. They tell me that she kept to herself and they sometime heard her talking to herself in English. The description of her eye color was the same as Emily's.

Leaving the Estate, there was nothing I could do, I had no clue where she was but hoped she had gotten back to the hotel or the embassy. I looked around my small house and wonder what I would take, nothing because this was a nightmare to me. "Emily, just to let you know, I'm leaving you and going back to my old wife and children," I told her in Lebanese.

She started to cry, and I could see she was worried that with me leaving, she might be killed. Because I had not given her any children as well as denied her the right to have children, the rest of the elders would think she was not worthy to be a wife for another man. I walked over to Emily and hugged her. "I will pay for your way out of the country and put you up somewhere."

The next morning, I put Emily on a bus and gave her all the money we had in our savings account. Her bus ticket was to a country where women were treated like other women, with respect. I also informed her that she would not have to get a divorce from me because we were not legally married, and I wished her luck in her new life.

With her safely out of the country, I decided that I would go to my mother's grave and say good-bye for the last time. There was no way I would ever come back to this country again, because I hated the way they treated the women and how I was being treated. My only problem was going to be getting out of the country without a passport, but if I could convince the embassy of whom I was, then I might have a chance.

*　　*　　*

After putting on some regular clothes, and a veil to cover my face. John took me to the grave site as my American tour guide and to watch for the police. As I'm walking toward Ryan's mothers gave, I notice in the distance a man walking back to a motor bike and I don't give it a second thought.

Once at Angela Gastons grave I place the rose I held in my hand against the stone and kneeling down I remove my face veil revealing my golden hair. I said my peace to her, "Angela, I wish I had met you. But I want you to know that your son Ryan gave you four beautiful grandchildren, one named after you. I want to thank you for raising a great son, I just wish he was still alive to be with me, please take care of both of you in heaven." Blowing a kiss to her stone I get up.

I head back to the car and once seated I weep silently since my mission is a failure. Except for going home with a serve lashing to my back and a swollen face. I hold both mine and Ryan's passports and cry.

*　　*　　*

I looked back and notice a car stopping by my mother's grave sight, as I am mounting the motorbike I watch and notice this woman leaving the car and walking toward my mom's grave. She kneels down and places a rose on the stone, then removed her veil to reveal her golden hair.

My heart stops. I can't believe what I am seeing. Could it be Daisy at my mom's grave. While I was still stunned by what I see, she gets into the car and they leave. I decide to chases after them for fear I may never see her again. I don't want her to think I am dead and move on; she is my wife, and I want her and my family back.

*   *   *

John doesn't say anything when I get back into the car; he knows I'm sad. As we are driving back to the embassy, I don't realize there is a crazy man on a motorcycle trying to catch up with us and eventually causes us to slam into a car due to John increasing the speed. A little shaken by the small accident, I go to ask what happened, "John, why did we hit another car?"

He looks at me, then into his rearview mirror, and back at me, "There is a man on a motorcycle following us, I fear he is working for the Gaston family." Trying to start the engine, John has no luck and says, "Run, Daisy! Get to the embassy fast. If the police catch you, you will never see your family again. I'll take care of this guy!"

Being that the embassy is a block away, I look back and the man in a motorbike is nearing us. Getting out of the car, I start to walk very quickly down the block. As I am getting further away from the car, I hear someone calling my name.

Looking back I see John stop the man by fighting him. Figuring that it is John telling me to run, I keep walking toward the embassy. Hearing my name yelled, I stop dead in my tracks and look back at the two men fighting. Something in the voice that had yelled my name sent a cold shiver down my spine. I see a man who has a full grown beard, long black hair, and very familiar eyes.

Instead of walking to the embassy and being that I'm within a few feet of the gates, I decide to walk back to the men. He has knocked John out and walks toward me. I am no longer wearing my vial being that I had removed it in the car so this man can see my face clearly. As I get within inches from the guy, my heart stops.

Looking at his face, I can see his eyes clearly, but his face is hard to see behind the beard. This man has aged, but his eyes are the same eyes that attracted me to him years ago. With tears in the corners of my eyes I whisper, "Ryan?"

I wasn't sure whether to believe that this man might be my long-lost and believed-to-be-dead husband. The man takes my left hand, placing a finger on my wedding finger. He slips my wedding band off my knuckle, but not off my finger. My heart stops. I stop breathing because I haven't been able to remove the ring ever, and only one man can do that—my true love.

The man shows me his left hand; he is wearing the matching wedding band. When he grabs my hand, I feel the warmth I haven't felt in years. This gentlemen places my fingers on the matching wedding band. I'm able to slip his ring off his knuckle, which as the belief goes, only your true love can do that. The tears that were in the corner of my eyes roll down my face.

John has gotten up from the pavement where Ryan had knocked him down. He comes over to us to tell us he hears the police and they will be here soon. I am not losing Ryan again. I grab his hand, and we run to the embassy gates. Once at the gates Ryan is worried and asks, "I can't make it over, I don't have a passport. The guards will have to detain me."

I smile at him then to the guard and hand the guard both Ryan's and my passport. I can see the amazement in Ryan's face.

Once we clear the gates and are free from the police, I walk to a bench and sit down, still letting all this come together in my mind. I had done it, I found my long-lost husband, the one who never gave up on me and whose love had bonded us in wedding bands.

Ryan sits down on the bench beside me and grabbed my hand. Feeling the warmth of our love, we looked into each other's eyes and pull into a passionate kiss. Ryan puts his arms around me pulling me into a hug as he chants, "Habibi, Habibi, my love."

Our hug seemed to last an hour, but John told us that if we wanted to catch my runway time, we had to leave now. Once on my privet jet, I had so many questions I wanted answers to. What happened? Why was he kept? How did he live the last ten years? But all Ryan wanted to do was hold me as I make a silent moan, and he remembers the whipping Frank had given me last night, Emily had told him about.

Ryan takes my hand and leads me to the washroom on the jet, running the cold water, and asking me to remove my shirt, he wets a cloth. While he treats my back, he whispers that he is sorry, and how he only wanted to protect the kids and me.

"Are the twins actually mine?" Ryan asks once his finished cleaning my back.

I turn around to face him, "Yes, they are."

Ryan smiles shows happiness and disappointment for not being in their life. "How'd you know Angela was my mom's name?"

"When you died, I wanted the girl to have your mother's name. So Sherri told me." Hugging Ryan, I kiss him on his furry cheek and tell him I need to make a call.

I call Matt to tell him I'm on the jet leaving, and the mission was a dead end. I'll be late because I will be checking in on one of the hotels I own in Vancouver. After the phone call I go join Ryan on the jet's couch, leaning my head on his shoulder. I close my eyes and breathe the first breath of happiness that I haven't felt in a long time.

Falling asleep on Ryan I don't notice him leave my side, but I awake suddenly and in a panic because Ryan is no longer with me. I start wondering if he was here in the jet in the first place or was that just a dream. Calling out his name is a futile since I get no answer. Becoming hysterical I head for the cockpit to ask the Captain if I had brought along another passenger.

At the door to the cockpit I hear my name and turn around to see Ryan emerging from the bathroom. He is clean-shaven, his hair cut, and looking like the man I had last seen the day I came to see him in Lebanon ten years ago. The only thing that was different was that he had aged. I run to him and hug him tightly, "Don't ever leave me again!"

Hugging me back, Ryan leads me to the couch again to calm me down. "How come you never remarried?"

After wiping my tears away and clearing my throat I say, "At first it was because I was too busy raising four children, then I was establishing my career. I did date, and some men were interesting, but then it got complicated when I was not being able to remove the wedding band. I also thought it wouldn't be fair to the children, I mean none of them knew you, Elijah was very little when you left and had few memories, the other three could have been easily excepted another man as their dad but I didn't think it was the right thing for them."

"I thank you for not marrying another man and honoring me." Ryan hugs me then punches the palm of his hand with the other. "Damn it, I hate that I have missed my children growing up. Here I am coming home, and I don't know them, and they don't know me." Starting to shed some tears, he then says, "We have to have another child so I can see what it's like to watch them grow up."

I give him a gentle laugh then say, "I'm too old to have any more children, and it isn't going to make a difference. Why not just get to know your children, and you can watch all the videos I had recorded of them." I hug him and kiss him then ask, "Why is it your weren't able to leave the country? And what have you been doing for the last ten years?"

Ryan pulls away from me. "Because I had gotten you pregnant while you were married to Mark, my family wanted to punish me, so they imprisoned me. I spent five years in prison, and when I was released I had read some article saying that you were happy. My older brother Frank had made a fake birth certificate and all that information.

"I was forced into an arranged marriage and threatened that if I left, my family would be killed, you and the kids as well as my new wife," He finished while pacing the floor of the jet.

I leaned back into the couch trying to digest all this information. So he was in jail, understandable. But why did it take another five years to finally try and leave the country? And what about his wife? I decided it would be best to slowly ask these questions. I still loved him but it had been ten years, and he probably had changed.

"So your wife, where is she? And do you have children with her?" Just saying your wife made me sad. I think Ryan wouldn't have wanted to remarry, but he did and the thought of his life with another woman for five years was disturbing to me.

Ryan could see that the knowledge of him having another wife bothered me. He sat back down on the couch and said, "It wasn't like I wanted to get remarried, and trust me I didn't treat her well. But it was the life my brother had given me, so I decided to go along with it. I was worried my brother might bring harm to you or the children, and that scared the hell out of me.

Here it was I knew you guys were alive and well, but the thought of you all being dead kept me going through my day-to-day life." He paused to drink some water. "Before you saw me chasing the car, I had told Emily to remarry and have a good life. I also gave her all the money I had and sent her on her away to another country where women are treated as equals. We don't have children!"

I was glad to hear that they didn't have a child, but still thinking that he slept with another woman bothered me. "Why did it take you five years to try and escape your new life?"

"I don't know! I kept seeing you in newspapers with men, and I thought you had moved on, so I didn't want to bother you. But then I saw you on TV, and that is when I e-mailed you. For some reason I thought if you could find our son in less than two weeks, you'd be able to find me," Ryan said while trying to hug me.

For some reason that answer wasn't good enough. I stood up and paced while saying, "Ryan, I can't accept that!" I scream, "You made me marry you while Runée was carrying your child and you knew! Forced me to marry you and wouldn't let me out of your sight. So you had to remarry and think it's all okay. Thinking that I had moved on, cheated on you, to conceive the twins. Why should I believe that you wouldn't give Emily a baby? That you wanted to return home when you never tried hard enough?" Now hurt and angry, I headed to one of the conference room's on the jet and locked myself in it.

Why was I so mad at him, when I had missed him for the last ten years he'd been gone. I guess finding out that it took him five years to come find me, or try and communicate with me. How much did he love me or was he just obsessed with me.

I hear Ryan pond on the door, "Daisy let me in!" He pauses then said, "Look if you must know. Emily came home yesterday telling me how she took care of an angel. She described you, but what was the trigger was the wedding band. I went to the mansion and found out that the new maid had stolen a ring and beaten up my brothers. Well that night I decided do or die." He paused again and said, "I'm sorry, baby, that I didn't try to get home sooner. But all that doesn't mater now because we are back together now."

He was right. We had found each other again. I should try and enjoy him again. So I unlocked the door and went back to the couch with him. We both fell asleep, and when the jet landed we went to a new hotel that I just purchased. Ryan walks in without me to the floor I told him to go to. I chat with the manager shortly, and have some food sent up to my suit. I take a shower to freshen up before Ryan and I eat.

While we're eating Ryan asks, "How have things been with you and the kids?" And before I'm to answer he adds, "I wish you had told me you were pregnant with the twins."

"Well it was hard to find out you were dead, and I was put on bed rest. The doctor told me that if I didn't take it easy that I would lose the baby. So I wasn't able to grieve your death and a part of me didn't want to believe you had died. After the twins were born I still wasn't able to grieve, my life had gotten complicated with having four children and no help. My mom spent a lot of time with me, and helped me raise the children while they were young. I think when the twins were four years old is when I was really able to grieve.

"My mom was watching the children while Matt and I went on a vacation. It was then that I actually grieved my loss. My brother helped me out and when we got back I decided I really needed to get my life in track. That is when I bought more real estate, a few more restaurants, and some hotels. I have property in Vancouver and Lethbridge so I go back and forth,." I told him while I cleaned my plate.

Ryan smiled and looked at me then said, "So what do you all own? I read some stuff in the papers and on the Internet, but I'm not quite sure."

"I bought another restaurant in Lethbridge, and the newest mall. So that makes two restaurants, one mall, some rental property, and the warehouse where I sometimes do videos. In Vancouver I own two restaurants, a dance studio, recording company, three hotels, and shares in a mall,." I tell him out of breath.

Looking at Ryan I could see he is feeling inferior and not worthy. It takes him some time before he says, "I'm proud of you, that you got your life back together and are the proud owner of much investments." He finishes his supper and gets up from the table. I can see that he's not sure what to do but is extremely bothered. "I just wish I didn't miss out on my children's lives. I should have tried to get home or in touch with you no matter what."

It brings tears to my eyes seeing Ryan feeling out of place and lost. "Honey, I video taped a lot of the important things going on with the children. And we are married so therefore the property I own is also yours. You can be the manager of some of the property. I know you are feeling out of shell, but there isn't much you can do but go forward." I go to hug Ryan.

He pulls out of the hug and walks away to the bathroom. Cleaning up the dishes I try and figure a way I can make it up to him. Wondering how the children were going to take to this intrusion on their life. Here they were use to not having a man in their lives and now their long lost dead father was back and they were going to have to respect him and listen to him.

This wasn't going to be easy on anyone and especially me. I would have to play the middleman more then once in their fights. Elijah had some memories, but the rest of the children did not know him and how they would react to him was going to be something.

Ryan comes out of the bathroom after spending half and hour in. Breaking my thoughts I look up to him and study his face; how I missed the sight of him. I go over to him and place my hand on his cheek, then through his hair, with my other hand I placed on his chest. For the next few minutes I traced all his features with my hands, feeling his skin, hair, and the outline of his features. Breathing in his scent, and feeling the warmth I hadn't felt for ten years was overwhelming.

He pulls me into a tight hug and picks me up, and I wrap my legs around his waist. I let him bring me to the bed. As he lowers me, I start kissing him and removing the towel he is wearing. With intense kissing and fondling, we make passionate love for over an hour. When we are finished I feel so exhausted and fulfilled being that I hadn't made love to another man since his disappearance.

Falling into a deep sleep in the arms of my true love was like floating on cloud nine. Waking up totally rejuvenated, you wouldn't think I had just been beaten two days ago. I had renewed strength and new motivation, as well as a new task at hand.

I couldn't have timed it any better with Sherri coming down for a visit to see the kids and me. Since they still had a few days left and knew I was coming back, Sherri and Renaldo decided to extend their visit a little longer. I get off the phone after making sure they'd be home for me. I wanted to share my unfortunate news with them as well as my experience.

Once in the garage, I told Ryan to stay in the car and that I would prepare the family for his arrival. I could see the fear and excitement in his eyes at the same time. Being that he was really nervous to see his twins for the first time, and his little girl and son, I was going to make sure the children made it easier on him.

I walked into the house and was greeted by Matt, "So how was your trip?"

I pulled Matt to a corner and asked him, "It's a long story, but what I really need you to do is take, Sherri, Renaldo, Montana, and Mom upstairs to the study and wait for me. I will be up in 10 minutes and I don't want any of you to leave the room till I come to it."

Matty looked at me strangely and then asked, "Daisy is everything okay?" Trying to hide any positive look on my face, but as it was slowly slipping he then said, "When you said your mission was a failure, you were just pulling my strings. You found him? Where is he?"

As Matty was getting excited, I had to put my hand over his mouth to quiet him, "Quiet! Let me break it to the children first. And don't say a word to anyone." And before I could say more, he grabbed me into a big hug, flinching in pain from my lashings, I enjoyed being hugged by my big brother. I had missed him on my trip and I also missed my children.

Matt gathers all the adults and they headed upstairs while the children came down stairs to the living room. I hugged the twins and they tell me, I'm not allowed to leave them again. Sonyia is happy to see me, letting me know how annoying the twins were with their whining and all. Elijah is most happy to see that I'm alive considering he could feel the beating I received.

Once the children are seated at the kitchen table, I go and break the news. "I want you children to know how proud I am with how you have dealt with having no father. You all know I went to Lebanon in search for your father. Well I want you to know that if I had found him, you would have had to listen to him, treat him with respect, listen to him and lastly love him to death as if he had never missed out in your lives."

The children looked up at me, the twins confused, Sonyia sad, and Elijah with a questioning look on his face. But Sonyia was the first to answer, "We would listen to him, and treat him with respect, and I would have hugged him every day. I would have told him how much I missed him, and love him," she finished crying, thinking that he was truly dead.

The twins were next to answer, "We don't know daddy but we would like to have a dad." I had to laugh at their answer.

Elijah was trying to figure out what I was up to, I could see his wheels turning, "Mom, you know we will always love dad. And if he were here, he would get the same amount of love and attention. What are you saying?"

And at the precise moment I told Ryan to walk into the house by saying, "I'm saying that I want to see the respect, love, care, and attention you have shown me over the years directed to your father." Ryan walked in right then.

The children's faces went from confusion, to happiness as they saw their long lost father. They had only seen his pictures, and what Sonyia and Elijah remembered of him, were faint memories. Alex and Angela screamed in delight, but all four of them ran to him. Ryan knelt down to the floor to receive his hugs and kisses, the children were so happy that they had a father. I just stood back and watched them all sharing in this precious moment. As it brought tears to my eyes, Elijah stepped back and came to me. Hugging me, he said. "Mom you did it! You found dad."

I hugged my son back, "Yes I did, I just wish I had gone in search for him earlier, then you kids wouldn't have missed out on so much of being with out a father." The tears were just streaming down my face, I still felt guilty that it took me so long. When deep down in my heart, I must have know he was alive for I wouldn't move on.

I had the resources, the manpower, if I had only been more persuasive, like I had done so when Elijah was kidnapped. Did that mean I didn't love my husband as much as I loved my children? But was it my entire fault when Ryan could have tried to get in contact with me earlier. As much as I wanted to give up on the matter, it was still eating away at me already, just as the whole Runée thing did.

Wiping the tears away from my eyes, I headed upstairs to get the adults. They asked, "What's wrong? What is all the fuss about? Why is there noise in the kitchen?"

I shrug my shoulders and tell them, "The kids were excited to see me and their presents. I also bought you guys presents." Sherri looks at me oddly, but she, Renaldo, Mom and Montana all head downstairs for the living room, to join the children. Matthew walks beside me, grabs my hand as if to tell me how proud he is.

Once Sherri gets downstairs and sees her brother she screams and runs to him. Renaldo, Mom and Montana are all excited to. I stand back with Matt and we watch as everyone hugs Ryan, while asking him a thousand questions.

Matt goes over and hugs Ryan, telling him how happy he is that he's home. Although I'm still unsure of many things, and feel not only sad but guilty. I try and push my feeling aside so that we can all party and celebrate.

Outside I start the barbeque, and have a smoke. Only then does my mom walk outside and to me, "Honey what's wrong? You would think you'd be happy?"

Perceptive as she is, she notices that I was stressed since I was smoking again after quitting a few years ago. I look at her and say, "I'm so confused, Mom. Granted he was imprisoned for five years, then forced into a marriage for the last five. What I don't understand is why it took ten years for him to get in touch with me. He says it was because I looked happy, but I don't believe him when he was so obsessed with me that we had to marry the minute I was divorced from my first marriage. He could have e-mailed me the minute he got out of jail instead of five years later!" I sit down, have a puff of my smoke, and put the stakes on the grill.

Mom sits down beside me. "Baby, I'm not sure. But maybe it was because he was afraid of causing harm to you or the children. Whatever his reason, I'm sure he meant you no harm. He was probably trying to gain the trust of his captors," she said with compassion.

I stand up, look at her with hurt and frustration. "That's not good enough! This man supposedly loves me to death, yet he will go along with this marriage, sleep with his wife whereas I never cheated on him, and the thought of being married to another man never crossed my mind!" I yelled in frustration.

My mom came to comfort me and quietly said, "Well you have to decide whether you want to forget all this and move on to be happy. Or whether you still want to be with him. Is this going to be something you can get over or not?" She hugged me, then went back to sit down.

I looked at her scared to admit what she was saying. I could move on now, the kids had their father back in their life. If I did leave Ryan they would still be able to know and build a relationship with him. Or I could try and move past this, like I had with Runée and that situation. But had I completely forgiven him for that, No! With all this information, I wasn't sure I wanted to be an obsession one moment and then forgotten the next.

Playing with the stakes on the grill, I said to mom under my breath but loud enough for her to hear. "The only reason he decided to leave was because he heard from Emily his wife, that a woman of my appearance was beaten and working at the estate. Once all the facts were there, that a woman with my wedding band and looks, he then decided to leave and break out of the country!"

My mom looked up at me stunned by the information I just delt her. I could see she didn't know what to say, or do.

Everyone gathered around the patio table, to enjoy their supper and Ryan being that he was home. I tell them about my trip and meeting Ryan and Sherri's older brother Frank. Sherri agrees with me, how much of a monster he is. I tell them all about my getting a server lashing for the idea of stealing. Everyone flinches in pain when I show them and my mom tells me I should get a doctor to look at it to make sure it doesn't get infected.

Elijah now understands the pain he felt on his back; what it was they did to me to caused his pain.

After supper, I make an excuse that I have to check on the steakhouse I own. But not only am I going to go, I'm also going to go the hospital to get my wound looked at. The doctor cleans my wounds, and puts a bandage on it, along with a cream to help it heal and not scar.

When I get back to the house, Sherri and Renaldo are in bed. Matthew and Montana had left along with Denis and Holly, their two little ones now seven and five years old. Mom also went home, but only after making sure Ryan would be all right being alone with the children.

Ryan was already in our bedroom, waiting for me. I ask him how things went when I was out. He tells me great. Explaining how he put the children to bed, and how much he loves the twins as well as Sonyia and Elijah. Once I'm dressed for bed, Ryan comes over to me and starts to kiss me. I tell him I'm exhausted, that it was a long day. He tells me I wont have to do anything. In the end we make love, but I'm not completely in it as I still have much on my mind.

The next morning I'm all dressed and ready to go to the office to finish my paper work for the trip. Ryan comes out of the bathroom and thinking he might be in a good mood I'm taken back by the ton of his voice, "Where are you going? I just got back and we need to talk about having another baby. I want another child! So therefore you need to take some time off, so we can work on having a baby."

Still upset about everything that I know, and now hearing him start to demand things from me. "I have businesses to run, the kids need to be taken to school, and I am not having another baby. I've raised four children alone and am not about to raise another." I tell him with a sharp tone.

He comes over to me, grabs my shoulders and says, "Fine take the kids to school. The businesses ran while you were away and can run with out you. But we are having another baby. I missed out on the twins growing up as well as Sonyia, not to mention Elijah. But now I'm home and I want to have another child." And with out letting me answer him, he started to kiss me with aggression. Trying to undo my pants, so that we could work on this baby, I managed to free myself of him.

I got away from him, and at our bedroom door. "Look just because you have been gone for ten years doesn't make you the boss again. I know you were use to bossing your other wife around, but I have been without a husband for 10years and will not have you telling me what to do!" I yelled at him before leaving the room.

I took the kids to school, leaving Ryan at home to do what ever he wanted. There was no way I wanted to be around him right now, so heading to the office I decided to leave Ryan a message telling him I'd be out all day. Was I crazy to leave my estranged husband alone in the house or city he was a stranger to now.

CHAPTER 11

Being a week from the day Ryan came home, my attitude toward him hadn't changed and I hadn't gotten use to him bossing me around. Granted he did tell me what to do or not to do while he was home before being missing for 10 years. But ever since he was gone, he'd gotten worse. It was like I was going to have to rebreak him of bad habits.

His relationship with the children got better and the twins loved having a father around. Sonyia was between being jealous and annoyed for all the attention his was giving Alex and Angela. Not only was he treating me like a second-class citizen, but he was also making Sonyia feel less of a person some times.

Elijah was so busy with school and his sports since it was his last year before his graduating year, that Ryan and him hadn't spent much time together. But even when Ryan was living with us before, they were never as close as him and I.

Ryan was still at me to have another baby, and every night he wanted to have sex whether I wanted to or not. This wasn't how I thought things would be with having him home. I guess I always pictured, the loving couple who missed each other.

I could see that I was getting under his skin with being obstinate, not wanting to make another baby, listen to him, and having an attitude toward him. And instead of being the wife who'd pine for her husband, I was being a distant and bitchy wife. I was fighting with him more than I was loving him.

So in June a month later when I missed my period, it came as no shock to me that I was pregnant. Going to the doctors to have my back checked, I found out I was truly pregnant.

It was a month from when I had first had sex with Ryan, and my back had healed perfectly leaving me a slight scar.

Going home with this information made me mad, confused more than I already was. I needed to resolve some things with my husband before bringing this child into our crazy life.

It was easy to make a decision before, stay with Ryan and put up with his behaviour and old ways of domination. Or leave him, and share custody, because spending the month of having him back was making my decision to leave him even easier.

Sure he had started to work at the restaurants, not wanting to have anything to do with the Hotels or Properties. He was still being demanding, bossy, treating me like a Lebanese woman, not an equal. Granted he was good with the kids, but I was not enjoying getting in trouble for coming home late, or not having supper prepared on time, smoking, dressing to sexy, and not wanting to have a baby with him.

So here I was a month pregnant, and leaving him was no longer an option. I would have to make him change his ways and start treating me with more respect or else he'd be raising this child alone.

As for the whole part about him not trying to leave Lebanon, that was still bothering me. I still hadn't come to terms with him not trying to escape till he had proof I was there. I needed more answers and to come to a resolution if I were to carry on being married to him.

The kids were watching TV when I got home, Ryan was with them. He gave me a look of disapproval when I am home late and missed supper. I tell him we need to talk and in our room.

Once in our room he decides to lay into me for neglecting our children. "Is this how you have been raising them. This is not how you be a mother! Come home when you want, have some one else prepare their food and put them to bed?" He demanded from me.

This is not how I wanted to start this news off with, but if we were going to get into a fight, so be it. "Look you have no right to judge me. I have done the best I could to raise our children. They need food, clothes, and money for all their activities. They have never complained about me working. Yes some times I have had my mother make their supper and put them to bed, but that is because I have been busy. I have never missed one important even in their lives, so don't start throwing accusations at me."

He walks up to me, grabs my shoulders. "Don't you raise your voice to me! It isn't my fault I haven't been in their lives for the past 10years. But in this last month I have done a better job then you have." Shaking me gently, he turns around then says, "I want you to become more of a mom to these children and stay home more. I can go to work and make the money."

Now I am fuming, who does this man think he is? That he can come back into my life, start getting aggressive with me, blaming me for his absents. "Well it sure isn't my fault that you have not been here. In fact if I hadn't come to your country you would not be here, because you weren't man enough to leave your new wife. No you say you weren't happy but honestly, you must have been. Because if you truly did love Elijah, Sonyia or I, you would have moved heaven and earth to come back to us. So let me ask you this, what would you have done if I hadn't come to your country? The way I see it is, you had a wife given to you and granted she was pretty. You slept with her, but maybe she couldn't give you a child even though you say you wouldn't get her pregnant." And with that said I walked up to him and slapped him.

I heard the crisp sound of my hand my on his face; I watched the blood rush to the spot my hand made as it hit. There was shock in his eyes, and hurt. He sat down on the edge of the bed then said, "I don't know. I had spent five years in prison for a crime that was not a crime. We had made love, and Elijah was the result of it. But they didn't understand, and there was no way I could leave the prison. I tried and every time I had to pay the price. I spent time in the hole, was beaten by whip or by fists. It got so bad that thinking of you and trying to escape was causing me more pain that it was easier to just allow them to brainwash me. Originally, I had a prison sentence of two years, but the more I talked about my previous life, or tried to escape, the more years they added."

He pause, wiped a few tears from his eyes. "When I was finally released, I wasn't truly released because they put an ankle monitor on me. I guess Frank still didn't trust me. Sure I was remarried, that was in hopes of satisfying me and make me forget my past life. But it took a long time before I slept with Emily, I felt so guilty. But when I saw you with another man in the paper, I felt a little better about doing it. Yes I had a job, but with the ankle bracelet on, I wasn't able to get to a computer without it going off."

Running his hands through his hair, he continued, "About six months ago they finally removed the ankle bracelet, but not without warning me that I was being watched. Feeling completely defeated, I accepted my new life. I thought you were happy and had moved on, heck I had seen that you had twins. Assuming you had moved on, I was shocked when I saw you on TV and heard that you hadn't."

Looking up at me he smiled, but then said, "Once I had that information, I wasn't sure whether to contact you or not. It took me a week to figure it out, so I wouldn't get caught and I felt guilty for having given up on you. But once you wrote back on the email, I felt a new hope."

He gave me a little chuckle, "I wasn't sure you'd come since I had told you never to come to the country. But I hoped you'd be determined as you were when Elijah was kidnapped, in finding me. Not hearing any word back from you for a couple weeks, made me wonder what was going on."

Ryan stood up, walked over to me, placing his hands gently on my shoulders he said, "But when Emily came home and told me she saw a angel with golden hair, green eyes and a matching wedding band. My heart did flips, and I knew you came looking for me. When my brother confirmed her story, I was hoping to either find you at the Estate or in town somewhere. But if I didn't find you I was willing to get shot, even though I hoped I could make enough of a fuss at the Embassy gates that they'd let me in."

He smiled at me, kissing me gently on the lips, "So when I saw you at my mothers grave. I knew fate sent an angel to help me, and when you were leaving in the car there was no way I was losing you a second time." Pausing he looked me directly in the eyes, "And the rest you now. But believe me when I say I'm sorry that I slept with Emily. If things had been different, I swear I would never have slept with her. I could understand if you had moved on, and had slept with other men."

I was taken back with all he had said. Finally I knew the story and with knowing, I couldn't hate him any more. But he was going to have to start treating me better.

"I'm sorry you went through all that. But I understand now and don't hate you. All I have to say is, you are back home where women are equals, so I would like you to stop treating me like you own me. I have survived very well without you, and if you keep it up, I will leave you."

He looked at me shocked that I had mentioned that. "I'm sorry. It was hard for me to treat Emily with disrespect, but I guess I fell back into my old ways. So I will try to get back to treating you as an equal, because you are right. You have raised four beautiful children, who show respect, compassion, intelligence, and are very healthy."

"Thankyou." I hugged him tightly then pulled away but not out of his arms. I kissed him gently on the lips, then said. "By the way Emily can't have children, because if she could, you'd have a few." He looked at me puzzled. "You got your wish. Happy home coming Papa."

Ryan looked at me intensely to see what I was saying, and with a questioning look he asked, "Are you?" All I had to do was smile at him, and he grabbed me and spun me around. He was so happy it was all over his face.

He showered me with kisses as I said with humour, "Just don't leave me to raise another baby alone."

As Christmas arrived, Ryan and the children were more comfortable with each other. I was in my seventh month of the pregnancy and wasn't feeling the difficulties I had with the other children. While we are opening our presents, there was a knock at the door. Since Ryan was helping the twins put together one of their toys, I went to answer the door.

Opening the door I was not expecting to see who I did. I was looking this tall dark-skinned man in the face. Seeing Frank clearly, I instantly felt fear in my gut. After clearing my throat, I ask him, "What are you doing here?"

He put his hands in his pockets and said, "I bring you no harm. I just wanted to see my nephews and nieces and brother. And I owe the two of you an apology."

Not sure what to think of this, if it is a trick or he is being serious, I welcome Frank into our home, but was prepared that he might do something dangerous. I brought him into the living room where everyone is opening their presents and having fun.

Once all eyes are directed to Frank, the room goes silent. Ryan gets up and demands to know why he is here, pulling Frank by the arm into the kitchen where the kids wouldn't be able to hear.

Ryan demands in a quiet voice, "What are you doing here? You can not do what you did to me in Lebanon here in Canada."

I can see Frank is uncomfortable, "I am serious when I mean that I came to see my extended family. I'm sorry for what I put you through brother. Your right, what goes on in Canada shouldn't reflect what goes on in our country." As Frank is starting to sweat, "I'm sorry for not trying to understand you and your love. And after reading up on Daisy, I give her credit for raising four children and building an empire." Frank smiles and looks to me. Right then he see my newly swollen belly, "Congratulations on the new baby."

We get things straightened out and then join the children. After introducing them to their uncle, we finish celebrating Christmas.

Being that I wasn't a young woman any more, I was happy that this pregnancy was going smoother then my previous pregnancy's. For the last seven months I was able to continue running the businesses full strength, work with some musicans on videos, and spend lots of quality time with my husband and kids.

Having Ryan back was hard to get use to, but after we got everything out in the open and he eased up on being controlling. We were doing almost better then we did before he was gone for 10years. I knew I was never going to break him of all of his controlling behaviour because that was who he was from the day I met him.

It was a beautiful sunny day in March when I gave birth to Zack. Ryan couldn't have been happier to have another boy, and the kids were so happy to have a little brother.

After bringing Zack home from the Hospital Ryan wanted to be a full time parent to him. I made sure to have enough milk pumped before going to work earlier in the morning, that way Ryan wouldn't have to worry about making bottles.

Spending so much time at work I hadn't seen the change in Ryan until Elijah brought it to my attention one night when I had returned home from work. "Mom, I know your busy and all but I wanted you to know that Dad has been paying more attention to Zack and forgetting the rest of us."

Taking my jacket and shoes off, I walk to my office while Elijah was telling me all this. "He's probably not forgetting you guys. He's just excited about raising Zack and enjoying all the little things he missed out on with Sonyia, Alex and Angela. I'm sure its nothing."

Elijah sits down in one of the chairs in my office and says, "Before Zack arrive and a month after Zack was born, Dad made our lunches, cleaned the house, spent time helping me to practice for my sports, did girl things with Sonyia and put the twins to bed. Now he doesn't do any of that and rarely acknowledges us."

I sat down in my leather chair behind my desk, sighed, and pondered for a bit before answering. Because I got home so late, the twins were already in bed, so I wasn't witness to Ryan putting them to bed. As for Sonyia she seemed more withdrawn, always said nothing was wrong. But she had asked me to go to the mall with her more. Yes, Ryan was spending tons of time with his favorite daughter, at first and I had not seen much of her, but now she wanted to spend time with me. I just figured she was getting older and needed her mom.

As for Ryan and my chemistry, we hadn't made love in a long time. Usually we always had sex before bed, but for some reason he always had a headache. I hadn't put much thought to his excuse. I just thought he was just trying to punish me for working so late. Because I was working long hours and making small trips to Lethbridge, Ryan and I hadn't done much talking. "I'll talk to your father, everything will be all right."

Turning the computer on to look at some of my emails, I then ask. "How is school going? Your grades still up? Any dates I need to mark off on the calendar? Excited about graduating?" Being that this was his graduating year.

Elijah looked at me and hesitated, "Schools good. My grades are still B's and I was wondering if I could go on a trip with the school? I want to know if I can have a grad party?"

I could see the anxiety in my sons face, "Well I would prefer A's and if you can pull off A's this last semester then I will allow you your grad Party. I'm glad you are getting B's but in order to get sports scholarships, you need A's. Where is this trip? And how much is it going to cost?" Even though money wasn't an issue with me, I still wanted my son to be brought up with morals and values.

"I still have time to improve my grades for college. The school tip is a week in France and we'd be studying the history of the country. It's a $1000. Plus any spending money if you want." Elijah told me with hope in his eyes.

I leaned back in my chair, glanced at some of the emails that Hillary had sent me for the report on the Restaurant, then glanced back at Elijah. "All right, I want your grades to improve, because this is your last semester. I'll pay for the trip, but the spending money you'll have to come up with. If you want a job to make up the rest, I can let one of my mangers know, but you'll have to work like the rest of the employees. Sure I'll probably send you down with some souvenir money for gifts for the family, but you can't spend that. Who's all chaperoning? And what are the sleeping arrangements?"

Reading another email, Elijah then says, "There will be four teaches going along and six parents. The girls and boys will have their own rooms, so you have nothing to worry about mom."

"What?" I looked up not quiet hearing all that was said, because the email was important.

Elijah got up from his chair, walked over to me and kissed my cheek. "Thanks Mom."

After telling him good night, I got back to my emails and business. Making a few calls before bed, I managed to fix a few small problems. I checked in on the twins and they were fast asleep. When I peeked in on Sonyia, she was still up, writing in her diary. Sitting on her bed, I asked her if she was having problems with dad. Sonyia told me she was too busy with school and dance to have time for dad.

I didn't quite believe her, but because I was preoccupied with work. I didn't give it more thought, kissing her goodnight I then went to check on Zack. Going into Zacks room, I wasn't expecting to see Ryan in their watching him sleep. Walking up to the crib, I placed my arm on Ryan's shoulders and said, "I'm sure he's fine. Come to bed with me." I kissed his forehead and left the room to get ready for bed.

Not realizing it had taken me almost an hour to get ready for bed, I stepped out and noticed Ryan wasn't in our room yet, so I thought I'd read a little.

As I was reading Ryan finally came to bed, and as he got under the covers I said, "What is going on with you lately that you are ignoring the other children?"

141

"Nothing, I haven't been ignoring Elijah, Sonyia, or the twins," Ryan said as he brought the covers to his chin then kissed me good night and turned off his lamp.

"Look, I know I have been very busy lately but the children have stressed their concerns with me. What is going on that is making you neglect the children?" I demand from him as I turn the light back on.

Ryan turns to me and with a raised voice says, "Damn it Daisy, that is it. You are never home. So how would you know what goes on. Kids don't always tell the truth, maybe they are making me look bad so that you will ease up on working so much."

As he glares at me, I fear to continue this fight would be a terrible mistake. Turning off the lamp, I roll over and try to sleep. Since attempting to sleep is becoming a hard task, I head for the kitchen.

Grabbing my smokes and a bottle of wine, I head for the patio. As I sit on the patio and sip my wine I think about what has been going on that I have seen. When I get up Ryan is always with Zack and when I come home from work, he is still with the baby. The days I have been home I have noticed that Ryan wasn't spending much time with the rest of us.

I finished my wine and went to bed. For the next week I pay more attention to what Ryan is doing and how he is behaving. After my week of observation I was going to confront Ryan, but I get called away on business. Asking my mom to check on the kids and Ryan, I feel more comfortable with going away for a bit.

With having to spend a week in Lethbridge straightening out my affairs, I headed home to have my mom, tell me that Ryan is indeed behaving oddly. He's very aggressive and is not eating much, spending all his time with Zack in the nursery.

I get a horrible feeling, one that is Ryan has forgotten all the other children so that he can focus on seeing all the little things he missed out on with Zack. "Mom can you please take the kids, including Zack for dinner?"

She didn't have to ask why, she knew just by looking at me. I put my suitcase down and took my jacket off, saying good-bye to the children and telling them to behave with Grandma. I went upstairs only to run into a confused Ryan.

"Where is Zack? He's missing. What have you done with my son?" Ryan yells at me.

I close my eyes, shake my head and head for our room. Sitting down at my makeup table, Ryan comes shortly to join me, but only to yell some more.

"Ryan, Zack is with mom. They all went out for supper. Because I want to know what the hell is going on with you that you need to ignore the rest of your family." I tell him as I start brushing my hair.

"Well tell your mom to bring him back. He could get sick or need me. How could you let him leave this house with out me? And I'm not ignoring any one, I'm just making up for lost time." Ryan said as he started to pace.

"You are Zack's father, not his mom. There fore you need to spend time with your other kids. Sonyia and Elijah know a bit of you, but Alex and Angela still don't know you enough." I told him quietly.

Ryan comes up behind me and grabs my hand with the hair brush in it. Squeezing my hand, he says angrily. "I have been deprived of many things, but this is one thing you are not going to control. So if you feel you need to work, then work. But don't judge me for my raising of Zack."

Trying to pull out of his grasp, I whimper. "Ryan your hurting me." He lets go of my hand and the brush drops. Standing up from the chair, I turn to face him and in doing so I see enrage in his face. "Your not well. You wont even have sex with me. We use to have sex every night. If I go out dressed sexy you don't even say anything. Elijah feels like you don't care enough about him, and Sonyia feels like she's not Daddy's little girl anymore."

I try moving out of the way because I can see that what I said has hit home with Ryan. As his hand comes out to slap me on the face, I fall to the bed. Feeling the sting of the slap, Ryan is on top of me and grabbing my arms to prevent me from fighting back. Turning my head away from looking directly at him. He lowers his face to mine, and I feel his hot breath and his racing heart as he says, "When I was gone for ten years you dressed like a slut anyway. You gave me what I wanted, and that is Zack. So call your mom and have her bring him back! The other children don't even respect me or care that I am back. They are using me, therefore they don't exist to me."

He lets go of my hands and pulls himself off of me. Not wanting to believe what he just said, I feel the tears built up. Here my husband is saying that his kids don't matter. "You don't mean that!" I yell at him. His answer is to hit me again. A back hand to the face, but I manage to catch my fall. Putting a hand to where he hit me, I say. "I want a divorce! And I will be taking full custody of Zack!"

Ryan comes at me, and I know it is going to be deadly. As I run for the door and try to open it, Ryan catches up to me and slams my head into our door. As my head is pressed up against the door, I feel the pain in my neck and back. Feeling his breath against my skin, I fear for my life for the first time being with Ryan.

And because I fear for my life, I kick him from behind and hit him in the balls. Ryan falls back in pain, I turn around and instead of running for my life I decide to beat him up for the first time in our marriage.

While he's on the ground I start kicking him. Ryan grabs my leg and flips me. As he gets back on his feet, I flip around and land on my feet. We are facing each other, and I know he's going to hit me again, so I punch him in the face. I hit him so hard that he goes down, hits his head hard on the floor.

Scared that I might have killed him, I check for a pulse and there is one. I call the police to have them collect my husband. I also tell them maybe to bring the Phyc ward.

Ryan is cuffed and being led out of the house while screaming for Zack. He starts to struggle and the Ambulance attendant give him a shot to calm him down. The kids come back with Grandma and I have to break the news to them, which they don't take very well. Sonyia takes it very hard and Zack seems lost without his daddy.

PART 4

CHAPTER 12

For the first week my husband is run through a bunch of neurological tests. But he shows no better progress with his behaviour and attitude. While he is in the confinements of his room, he screams for Zack. I go to visit and he doesn't acknowledge me, and tries to harm me, but the nurses step in.

The doctors decide to run Ryan through x-rays and other tests to see if there is some form of tumour or cancer that may be causing the change for his behaviour.

With Ryan being locked away in a phyc ward, I had to spend more time at home with the children and especially Zack. He was so confused with not having his dad around, and because I wasn't the primary parent I was a stranger to my son.

While I was making us supper, Ryan's doctor called me, "Mrs. Gaston? Is there any way you can come to the hospital?"

"Well right now I am making super. Is there anyway this can wait till tomorrow?" I asked the doctor a little shaken.

"I'm afraid not Mrs. Gaston!" the doctor said sternly.

Just hearing the tone in the doctor's voice send a dagger to my heart, "Is my husband okay?" I asked trying to stay calm.

"He's fine for now, but I really need to speak with you." The doctor said before having to attend a paige.

I yell for Elijah to watch the children and finish making supper, he can see that I am bothered and asks, "Mom what's wrong? Why do you have to go to the hospital so soon? Is dad okay?"

As I'm trying gather everything, to rush out the door. I say, "Please Elijah, just do as I ask! I can't get into it now." And on that note I leave the house, not sure what to expect from the doctor.

Once at the hospital I had to wait for the doctor to get out of the room of the patient he was seeing to. After thirty minutes of waiting I am starving, very stressed and concerned for my husband. Finally the doctor comes out to speak with me.

Going into a privet office, Ryan's doctor went straight into what he needed to tell me. "After looking over your husbands x-rays and ultrasounds, we have spotted a tumour on your husbands left temple. This is what is causing the erratic behaviour in him. Because the tumour is so large it is interfering with his memory and reasoning." The doctor sits down at his desk.

I am shocked. It makes sense, but at the same time the thought of a tumour on his brain frightened the hell out of me. "What is to happen to him?" I ask holding on to the last bit of nerves I have left in me.

"We will need to operate on him immediately. When we operate, we will find out if it is a malignant or benign tumour." The doctor passes me a piece of paper. "I'm surprised this had never shown up earlier."

Looking at the paper, I see it is a consent form. Swallowing the large lump forming in my throat, I read on to understand that I will be allowing the doctors to work on my husband, and the surgery may have consequences, especially because of the size of the tumour. "What do you want me to do?" I ask.

"I need you to sign the consent form, allowing us to do an emergency removal. Just like any other surgery there are risks, but I feel your husband will be better after we remove the tumour." The doctor told me with a little more compassion.

After signing the form, I went to look in on my husband. He was asleep in his room, calm but not for long. I was going to have to tell him what was going to happen to him tomorrow.

When I got into his room, and woke him. Ryan didn't seem to know who I was. "Honey, tomorrow you will be going for surgery. The surgery is to remove a tumour on your brain." I tried to hug Ryan but he seemed bothered.

Ryan wondered around his room muttering Zack's name, disturbed by this I lightly touched his arm and say, "After the surgery, you will be able to see Zack. He misses you and so do the rest of the family."

Leaving the hospital I was feeling drained, empty, and scared not only for myself but for Ryan. I wasn't sure if he was sane enough to feel scared or worried. Heck I wasn't even sure if he was going through a slow nightmare, one that takes forever to get to the end or seems hard to wake up from.

Never having experienced any of the pain of stress Ryan was dealing with, I wasn't sure how to deal with him or his treatment. Even though the doctor's said the surgery is something they perform all the time. I still worried that they might find more when they opened him up.

The drive home seamed to go so slowly that I felt like I could open the door and step outside to walk the speed I was going. Things were going through my mind, going faster then I felt they were.

Once at home I break the news to the children, and they all reacted emotionally. Elijah calls my mom to have her come to the house, while I make the calls to Ryans sister Sherri and to Frank and his brother Marshall. Sherri tells me she want's to be there and they will take the next flight out, but I insist that they just get what they need and I'll send my jet.

Frank says he really can't do much but does wish Ryan the best.

The twins are confused and they mostly want dad to be all right and come home to play with them. Zack doesn't know what's going on, except his favorite parent isn't home. Elijah understands what is going on and says he will help out in any way he can. After Elijah hugs me, I go to Sonyia's room to see what's up with her.

Sonyai is sitting on her bed, back against the bed frame, and she is writing in her diary. "Honey we should talk." I move to her bed and sit beside her, I start playing with her hair and then say, "I know that you are really close with your father and that you and I are not as close. But we were close when your dad wasn't here, so I'm glad you now have a father to give you the attention you were deprived as a young girl."

She finishes writing and puts her pen and diary down. "It's not fair! Uncle Frank imprisons him so we grow up with out a father for ten years and you become busy with all your businesses. Then you find him and brought him home, and we weren't enough. You guys had to have another baby, a baby who is cuter and takes our returned father away from us, the ones who have suffered ten years with out a dad. Why does Zack get him, and why'd he have to get sick?" Sonyia finished with tears streaming down her face and her voice whinny.

I bring her to me and hug her. Petting her hair I gently say, "I know it's not fair. Because your dad missed out in you kids' upbringing, he wanted another child so that he could see what he was missing out on. I'm sorry that I haven't been the proper mother to you as well, but I will try harder for you, sweety." Sonyia pulls away from my shoulder she was crying on and looks in my eyes. "Daddy will be all right, and when they remove the tumour, I promise he will be back to his old self spending time with all you children, not just Zack."

As I wipe her tears from her face Sonyia says, "I hope so Mom. I missed him so much and I pray that he survives the surgery." We hug once more, before I head to my room to have a moment to myself.

On the patio off my master bedroom, I sit and have a smoke. Listening to the birds chirp, the smell of the air, and the colors of evening spring, I ponder everything. Lost in my thoughts I don't hear Elijah come up behind me, "Mom! You know dad would kill you if he saw you smoking." I look toward the smoke in my hand and laugh.

"Well there's a lot of things your dad would love to kill me for, but I don't think he is in that position to kill anyone." I comment.

Elijah sits down in the patio chair next to me, "I know, I was just trying to be funny and cheer you up. Dad will be all right, I'm sure its just a small tumour and not spreadable. If you are worried about us children, we will be fine and help out around the house." My son then puts his arm around my shoulders and hugs me. We sit on the patio for what seems to be a very long time. Elijah leaves before I get up and see to the twins and Zack.

Sherri and Renaldo arrive three hours from when I called them. My mom is at the house and is helping me with the children. I call my secretary to have her reschedule my appointments and let her know that I'll be away from the office for two weeks at least.

149

The next morning as Sherri, Renaldo, Matty, Montana, Elijah, and I are in the waiting room while Ryan has been taken into surgery. My mom is watching the twins, Zack and my brother's two children. I tried to hug, kiss and say I love you to Ryan before he went into surgery but he still had a confused look on his face, as well as was still talking babble.

Waiting for the doctor to come out after the surgery felt like hours. We talked very little between us and I don't know who was more nervous Sherri or I. While I am flipping through a magazine, the doctor came out of surgery. My heart froze as I awaited the news, "Mrs. Gaston I want to let you know that the surgery went well. The Tumour was pretty big and it's a good thing we got to it before it was too late."

Hearing that, "before it was too late." Made my body go stiff as I waited to hear the rest of what the doctor was going to say. "Because the Tumour was still growing, it had also grown into the speech part of the brain and we had to remove a small part of the speech tissue. If we hadn't he would be back in here to have another tumour removed and then who knows what kind of damage the tumour would have done." The doctor paused for a second before continuing, "Ryan has survive the surgery with no more traces of Tumours. He will have to have speech therapy to help him regain what speech he has lost. He is out of the woods for now, but still has a lot of work ahead of him."

My heart started to beat again, my body got less tense and I stood up to hug the doctor for saving my husbands life. Then the whole family and I all hugged each other. While we waited to see Ryan in recovery, the family and I went to eat.

Before the food arrived, I called my mom and told her what the doctor told us. I was finally able to relax and enjoy a meal with piece of mind knowing that things were going to get back to normal for a little while. It was going to be hard at first with Ryan since he wasn't going to be able to speak. I knew this would kill Ryan but at least he would be home with his family and could live as normal as possible.

I let everyone go and see Ryan first, cause I wasn't sure how Ryan would react to me. Once Sherri, Renaldo, Matthew, Montana and Elijah were done visiting Ryan, I step into the hospital room. Ryan looked at me, I could see he was tired so I wouldn't stay to long.

I stood at the foot of the bed, still nervous. Ryan extended his hand out to me. I move to the head of the bed to grab his hand. We hold hands, and Ryan strokes my hand. It was the first form of affection I had received from Ryan in the last couple months. I knew then that my husband was going to be better, except for the fact that he might not be able to speak again.

I stat on his bed and leaned in toward him. Kissing him on the lips, I patted his hand and told him that I loved him very much. Spending five minutes with him, we just cuddled. In the end Ryan drifted off to sleep, and I kissed his forehead and left to go home.

The next day when I went to see Ryan, I found out he'd been induced into a comma. Finding out that during the night he was having complications from the surgery, so the doctor on call thought it would be best if he was put into a comma so he wouldn't get an infection and his brain would have a better chance at healing.

For the next month I spent most of my time in the hospital beside his bedside. The children came and visited him when they were up to it. Ryan's room was becoming very homey with all the drawings, pictures, cards and flowers in it. Sherri decided to stay at the house to help me with the children while Renaldo went back to take care of his businesses. Hillary was getting a work out having to take care of all my affairs. I was only able to take care of the affairs in Vancouver, that way I was still able to see my husband.

The doctor informed me that his brain waves were excellent, his surgery scar was healing, and the doctor felt very confident that Ryan would awake from his comma pretty soon. But the next step would be physio and speech therapy. The doctor warned me that this would be a long processes and very hard.

I awoke to someone petting my hand, looking up I saw Ryan staring at me with a smile on his face. I smiled back at him and said "hi." He goes to say hi, but nothing comes out of his voice, trying a few more times to say "hi." I can see that for him trying to talk and having nothing come out is making him scared, and angry. Before he can freak out, I call for the doctor so that Ryan understands what's happened.

The doctor tells my husband about the surgery, the tumour and how a small piece of his brain had to be removed. The Doctor informs Ryan that he will be able to talk again, but needs to have speech therapy. As Ryan is hearing this information, I can see his wheels turning. He is trying to figure out when this all happened, and after handing him a pen and a pad so that he can communicate with us.

Writing down on his pad, he tells us that he remembers spending time with the children and then having head aches. Being that is all he can remember, the doctor explains that this is part of the tumours doing.

Ryan has to spend another week at the hospital to regain the strength he lost while being in a common, when the doctor gives him the okay to go home, I pick him up. The kids are so happy to have him come home that they throw him a party two weeks from his homecoming. Ryan has gotten use to having to write on his doodle pad, but hates having to do so.

While everyone is having a good time talking to Ryan, I go have a smoke on the balcony. I didn't hear my mom come out, "Honey you need to quite smoking. Your husband is home and everything is fine now."

I roll my head from side to side, frustrated by my moms intrusion. All I wanted was some time to think about my new life and how I was going to handle it. "Mom its not like I'm a chain smoker. I just have a smoke when I feel stressed, and right now I wanted to have a moment to my self while everyone entertains Ryan."

"Why don't you spend some family time with everyone, they didn't just come to see Ryan, they came to see everyone. You're being selfish!" My mom snapped at me.

I take a long deep inhale of my smoke then turn to look at my mother with enraged eyes and say to her with a harsh tone, "You have not had to spend the last two weeks glued to your husband! I can't do anything on my own, and Ryan hates to be alone. I understand he can't speak and is frightened, but my staff needs me to get back to work. Hillary needs me, she is very stressed with the restaurant, and with her being pregnant again I can't be tied down to a cripple."

Looking at my mothers face I could see I just disappointed her. "Mom, I never thought in my wildest dreams, I would be raising five children and a handicapped husband."

My mom isn't sure how to react but says, "I know it is going to be hard. But Ryan is going to therapy and will be able to speak in no time. You just need to be stronger and more patient. It will all work out just fine and as for your businesses, you should just hire more people."

I finish my smoke and put it out, then walk around on the deck before joining mom at the railing before saying with a laugh. "It would be great to hire more staff, but I'm kind of busy with a speech impaired husband." Then adding with a chuckle, "First the horrible way in how we got married, then the Mexico thing, Elijah being kidnapped, then almost losing Sonyia and shortly after that having Ryan's mom die and his family sentence him to jail." Not laughing anymore, starting to well up with tears,

"So then after ten years I go to rescue him, my children have grown up most of their life without a father and they finally get one. But no Ryan wants another child and then gets a tumour." As tears are breaking free of my eyes I then say, "So here I have four children that feel their dad doesn't really want to get to know then, he would rather see what he missed out on with having Zack around, rather then build memories with them!"

My mom puts her arm around me and pulls me into a hug. Hugging for a long time, I didn't see that Ryan had come outside to talk with me. I look over my mom's shoulders and see Ryan heading back into the house. My heart drops and I feel sick to my stomach with thinking how much Ryan might have heard. Taking my right hand that was on my mom's back I bring it to my eyes and close them in pain, for Ryan had overheard me and I didn't say anything nice about him.

Once the guests had left and the children were in bed, I got ready for bed. Since Ryan had been sleeping in the guest room since he got back, I always went to him and said good night. Ryan had no memory of the last few months before his surgery, so he didn't know how uncomfortable I felt with having him back in our bed.

He was in my office on the computer. I asked him if he was going to bed soon and he gave me a thumbs up. So I went over to him and kissed him goodnight.

On the balcony in my bedroom, I had a quick smoke while thinking how I was going to apologise to him. Sure I had meant what I said, but it wasn't fair that he heard me with out explanation to my opinion. God, I hated myself for being so negligent, and not knowing he was there to over hear.

I decided to quite stressing about my problem and go apologise to him. Back in our bedroom, I saw Ryan sitting in one of the chairs in the room. With widened eyes

I wasn't sure how long he was in our room and if he had seen me smoke. He must not have or else he would have been on the deck putting it out and yelling at me for doing it. But then again he couldn't yell, so why get mad at me for smoking.

I was really feeling like crap now. Seeing a folded paper on the bed with a rose, I looked at Ryan who smiled and nodded down toward the paper, indicating I read it. Sitting down on the edge of the bed, I open the letter and read the most heartfelt and romantic letter he had ever written me.

My dear and loyal wife, I want you to know how much I understand your pain. Yes I did over hear what you told your mother, and I'm glad I did. I am truly sorry about my being kidnapped and if I could change things I would, but I didn't not know how the children were feeling. And I am glad I overheard. I never thought about it from their point of view, just my own.

I want you to know that this speech impediment will not be forever, for I cannot stand the idea of not yelling, talking, whispering, and laughing with you. I also want you and the children to know that I am not going anywhere. I want to make it up to all of you, the kids need me to share their future with them and not dwell on what I've missed out on.

As for you my love, I have missed you so much. I know I have spent my time back in the guest room, because I was horrible with you. I want to make it up to you, by not demanding you spend all your time with me, because I am not handicapped. I just can't speak! So I want you to resume life as if I were able to talk, I can even get back to work too, by doing the paper work.

Not being able to talk has bothered me so badly, that I have made it my goal to learn to speak faster then the doctor said I will. I have also made it my goal to treat both you and the kids with more love and I plan to start now.

There are tears sliding down my face and I look up from reading the letter. Ryan is standing over me, looking down at me. He grabs my hands, the letter drops to the floor, standing face to face, he wipes away my tears with his right hand. I say to him very quietly, "I love you and I am so sorry for everything."

Ryan's answer to my apology is to kiss me. We kiss on the mouth as I run my hands through his hair, before he slides his hand over my breasts. Slowly lowering me to the bed, he removes his PJ pants, and slides my nighty above my waist. We are kissing so heavy and caressing each other that I don't realize my legs spreading so that he can enter me.

As I am kissing him and moaning in delight, I feel his hard cock enter into my wetness. We kiss, pump each other and moan while rolling on the bed. Our sex session lasts almost an hour, while I orgasm at least ten times, before he blows his warm sensual load in me. Collapsing in exhaustion, I just whisper how much I love him and miss him. Ryan's answer to this is just to cover my body with sweet delicate kisses.

153

The next month is hard at first, but gets easier with Ryan coming through with his promises to the kids and I. Ryan tends his Speech therapy appointments, and starts getting back into his routine of work. Just like he said in the letter he does all the paper work and helps with raising the twins, Sonyia and Elijah.

Unfortunately, Hillary is having a hard time at the restaurant that I have to make a trip to Lethbridge to straighten out the problem. Informing Ryan that Hillary is having some trouble with someone trying to put the restaurant out of business and that I have to go and take care of it. He surprises me by telling me on his doodle pad that he will come along encase I need a strong male influence.

I shake my head and laugh, if only he knew my secret. My mother agrees to watch the children while we are gone, but Ryan and I have to promise the kids we will go on a family vacation the minute we get back to town. As well as we wont be missing Elijah Graduation.

Once in Lethbridge I go directly to the restaurant and see that I have lost some very good workers and they have been replaced with shady works. Confused at why my restaurant is gone throw these changes. Reading the customer complaints, I grow angry but not as angry as I get when I see the document about a small company who wants to take over my restaurant at what cost.

Calling Hillary immediately I want answers from her and I demand she come to the restaurant now. Once she gets here, we sit down at a table while Ryan is out visiting his sister.

Looking Hillary in the eyes, "What is going on? We have lost extremely good cooks, waiters and servers. Why is this restaurant getting poor reviews and who is this company trying to take over my business or put me out?"

Seeing the fear on her face she says, "Look you made me manager of the new mall as well as help out with Dooley's, so I have put most of my time there. But you have asked me to look in on the restaurant while you have been taking care of Ryan, so I have dropped by a few times. I too have noticed the staff leaving and new ones coming. I asked the assistant manager and he said it was because the old staff were not performing to par. And that is when the complaints started coming in, even though we started getting some before all the good staff were fired or left.

Not sure what to think or say, I just sit in quiet. With Ryan being sick and not able to take care of the businesses in Lethbridge and because I also haven't been able to get to Lethbridge and check up on things, I had lost very good staff. People whom have been with me from the beginning. So who ever it was that is trying to put me out of business was doing a good job. My old staff had been through a lot with Ryan and I running the place.

"Hillary, I'm not mad at you, it's not your fault. One thing I know is that my assistant manager Bob has to been in cahoots with the guy trying to take over the restaurant. I'm going to get a hold of some of the old staff and see if I can get them back as well as meet with this guy." She goes to get up from the table.

Standing up with her, I walk over to her and give her a big hug, "Thank you for checking in on the restaurant while I have been distracted."

She hugs me back and says, "No problem, if you need any help with getting the old staff back, let me know."

When I go to my office in the restaurant, the new cook comes in and asks, "Who are you and what are you doing in Bobs office? I'm sorry but you have to leave!"

I smile to myself, look at this cocky young man with annoyance before saying, "I beg your pardon. Do you not know who I am and who you are working for?" The young cook looks confused but try's not to lose his ground. "Bob is the assistant manager, and this isn't his office and nor should he ever be in it. This is my office, I, the manager and owner of the restaurant you work in."

The cook is baffled about what he is hearing and says, "Sorry, I have never met the owner or managers."

I smile at him and say, "Well now you have, but the other manager, he's worse 'cause he's my husband!" I finish in a sharp tone.

The young cocky cook leaves but not as sure of himself as he was when he tried telling me off. I look into the paper work and see the complaints that were made while my old staff was still working. Complains about food quality, appearance of the staff and restaurant. I noticed there was a consistency with the type of complaints, the times the people came in, and the style of writing.

I hadn't had a mystery shopper in the restaurant in a long time, cause I was so busy with Ryan's recovery and Illness. Reading the paperwork from Stan who was the Health Inspector. His paper worker seemed to be dated shortly after the complaints were issued.

It was like who ever was complaining thought they would get the Health Inspector involved.

There were warning notices, fix it notices, fire staff suggestions, and now a shut down notice. Just reading the paperwork from the Inspector made me so fumed, that my Assistant Manager Bob didn't get in touch with me about the Health Inspector.

I knew this wasn't just a mistake. It was all a coincidence. There was a reason I wasn't receiving word about my restaurant and how it was starting to crumble. Gathering all the paper work and phone numbers, I needed to get out of this place before I fired all the staff and make a huge scene.

Sitting in my car, I called up a few of my better staff. Finding out that Bob the Assistant Manger hooked up with a business partner and ever since had been acting weird. Then there were all these complaints that had never come before. Bob started freaking out at all the staff and that's when the firing started. Gathering all this information I was starting to draw a conclusion.

I asked my old top chef, if he still wanted to work for the restaurant and he did. I also had asked him if he wanted the position of Assistant Manager or if he could recommend one of the old waiters or servers. He recommend a waiter who I had noticed great things from in the past, so I told my chef that the Assistant Manager Bob was going to be fired along with a lot of staff.

I wanted the complaints handwriting tested and finger printed, so I shipped them off to my brother. Calling up some of the other business owners in town, I arrange to have nightcap with them.

Ryan came along with me to this nightcap with some of the other owners in town. We met in the historical water tower restaurant lunge, with a view of the city lights at night. Excellent food and wine, as well as a cozy atmosphere made the meeting go really well. There are owners from a liquor store, grocery store, clothing store and another restaurant. Everyone is enjoying the food and the conversation is interesting.

One of the clothing retailers says, "I've heard a rumour that there is a guy in town who is running owners out of business."

Another gentlemen from the local liquor store adds, "That's not a rumour. I have a friend who's business was shut down, and it was going to cost to much to repair so he sold it to this guy who was determined to buy his business."

Then one of the ladies who owns the Safeway grocery store says, "Yah, I heard that too. This tycoon supposedly goes around and asks to buy businesses. If they don't sell, well later on the business starts to have problems, and if they can't address them, then they sell or foreclose."

Hearing all these owners talk about the same problem was interesting. "So does anyone know how to get a hold of this guy? Or has anyone even seen him?" I ask while sipping my wine.

The restaurant owner speaks up and says, "Supposedly he likes to hang out at the Italian club on the west side of town. I haven't seen him, but I hear he looks like a New Yorker, very stylish and clean cut, wearing expensive suits."

After the nightcap with all the owners—they agree that they enjoyed themselves and would like to meet again in a month—Ryan and I head back to hotel. Ryan wants to know what I'm up to. I tell him when I know then I will inform him. I can see that he is not satisfied with my answer but is tired, so he isn't going to argue with me.

I go and check my email to see if my brother had found any similarities in the writing and if there were any fingerprints that were consistent. Since I wasn't near a lab and hadn't brought my resources I had to have my evidence sent away. Getting an email from my brother stating that the writing's were all used with the same pen and penmanship. I just knew this had to be an accomplice to this guy who was putting owners out of business for his own gain.

My brother also put into the email how he noticed the same fingerprints on all the complaints. Attached to the email is a file with the name of the guy who the fingerprints belong to. And there is a rap sheet on this guy, it seems Malcom is a Harvard drop out who has been working for other companies to put business out, or buy them for the client.

Now I had a name for this guy in town that was putting owners out of work and now trying to steal my restaurant. Malcom was crocked and working for crocked people and this Malcom guy had just messed with the wrong business.

I send an email to my brother, thanking him for his help and I also filled out a report since I was going to take this on as a case. I sent my report to my supervisor explaining how I was going to get this guy with a tape recorder. I close the laptop and join Ryan in bed, who was already fast asleep.

CHAPTER 13

Being that Malcom hadn't met me, arranging for an interview wouldn't be so hard. I would just pretend that I was from a corporation trying to put another business out of business, and that I needed someone's help in persuading this company.

Malcom asked me if I would mind showing up for the interview at the west side Italian club where he was known to hang out.

I bought a tape recorder with a hyper sensitive Microphone. Ryan notices me running around and gathering information. He wants to know what I'm up to, "I have scheduled a meeting with the guy who is trying to ruin our restaurant and is also putting other businesses out of business."

Ryan looked irritated and scribbles down, "I do not approve! I'm coming with!" I laugh to myself but it was actually out loud and Ryan does not take to me mocking him. So I agree that he can come, but Hillary has to come and sit with him off in the distance. Cause if Malcom sees Hillary my case is busted.

The Italian restaurant is beautiful, with the upper level wrapped up by a black iron railing. "Bob" my Assistant Manager who didn't know it yet but was fired, and Malcom were awaiting me on the second level. Because Bob was here, I headed to the car and in the trunk I opened up my black bag. Getting into the car to change. I didn't want to take the chance of him recognizing me from one of my pictures at the restaurant.

With our restaurant being a family-owned business, there were a few pictures of Ryan and me, as well as a recent family picture. Being that Bob had made my office into his, he'd of course had to have looked at the pictures. I knew he also was aware of what Ryan and Hillary looked like, so I prayed they were in a dark cubby.

After spending ten minutes putting on a disguise, I step out into the parking lot and walk back into this attractive club slash bar. Ryan and Hillary look at me strangely, trying to figure out if they know me or not.

A waitress led me upstairs to the second level. Malcom and Bob have a table by the fireplace. Not that there are many tables to chose from. The second level is mostly used for two pool tables, a wraparound bar with stools, a small dance floor, and six tables with chairs. One table had my rival and soon-to-be-fired assistant manager sitting at.

Malcom stands up to properly greet me, shaking my hand gently. A sign of weakness. Bob wants to shake my hand, and in doing so, looks into my eyes. I can feel the hairs lifting on my back 'cause I know he is trying to figure out if he knows me. Since Bob was not hired by me but by Hillary, we had not met personally. He had seen a picture of me and Ryan in my office, but I had never had to deal with him, being that he was hired just when Ryan had gotten sick. Hillary still checked up on the restaurant for me while I was detained.

As Bob was clearly studying my face to see if he reconized me, I knew that the low lighting would make it hard for him to see my eye color. As for my hair, I was wearing the black wig again. Remembering how hard it was for Hillary to recognize me last time I had it on, I knew Bob was fooled.

Once we take a seat, I start the conversation off by saying, "I have heard word, that you are the guy to get in touch with if you need some taking care of. Am I right?"

Malcom sips some of his beer and chuckles, "Depends on the kind of taking care of you are talking about."

I give him a devious smile to which I reply, "Well you see, my boss is looking at a mall owned by some woman business tycoon. And were having a little bit of a hard time negotiating with her."

Bob looks at me with creepy eyes and says, "I know who you're talking about. She is the same owner who owns this restaurant we are taking over. She is very busy, and way to wealthy for her own good." Still looking at me with eyes that are taking me all in. I divert my eyes away from this man.

"Well that is good, what is it that makes you guys the ones for my boss to chose. I mean we have a few other prospects to help us work on this Mall project." I sip some more of my cocktail and get more comfortable in the leather chair I am sitting in.

Malcom leans over the table, and says to me quietly, but not quiet enough that my microphone can't pick up the conversation. "Well Mrs. Gaston's restaurant is been closed down for repairs and extermination of the rodent problem. Her husband has been retarded by a speech impediment, so she is overwhelmed with his recovery and her other businesses. This lady has a large family, businesses in her current place of residency, so we are kind of doing her a favour."

I interrupt him by asking, "Well my boss and I have made offers to her company for the Mall. What is it that you can do differently? And this is a bit bigger then a restaurant."

Still leaning over the table Malcom chuckles and says still in that quiet tone, "Don't worry about it. If your boss wants the Mall, we can get him the Mall. Bob and I got the restaurant for one of our clients, so the mall maybe a little harder to get, but give us a date that your boss wants it and we will deliver!" Malcom then leaned back and finished his beer before the waitress came by our table.

The waitress asked me if I wanted another cocktail, but what I really wanted was to get the hell out of this lounge before I jumped over the table and beat the crap out of this cocky man. Who had chosen a career of putting business out of business whether it was with integrity, or using unethical measurements.

Swallowing the lump of frustration and anger in my throat, I put a friendly smile on and said, "Well I thank you for meeting with me as well as all the information you have provided. I will talk to my superior tomorrow and will be in touch with you later." Standing up I shake Malcom's hand, and in doing so I feel sick to my stomach to shake hands with a criminal.

Bob asks with a sly tone, "Well just because the business is done, doesn't mean you have to leave. Stay have another, the night is still young." He goes to grab my hand and smell it, then place a kiss on the palm.

I pull my hand back quickly and say, "Sir, I did not come here to mix business with pleasure." Trying not to show the fear and disgust I have on my face, I say, "I really must be on my way now."

With my heart pounding in my chest, I turn on shaky legs and walk away as gracefully as I can. Closing my eyes briefly I make my way outside, take a deep breath, then head for the car to remove my disguise and join my husband and friend who have been entertaining themselves for the last forty-five minutes while I was being ogled by Bob, and insulted by Malcom with his crooked ways of business dealings.

Walking around the corner of the building and heading to my car which is not to far away. I hear the Lounge door to the entrance open and close. Not thinking anything of it, I continue my way to my car. As I get to the door of my car, I can hear the voice of a man and it is getting close to me. Looking over my shoulder I notice Bob walking toward me.

Searching my pocket for my keys so that I can hit the alarm on the Jeep I'm driving. I ask with a shaky voice, "What do you want Bob? I thought we talked about all there is to discuss. As I told your partner, I will talk with my boss and be in touch with you later!"

With my back up against my car, so that I can see Bob and be prepared to defend myself should anything arise, he says, "Yah the business is done. But I'm out here to collect you. I saw the looks you gave me. I see how beautiful you are and I know you want me."

I hadn't thought I gave him any looks, and was pretty sure I hadn't as much glanced at him. He steps closer to me and I am struggling to find my keys in my purse. I quickly look down to figure out where my keys are and when I look up, Bob is right in front of me. So close that I can breath the beers he was drinking and the smell of his cheap cologne.

I tense up my body and look him straight in the eyes, "Get away from me, I have a husband." Hoping he hasn't heard the fear in my voice.

Bob steps into my personal space and whispers in my ear, "I saw that you were wearing a ring, but baby I know you want me."

Taking my hand out of my purse I go to shove him away from me. Once my hands are on his chest so that I can push him off of me, Bob goes to grab my wrist and place them beside my shoulders up against the jeep. As this man is using great power on my arms to keep me from hurting him I scream, "Get off of me!"

Bob takes that as a sign to cover my mouth with his and kiss me. As I am trying to squirm under his weight and up against the car, Bob then starts to take his mouth past my lips and down my neck to my chest.

Feeling his hot breath on my flesh makes my stomach sick. Trying to yell again, but getting cuffed really hard with his right hand. A rush of pain comes to a newly swollen face, and my sight starts to get darker. With one more attempt, I try to kick him in the groin but miss, and he cuffs me in the face again.

Feeling the pain in my face, and blurred vision. I am not able to fight him as he places his left hand under my skirt moving toward my vulnerability. Because he has hit me twice and in the head, my vision is poor, and the pain in my head is overwhelming and numbing.

He is kissing my mouth and drops my right arm to start to unzip his pants. Being that I am parked where people don't normally look, and where there is no streetlight, I am on my own to defend myself. Bob's body was up against mine, which was up against my rental Jeep. The pain running through my body, my vision blurred, and my feet cemented, I look to the clear black sky as I can't look while this man moves in for the kill.

With my back up against my car so that I can see Bob and be prepared to defend myself should anything arise, I hear him say, "Yah the business is done. But I'm out here to collect you. I saw the looks you gave me. I see how beautiful you are, and I know you want me."

I shake my head after the vision I just foresaw. There was no way I was going to allow that to happen. "Come any closer, Bob, and you'll be hurt!" I yell at him.

I find my keys and place my finger on the alarm button. "Do you think I'm afraid of you? No. But you and I will get to know each other better," he goes to say while continuing to approach me.

I hit the car alarm button, and this only makes Bob come at me faster than I anticipated. He hits me with his right fist, and I fall to the ground. While I am scrambling to my feet, he comes at me. I start punching him and fighting him off just as much as he is doing with me. The only difference is he is trying to knock me out so that he can rape me.

As we are tussling on the ground, I feel the weight of his body being removed off me and see Ryan pulling him away. Ryan starts beating the crap out of him while Hillary is helping me to get to my feet. "Are you okay, Daisy? Did he do anything to you?"

"No I'm fine," I say with fear in my voice, "But I have to help Ryan." Getting to Ryan's aid, I start grabbing Bob's wrists while Ryan is still punching him in the gut. Telling Ryan to go get some rope in the back of the Jeep,

Once he leaves to do so, I drop Bob's one arm putting him into an uncomfortable lock before putting him into a sleeper hold and knocking him out. Ryan comes back with the rope, I can see he is confused on why the man's knocked out, and why I have rope in my jeep.

Ryan looks back to Hillary for answers but I can see she isn't going to tell him anything, while I smile to myself.

The police arrive and restrain Bob. After the police take all the important information down for their report, Ryan wants me to go to the hospital but I tell him it is not necessary since I only have a few minor cutes on my face.

Being that I have all the information I need from Malcom to put him out of business and in jail, I want to get back to the hotel quickly so that I can get in touch with Matt, and have Malcom put away for years. Knowing there is no way to help the other business that have gone under, I can still feel better with that fact that I will be able to help the business who are being tortured by this man, and they will not go under.

Spending another two weeks in Lethbridge to fix up all the problems Bob and Malcom created so that they could try to steal my restaurant. With spending as much at fourteen hours at the restaurant, I am not paying attention to Ryan and the noises he is now able to make.

But I have straightened out any problems with the Mall and the restaurant is in the hands of my trusted Chef who I loved. He was a great cook and would run the place like I was actually there.

Once back home, I rarely saw Ryan not only because I was very busy with music videos and meetings with some new clients, but because Ryan was spending more time with Elijah. Assuming my husband is just trying to help Elijah with his final's, I asked no questions. Since Grad was approaching, I figured maybe they were having the birds and the bee's talk.

It's the night before Zack's first birthday, and I'm sitting at my vanity brushing my hair and thinking of how fast this last year has gone by. First having Zack, then being so busy with work that I don't see that my husband is getting sick. But to find out he has a brain tumour and needs immediate surgery in order to survive. The only downside is that my husband had lost his speech, and I have to discipline the children while running our investments.

Ryan comes up to me taking my brush from my hand and starts brushing my hair. I smile and look up to his eyes in the mirror. "I love you."

Not quite sure what I just heard, I look harder at him in the mirror. And Ryan says, "I truly love you, Daisy."

Tears are falling down my face because not only did I hear him say that, but I also saw his mouth move with words coming out of it. My husband can speak! How much I have missed the sound of his voice.

"Don't cry. I have missed telling you every day with words how much I love you. I have missed the fact that I cannot yell at you or laugh with you," Ryan says with a chuckle and big smile on his face.

Pulling me up from my vanity stool, we kiss passionate and then make love for the night. While making love Ryan wants to whisper sweet nothings into my ear, so that I know how happy he is that he can speak again and make our love making more passionate.

When we wake up, Ryan wants to keep his voice secret from the rest of the family until we sing "Happy Birthday" to Zack.

While Ryan is showering, Elijah comes into the bedroom and I hug him for helping his father find his voice and his new found determination to help the deaf people find their voices in whatever way possible.

As the cake is being severed, candles are lit, and Zack sitting on my lap. We all start to sing Happy Birthday to Zack. At first the children don't notice anything, but when their dad raises his voice and uses a deeper ton, they all silence their voices and listen as Ryan finishes the song.

Zack's not sure what all the commotion is since he is turning one, but all the kids get excited and hug their dad, asking him when he got his voice back. The rest of the night is filled with laughter and lots of fun having little Zack start a cake fight, but being a baby he gets away with it.

It is the end of June, as Elijah is walking down the carpet to receive his scholar for Graduating with Honours. The whole family was there and proud of him, his grades had improved and he was noticed for his athletic ability to be awarded a grant for University. Since he wanted to attend a good University with an outstanding medical program. Taking as many pictures as I could, and trying not to cry too much, my little boy who started all this life with me was all grown up.

I did keep my promise to have one of the hotel available for his party. Ryan was so happy to see his oldest graduate. Sonyai was jealous that her brother was getting a kick ass party. But I told her if she got her grades up and a job, then she too would allowed a party for grad.

Ryan was holding Zack while I was busy with pictures and the twins. My mom was so happy to be seeing her grandson graduate. Matthew, Montana, Holly and Denis were also attending the grad and after supper.

After the party, we allowed Elijah to go on a vacation without us to a place of his choosing. He chose to see Africa, said he wanted to see what types of medicine he might also want to study so that he could join Doctors Without Boarders.

The rest of us thought we might also enjoy some time off and went to Disneyland.

Five years later, things were going great. Elijah is twenty-two, has a bachelor of science degree, and now working on getting his medical degree while dating a really nice young lady with similar interests.

Sonyia is twenty and attending police academy, which her father disapproves. Me, I am not to worry. She could be joining a more aggressive law enforcement agency.

Angela and Alex are fifteen, and Zack is six. All three children were receiving more attention from both parents now that the older two were out of the house.

The businesses are flourishing while Ryan's relationships with the children has become just like any other parent's relationship with their children who have been with them their whole lives.

I answer the front door after it won't stop buzzing and am shocked to see Mark at my door. It has been twenty-two years since I last saw him. "Hi, Daisy. I know it's odd to see me here, but I desperately need your help, my wife has gone missing."

Seeing the grief in Mark's eyes, I let him in. "I'm sorry to hear that. Maybe she left you," I say with some compassion in my voice.

"No! We were very happy, I think she has been kidnapped. In Edmonton, there has been a high increase in wives and young women disappearing." Not sure what to think of this information, I guide Mark to the living room so that we can talk further.

After sitting down on the couch I ask, "So what can I do to help?"

Mark claps his hands together and looks me square in the eyes and says. "I need your FBI help."

I unexpectedly swallow, how is it he knows? Looking around the room to see if Ryan has entered and maybe heard, I nervously say. "What makes you think I am FBI?"

Mark looks around my house as to take in all the furniture and see how I'm living, "Let's not play games, I am a cop and I am privy to that kind of information. Why did you never tell me that while we were together?"

And right then Ryan walks into the living room. In a shocking ton he say, "Hi Mark. What are you doing here and what did my wife not tell you when you two were together?"

Just listening to Ryan address Mark, made the hairs on my neck crawl. Especially when he said wife and referred to Mark and I as together not married. Feeling the blood rush to my cheeks, I pray Mark not reveal what I had still not revealed to Ryan.

With Ryan sitting down next to me, "Mark that information is wrong and it's not true." I tell mark with a sharp tone, hoping he gets the drift that I don't want to talk about my being FBI.

"Daisy, I just looked at your file two days ago. You signed up for the FBI when you were 17 and have never quite. As a matter of fact you are still active, helping in cases from time to time. Look enough about that, I need your expertise, will you help me?" Mark pleas with me.

Turning my face away from Ryan, I feel him squeeze my hand. Feeling his eyes burn into my sole I hear him ask, "Dear is this true? Are you FBI? What is going on?"

Feeling my body heat turn up a thousand degrees, I look over to Ryan on my left with only my eyes and not turning my face to him. But not looking at him square on isn't good enough. He is not happy for I can feel his anger through the grip he has on my hand and the glare he is using. "Some of what Mark say's might be true."

Mark interrupts before Ryan has a chance to get into it with me. "Look I need you to pose as my newest love interest, do some detective work, and just help me find her. Heck maybe we can solve the case on the missing women of Edmonton as well."

With Marks proposal on the table, Ryan jumps up from the couch. I can see that he is still trying to process the information that I may be FBI and why I haven't told him. After pacing the living room a bit, he stops directly in front of me, saying with aggression, "Are you FBI and still active? And how is it you never told me?"

Seeing that Ryan is towering over me while I sit on the couch, I decide to stand up so that I have a better chance of telling him what I have dreaded telling. "Yes, I am FBI! I joined when I was young, as soon as I graduated, to avenge my father death. No, I never quite, my mother knows, and Matthew is one of my colleges because he joined up after finding out I decided to follow in my father's footsteps."

Pausing for a minute to let the information sink in. I then went on being that Mark just blew my cover, "How do you think I was able to find Elijah with in two weeks? How do you think I found you? My only weakness has been you Ryan!"

Watching my husband try to absorb all this information, I look over to Mark. "Yes I will help you. It may also have the same connection to some of the missing women from Vancouver. As to why I never told you I was FBI, well I was trying to start a new life. My mom thought I quite and had moved on with my life in a new city. All was true except the quitting part."

Ryan turns me around violently, so that I can face him. Looking into his now dark black eyes, he says. "I will not allow any wife of mine to be FBI and let alone have you working and staying with your ex-husband!" But more like yells at me.

Swallowing back my anger, then looking at him sternly, "You know I may be FBI, and I have put up with a lot of your aggressive behaviour, but know this. At any moment I could drop you like a ton of bricks! I'm not as weak as you would like me to be, or have been in the past." Turning around to look at Mark I say, "Give me a few hours and we will fly out immediately."

Mark gets up and hugs me while thanking me for deciding to help him. Ryan storms off, trying to figure out how to deal with all this information and the fact that his wife is going out on a job.

*   *   *

I couldn't believe it, my wife is FBI. I wasn't sure how to take it, I surely was not happy to hear that. And I did not want her to put her life on the line for other people, let alone her ex-husband.

Thinking back to when Elijah was kidnapped, I guess it made sense that if she wasn't pregnant, she would have found him much faster and I would not have had to go and see Runée in prison.

But she did marijuana after having Sonyia, surely they would have fired her for that?

I know that I was imprisoned in jail for 5 years, why then did she not use her resources to find me earlier? Granted after I e-mailed her, she did come to my country rather fast and search for me. Although she found no traces of me, we still found each other.

She said she was still active. So then when she claims to go away on business trips, for the hotels, restaurants, and music videos. Was she really doing what she said or was she working on a case?

Feeling a lack of trust, I was so confused and angry. My wife was admitting her self to help another man, let alone the man I stole her from. There was no way I was going to let her go and do this.

But just hearing those words, "You know I may be FBI, and I have put up with a lot of your aggressive behaviour, but know this. At any moment I could drop you like a ton of bricks! I'm not as weak as you would like me to be, or have been in the past."

She was right, she had put up with my Arabic ways and aggression. But Daisy had not slugged me, or done anything about it, except the time before I was committed. I wasn't sure how to take that, even now thinking back to Bob in the parking lot, while he was trying to take advantage of my wife. She had handled herself very well and really didn't need my help.

Specially when I had retrieved the rope she asked for, and he was knocked out cold. Daisy must have used a fancy move to knock him out while my back was turned.

Now it was all making sense when both her mom and brother said I didn't know Daisy as well as I thought. That she wasn't as weak as I thought and could handle herself.

Just like I said to Mark, in four hours I had taken care of business. I called all my managers informing them to take care of matters till I returned from a trip. I inform my secretary that she will have to move all my appointments with musicians back as well as the videos I was choreographing. The kid's knew I will be away for some time but would be in touch with them via phone. It wasn't new to them that I would go on trips for business or "other business" as I called it.

Elijah knew I would be coming back for his university graduation and that I was going on an FBI mission After he found out I was FBI when he overheard Matt and I talking about me going into Lebanon to search for Ryan. I was very impressed with him for keeping my secret a secret from his father. Although Ryan wouldn't be happy if he found out his son knew and he did not.

With in the four hours I had allotted myself to get ready, Ryan was no where to be found. Or wasn't following me around the house like a puppy dog, snapping at my heel.

I had the car packed with my suitcases of clothes, since I would be dropping by the office to pick up some equipment. Feeling this fear in my gut that Ryan might have left me, I go back in the house to say good-bye to the twins and Zack one last time when I run square into Ryan's chest.

Grabbing me by the wrists and pulling them into his chest, "I don't want you to leave! I still haven't digested all this information and I need answers."

Looking into his now softened eyes I say, "I might not have all the answers or at least the answers you are looking for. I just know that we have been working on a case of missing women that are married and young in Vancouver. And since Mark's wife is now one of them, this may help not only the FBI, but all the police and grieving husbands and families. Put your self in Marks place, you'd ask the same. Heck look what you did in order to try and find Elijah when he was taken away from us."

Ryan pulls me into him and hugs me tightly. "You are right." Pulling away for a second, he looks into my eyes, "I love you so much." Then kissing me, he says, "Take care of yourself and stay in contact. If not I will harass Matt so much and when you get back I making you quite."

After saying good-bye to Ryan and the children one last time, I head to pick up Mark at his hotel. We then head for the FBI headquarters and I gather the things I would need for the case, including my gun.

CHAPTER 14

Landing back in Edmonton brings back the memories of retrieving Elijah and how it came close to almost losing him to Mandy's crazy sister Michelle. Arriving in Edmonton, I go directly to work with my investigation. I check all the places Sally hung out, her shopping centres, and place of work.

Some of the neighbours come to see who the new lady is in Marks life, and he tells them that I am his new wife. But the friend that is the most interested is a male co-worker that comes by later in the day while Mark is at work to introduce himself.

Greeting him outside while I am pulling weeds out of the garden, Philip comes up behind me and says, "Hi, I'm Philip. I workout at the same gym with your husband."

Getting up from the ground, I go to shake Philips hand, noticing it to be weak and cold. "Daisy." After shaking his hand, I'm noticing this man checking me out with his gawking eyes.

"I'm surprised that Mark got remarried so soon." Philip says as if we have been the closest of friends.

"Well he told me his wife and him had been having troubles, and he was glad to see her go. He just pretended to be sad so that he could keep our relationship a secret." I tell him with confidence in my voice.

"Yah I had heard from Sally that she was upset with him and planning on leaving. How did you two meet, if he married you so soon." Philip asked.

Taken back a little by Philip knowing that Sally and Mark were having troubles. But then Philip was one of Marks closest friends. "We met on the internet and it kinda went from there." I told him with a smile of happiness.

After meeting Philip, I went back into the house and file a report on him. While working on the computer, Ryan calls to give me grief. It seems he is still very mad at me, and that when I get back I will pay for lying to him. I inform him that I have a feeling this case will be very easy to solve.

Once I finish typing my report on the latest information I had gathered, I send it back to the office to be processed by Matthew.

When Mark comes home from work later that night, I decide to have chat with him about his wife. While we flew to Edmonton, we didn't really talk about him and Sally. I mostly outlined the case and how we were going to make it look like we were married.

Not that that was going to be very hard, considering we were married and in a relationship for three years.

Once Mark got home and I had supper on the table, I thought we should cut the air and possible tension. Since the last time we were together, he was packing up his things, and divorcing me. If we were going to make this fake marriage seem real, were needed to get past the past.

While sitting at the dinning table I start making way in our old relationship, by starting the processes. "I'm just wondering. Do you always get home this late?"

Mark looks up from his plate, "Well my work takes me late into the night. Why the question?"

Just looking at Marks features, his salt and peppery hair once jet black has thinned with time. How much he looks like his father, in looks and body strength. But also looking at my old husband I can see he has been stressed with the disappearance of his wife. "Well I had a nice but creepy chat with your friend and neighbour Phil. I know that you and Sally were having problems, but I was wondering if your coming home late at night might be one of the reasons you too were having problems."

He finished his plate and stat back in his chair, putting his hands together to prepare for a long conversation, that I think he knew was due. "Sally was bothered by my hours, but with her working different days and hours as me. We rarely saw each other, she wanted to talk about it but I kept brushing her off. When ever she wanted to spend time with me on our days off together, it never really happened."

Sipping my wine I then said, "So could I assume that on your days off, you did the same as with me. Spent your time alone, on the computer or watching Science fiction shows?"

Watching Marks brows raise, I could see he didn't like my assumption, but looking away, "Yes. I did the same as I did with you. All I ever wanted was to spend my free time alone, and to relax. I didn't want to have to be around her or the children, so I guess I pushed her away."

Looking at Mark I could see there was something else behind just pushing Sally away on his free time. "And then if Sally went out with her friends and didn't come home until late. I would accuse her of having an affair, so I guess that might be why she left me, I don't know." Mark finished with sad eyes, and a defeated look.

Massaging my forehead, I felt guilty because of what happened with Ryan and I. Mark felt he could not trust his wife, even though he loved her dearly. "Mark I want to start off by telling you how sorry I am about how we ended. It was not planned, heck if I hadn't slept with Ryan, I would have been raped by Shane and maybe gotten pregnant by him."

For the first time I could see that Mark understood me, and felt a bit sorry for how things ended. "Daisy I know I was harsh at the time with you. And I want you to know that I too am sorry for the way I ended it. You are right, you never cheated on me. It was just a situation of bad timing on both Ryan and your part. I have come to the conclusion that if Ryan was not there, Shane would have rapped you and if you had gotten pregnant, the child would have either looked closer to me and we may or may not have stayed married while raising the child. If the truth had come out with him drugging you, Shane would have probably abandoned you to raise the child alone or maybe worse."

I looked into Marks eyes, still the rich dark brown, and for the first time it was like we were connecting again. Seeing the passion and sincerity made my heart sputter. "Thank you! Mark, that means a lot hearing that, and you're right. This may sound trite, but I'm glad that Ryan was there, and we had had sex. 'Cause I'm not sure how I would have handled knowing I'd been raped."

Mark got up from the table and came to my side. Pulling me up to him, he held my hands together and brought them to his chest, kissed my forehead, and put his arms around me. I could feel his warmth and compassion from within. It was like the first couple years we were together before things started to go awry.

Interrupting our moment I say, "Do you feel the connection between us? I bet this is what was lacking in your marriage. I am sorry that you used what happened with us against Sally. Mark we talked about this before, you can't blame one woman for the mistakes of a old relationship!" I finished with a more aggressive tone.

After hugging me, Mark gathered up the dishes and together we did them while finishing our talk. "And I know that. Since Sally has been missing and my mother has the kids, I have had a lot of time to think about everything. The mistakes between us and the mistakes I made with Sally."

I was impressed to hear all this from the man I use to love or thought I loved. "Well I am glad to hear that. So now that you have that figured out, what are you planning to change when Sally comes back?"

Mark thought long and hard about that while doing the dishes and then informed me of how he was going to woe his wife and treat her like the queen he should have been treating her. How he was going to cut back on shifts and spend more time with his family.

After dishes Mark went to the Gym to work out, while I checked my mail to see if there were any problems with any of the businesses. After finishing with my emails and house cleaning, I went outside and started a fire. While sitting by the fire, watching the colors of the sky changed as the stars started to appear and the pretty sun setting sky left for another night, I pondered what my life might have been like had I stayed married to Mark.

And if Mark had been reading my mind, I hadn't heard him sneak up behind me, "Nice fire! Sally and I haven't had a fire in the backyard in a long time." He paused a minute and found a chair to sit in to the left of me and a little farther from the fire. With a chuckle he said, "Your going to think this is funny but at the gym I was wondering what life might have been had you and I stayed together."

I laughed at the thought too, "Actually I was just thinking that. Granted I probably more then you have given it more thought. I think we would have stayed married longer, I would still continued to party and shop and I think we would have continued to do our separate things and in the end if we had not gotten counselling I think we would have divorced." I didn't like that I had said that, but I truly felt it in my heart.

Mark looked over to me, smiled and said, "I kinda came up with the same conclusion. I mean, sure we loved each other but had so little in common and when we were alone, there was nothing there. And I hate to say this, but I think it was fate that things turned out the way they did. You are happy with Ryan and I was happy with my wife. We would never have lasted you and I."

I looked at him, the flame shadowing on his face, feeling the warmth of the fire I smile genuinely at him. Mark was right, it was fate and it had to be or else my wedding ring wouldn't have the magic of true love. "I totally agree and at least we can still be friends."

Sitting back in the chair I felt good. Mark and I had broken the tension and gotten through our past. Now all that was needed was to find his wife. But tonight I was going to enjoy this fire, the stars in the sky, and Marks company, for tomorrow was a new day.

And that it was. Mark went to work early in the morning, and I cleaned the house. At lunch I prepared food for Mark when he came home. Then after lunch I was back in the front yard pulling weeds and pruning.

I didn't think about the clothes I was wearing and who might see it. But as if my shirt was a magnet, Phil stopped his car in our driveway and felt the need to talk with me. As we were talking he noticed a few scars on my back from the lashing I received while in Lebanon in my search for Ryan.

Phil came into my personal space immediately and places a hand on the flesh of my back, "Oh my god. Did Mark do this to you? How can you be with a man like that?"

Pulling away from him due to his creepy touch and clammy hands, I look over my shoulder briefly then say, "It's nothing, that was a long time ago."

Leering into my face Phil says to my quietly, "If there is a chance that Mark is harming you and you feel your life is in danger let me know. I can help you how ever you need it." Standing more straight and with some distance between us Phil then said, "I hate to see such pretty women in abusive situations. Heck I hate to see them even miserable."

The fact that this guy bothered me and was saying such things, made me consider him a suspect in helping Sally run away. But when he said the last thing, I was sure this guy knew where Sally was. I thanked him for his generosity and asked him to leave because I would not want my husband to come home and see this man, his friend flirting with me.

Later that day before Mark came home from work, I checked with Matt as too see if there was anything on Phil. But so far the computers have come up with nothing. Thinking that maybe Phil isn't his real name, I know I need to get finger prints from him.

At supper I feel the need to ask Mark about his friendship with Phil, "I was wondering about you and Phil. How long have you been friends with him? Where did you meet him? And did you notice anything odd between him and Sally?"

Mark looks up at me oddly and while eating, then says, "I met Phil at the gym about a year ago. I never really thought about it, but yah Sally made friends with him to. Why the questions? Do you suspect him?"

Nodding my head up and down gently I say, "I know he's your friend but he gives me the creeps and I have a feeling this man knows where you wife is. He told me today that if you harmed me, that he could help me get away."

"Why would he think I harmed you or would harm you?" Mark demanded confused.

"He saw the few scares on my back and thought you did it. Then he offered me help and the day before that had mentioned there were problems with you and Sally. Now whether you talked to him about that, I don't know. But I honestly feel that he had something to do with Sally leaving you. And if you say that your wife and him were friends, who knows what she told him." I told Mark with sincerity in my voice.

Mark stopped eating. I think he was shocked to hear that his friend was a hero to women, but it came from disturbing families. For a long time he just stat at the table, not finishing his plate. I could see he was trying to do his own conclusion. Once I started to remove the dishes he asked, "Have the FBI come up with anything on Phil?"

As I gently place the dishes in my hand on the counter, I turn to face Mark then say, "Nothing bad is in his file, but I don't think he is who he says he is. I was thinking to get finger prints from him and in order to do so, I want to take him up on his offer of help."

Looking at me with sadness in his eyes, Mark asked, "When do you plan on this?"

"In a couple hours. I need to finish up some paper work and send my plan to Matt. Then put my tracking device on and bracelet for finger prints, that kind of stuff." I told Mark.

For the first time my ex-husband was out of words and I think it was because he was still trying to digest all the information I had given him as well as my plan. While he pondered his thoughts, I got straight to work.

Typing up a email to my brother and one for my supervisors, which stated that I was going to make it look like Mark was Evil and take Phil up on his offered. With doing this I would be wearing my tracking chip in case something went wrong. This chip was capable of reading my pulse rate, knowing my location and being so small it was undetectable. I also explained in my letter that all I was planning on getting out of this was more information on Sally if possible and finger prints from Phil. The project should last 8hrs, because then I would tell Phil that I was happy with Mark and wanted to work things out with him.

Placing the chip in the inner cavity of my ear where there is strong cartilage, which is the little pocket you have above your ear hole. Sometimes you can pierce it, but it's rarely done. I write a little note to Ryan and place it in an envelope, asking Mark to send it if anything should go wrong.

When I'm done all that is needed to be done, I tell Mark that we need to get into a fight in case Phil is outside. I also tell Mark that he will have to hit me, so that I have a mark on my face and it is more believable.

Mark looks at me strangely, not wanting to hit me but then knows my plan is in motion.

Mark does hit me and as he's about to, I tense up thinking how much Mark might actually want to hit me for the past mistakes. Instead of a harsh painful cuff across the face, he just slaps me hard. Feeling the sting to my face I look up at him with wide eyes astonished that he actually hit me.

Knowing that the hit had to have left a mark on my face I make for the door. Outside it is starting to poor, I make myself cry by thinking of how I lost Ryan once and if I were to lose him again, I would die.

As I am crying and wondering the street in the pouring rain, I hear a car slow down and roll its window down. "Daisy are you all right?" Phil asks. Feeling chills go through my body, I look over to see Phil sitting in the drivers seat of his BMW. "Mark and I got into a fight, its nothing."

Phil puts the car into park and turns off the engine, "Your face is red. Did he hit you?" I put my hand to my face where Mark had slapped me. Being shocked that he had gone through with my crazy scheme to hit me, it wasn't all his fault when I told him to. "Its just a little slap. Don't worry about me, he went to the gym to cool down and I thought I'd take a walk to work off some steam."

"Well it's raining pretty good, you should get in the car. We'll go for coffee and chat about it," Phil said.

Taking the bait I get into Phil's BMW. As he starts the engine and we drive off to presumably one if his favorite diners, I can't help but notice the smell of detergent and bleach. Sitting in the passenger seat warming up, I wonder where we are going. Looking over to Phil, I can see he senses my question.

"You know no man should hit a woman, I don't care what the crime. If you say this is the first time, I won't believe you. That's what all abused women say, and I know it's a lie because they are afraid of their husbands." Looking at Phil strangely, pondering why he's going on like this and where it's leading to, I allow him to continue his rampage. "Don't worry, Mark may be my friend but he will not hurt you again. I promise you that! You will be safe, I'm taking you to a place for battered women where you can get counselling and be around other women in your position."

And with all that said, Phil was quiet for the rest of the drive. Well maybe I was wrong about this guy and he was a local female hero. So he probably saw Sally in distress and thought to take her to this women's shelter. Once inside the shelter I would be able to find Sally and get to the bottom of this matter.

I noticed we were driving into the transportation airport hanger, finding it strange for a women's shelter. On the flip side it made a lot of sense. Who would think the area of a Airport Hanger to be the place of safety.

Phil parks in front of a warehouse door, shutting the engine off, I decide to tell Phil that I have changed my mind (just as planned). Granted I never agreed to go along with his idea, but now I knew where Sally could be found. "Thank you Phil for thinking of my safety, but I really don't need protection from Mark. I said something about his parents and he got a little mad. So if you could take me home and we could all look beyond this event?"

"Daisy, I will not take you back. Once we get inside you'll understand that there is a better life ahead of you." Phil opens his door and gets out into the cool night breeze.

Feeling uncomfortable and out of my shell I too get out of the car. The cool damp breeze hits my face. With closing my door I tell Phil, "I'm just going to walk home, I'm really not interesting in being helped."

Phil comes around the car to my side and says aggressively, "You have no choice! I'm helping you and that is that!"

Confused by this sudden burst of authority and hastiness. Turning from Phil to head in the other direction, I am detained when he grabs my right arm and pulls me back to him. Looking him in the eyes, I see anger and authority.

Noticing the door to the Warehouse is now open. I see men emerging from the bay of the hanger, but that's all I see before feeling a throbbing pain to my temple. The air gets heavier, its darker and my body becomes putty.

I wake to a throbbing head ach and foul smell, in what appears to be the back freezer part of a semi trailer, which makes no sense when the last I remember is being at a Cargo airport warehouse. It is not cold like a freezer, but I notice other women who are scared, beaten.

I see Phil through the bars that have us women caged back here. I can hear him say on his cell, "The shipment's all here." After finishing up with his call, he turns to us women and says, "The next time you lady's take what you have for granted by cheating or being upset with your husbands, maybe you'll learn and that is if you get out of what your getting into." And after his grand speech he pops a tape into the VCR that is attached to the TV unit on one of the walls. Then he closes the doors to the crate and locking us in.

With dime light we are able to watch the video playing and it shows us as well as explaining what our new life will be like as slaves in Lebanon, Ryan's home country.

My heart drops and my back burns from the few scars I still have after the severe lashing I got the last time I was in this country from my brother-in-law Frank.

The other girls cry. I notice they are foreign, and I don't understand their languages.

A skinny blonde girl speaks in English, "Are we going to die?" She is young, can't be much older then twenty-four, slim, fair skinned with perky breasts.

I tell her, "We might if we don't obey the law of our new masters, but if you stay strong and listen, you will be able to get out of the situation."

She asks, "How is it you know so much?"

I look at her with sad eyes because I promised myself I would never step foot in Lebanon again. "The last time I was in this country was seven years ago looking for my dead husband, I became a slave for his family in order to see if my husband was truly dead, and being in this country I found out how bad it was to be a woman slave."

*   *   *

After putting the kids to bed and feeling very nervous and anxious, I just knew something was wrong with Daisy. After pouring myself a brandy and turning the TV on to the news, the phone rings. Thinking it will be my wife since this was the same time she called last night, I am shocked to find out that it is her brother Matt calling.

"What's up, Matt? How are you and your family?" I ask my brother-in-law.

"Not much, Montana is in bed as well as the kids. I was wondering if it's too late to drop by?" Matt asks me with some restraint in his voice.

Not paying attention to the news, and hearing Matt's uncertainty I tell him that he can drop by any time.

After hanging up the phone with Matt, I try to get back to watching the news, but I can't seem to relax. With talking to Matt I know something is wrong, I try to watch some comedy but nothing seems to work. Getting up to pour another brandy, the doorbell rings.

Hoping the children don't wake, and finding it rather odd that Matt could be here already being that his house is fifteen minutes drive from ours. Opening the door I am shocked to see Mark, Daisy's ex-husband and my old best friend.

With letting Mark into the house I casually ask, "What are you doing here? Where is Daisy?" I look around the porch for her but do not see her. "Aren't you and Daisy working on your missing wife?" I ask finally, trying not to let my anger arise.

Watching Mark fidget in his place, then break down, "I am so sorry. Things were going well, but Daisy wanted to go through with her crazy scheme. Having me hit her and then run out, so that a friend would find her and take her to where Sally was taken. It's been two days and I haven't heard from her, so I thought maybe she came home or her planned worked." He finished while lowering his eyes in shame.

I could not believe my ears, Mark was in my kitchen and had the balls to tell me he hit my wife, then let her take off with some hair brained scheme. Now she was missing like his wife. Without hesitation and much thought, my right fist connected with Marks left jaw. This man had the edacity to tell me he hit my wife and she was missing.

Now I knew what Matt was coming over to tell me and why his voice was so shaky. Looking down at Mark on the floor, as that is where he fell after my hitting him.

Mark put his hand on his jaw and rolled it around to see if it was broken. Then getting back to his feet he said, "I am so sorry, I only slapped her because I did not want to go through with her plan of cuffing her and she provoked me."

After getting another glass of brandy for me and one for Mark, "You are not her husband, you have no right to hit her. And you should have called me about her plan."

"Ryan! She will be all right, and its not like you haven't hit her." Mark said with attitude.

Downing the rest of my drink I could not believe the nerve of this man. But before I could deck him again, Matt came in through the front door. "What are you doing here, Mark?"

"I came here to tell Ryan that Daisy has gone missing after putting her plan into motion, and to deliver this letter to him personally."

My wife had written me a letter, what was going on? "Well, can I have the letter?"

Mark handed me the letter and turned to Matt to tell him that Daisy had not returned after eight hours as planned. "So after some more time, I went over to Phil's and he told me he had not seen her since the last time she was in the garden. But I knew that was a lie when I watched her as she was walking down the sidewalk when he picked her up," Mark said to Matthew.

"What? You watched this man pick my wife up, and this Phil guy is not arrested?" I yelled at Mark before reading my letter.

Matt gets in between Mark and me, feeling the tension. "Ryan I came over here to tell you that Daisy is alive, and that we are tracking her." Matt tells me while using his arms to distance Mark and I.

Feeling a huge sigh of relief, I go to open the letter while asking where Daisy is. But hearing that she is in Lebanon my just heart drops. "What do you mean she is in Lebanon?" I demand.

"Well after she sent head office her details of the mission and her plan, we watched her tracking device. Which by the way Mark lead to a cargo airport warehouse. The FBI is moving in on the site as we speak. I happened to notice her heart rate speed up and then saw that she was moving really fast. While our team watched her micro chip locator we saw her heading into Lebanon." Matt told me gently.

All Mark could say was Wow! "Do you think that there is some kind of female slave trade?"

"I'm afraid so." Matt replied.

Sitting down on the couch, I just didn't know what to do. My wife, an FBI agent since she was seventeen years old, was on her way to Lebanon. I wondered if she was going to be able to get out of my country again. If I wasn't afraid to go back, I would be leaving as we were wasting time speaking. "So let me get this straight. As my wife was trying to solve the case, she just happened to have gotten herself trapped and is now on her way back into a country that she has once received a lashing for."

Matt chuckled but then got serious, "She is indeed heading for your country, but the FBI will be there looking for her. The only problem is that she might still be a wanted woman from when your brother made her a wanted woman. But I wouldn't be worried, she knows the country and was able to get to the embassy."

Not wanting to hear any more being that I was getting a headache. I directed my attention to the letter Daisy wrote me.

> *To my habibi,*
>
> *As you have found out I did not return home as planned. Meaning something changed in my mission. But don't fret, I know you just found out I am FBI, but I am also highly trained. Besides the equipment that will be tracking me, you can track me and know I am alive by trying to remove your wedding band. Both you and I know that we cannot remove our wedding bands unless by our true love or well you know. Any way take care of the children and I'm sure I will be home shortly.*
>
> *Love to you and the Children,*
> *Daisy*

Folding the letter, I smell it and breath in her perfume. Bringing my hands to my face I take a deep breath and wipe the tears that formed in my eyes as I read the letter. And exhaling my breath I try to remove my wedding band. Thankfully it does not remove. Getting up from the couch I grab the phone and dial my brother Frank's number. He owes my wife a favor.

Once arriving in Lebanon we are introduced to the buyers, all with dark hair and skin. None of them looks poor, all wearing expensive suits and smelling of exquisite perfume. They're all speaking Lebanese, which I understand very well after my husband taught me and the children, and after being in his country previously.

I have been around Ryan, his sister, and Renaldo as they teach the children their language, not to mention when he gets mad at me and curses me in Lebanese. They are talking about the shipment, us. The men are asking if we are damaged, what are backgrounds are, whether we will be traceable, and if we are of good breeding or working stock.

I also hear one of the buyers say that he wants to try the product out first, meaning sex, well in our case rapping us. And if the women are of great sex, but not worth breeding, they want us castrated so that no children can be born. Just hearing the one man talk about how children can not be a result of these men's rapes, make my blood boil. I know how it is a disgrace to have a bastard child in this country and let alone a child with in another race.

They take some of the younger girls who do not speak English but maybe Chinese or Indian and I hear their screams as the men force themselves on them. I yell in

Lebanese at the men to stop what they are doing for the consequences will be far worse then what they are doing, which gets the attention of the boss.

The boss is tall with broad shoulders, deep brown eyes, a full-grown beard and a smell of Cuban cigars. He looks at me with eyes I've only seen on Ryan when he's mad at me. Feeling the common fear in my gut, this guy comes into my face and freaks at me in Lebanese. He yells, "How is it you know our language? You think you have power! For someone who knows the word, must also know her place. You must be punished!"

This man grabs me, pulls me into a dark fish smelling room as he has full intentions of rapping me. I fight with him to get him off of me and to prevent him from taking my clothes off while yelling some more in Lebanese. This only angers the boss some more, but seeing that I have put a little fear in him, the man goes to smack me and telling me that I will pay and die at the hands of my new master.

Not sure who my new master is, I'm taken away as other girls are still screaming. I want to help, but the men are too strong. Conflicted with wanting to help and wanting to solve the crime. I could bust the current situation or let it go to the final stage and bust all party's involved in this abduction of women from both Canada and the U.S.

Riding in a van with my arms bond I recognize little of the country side. But when I get closer to where I will be living, I notice it is a rich part of the country. Arriving at a hug Mansion, and I am introduced to my new master Marchello

Marchello is not Lebanese like I assumed, he is Italian but speaks fluent Lebanese. Standing 5'6", with dark hair, green eyes, olive skin, and mustache. Being that he is short, and equal to my high, he makes up for it by strength. I can see his muscles through his clothes as he moves closer to the van to view me.

I'm taken out of the van and shackles are placed around my ankles. Once my arms are released of their bindings, he demands I strip. Taken back by his demand to strip right here in the courtyard, where the gardeners, and other on lookers could see my nakedness.

Not liking my hesitation, he hits me across the face. I drop to the ground with pain to the jaw. I hear from the guards who have dropped me off that I argued with the boss and speak Lebanese. The guard also mentions that I have a spirit and threatened the boss.

Once I get up off the ground, I look at Marchello and he once again demands I strip while raising his hand to get ready to cuff me again. Slowly I remove my clothing, leaving only my panties on since that my ankles are shackled. Marchello walk around me, looks me over, up and down.

When he places his hands on my breasts, I try to fight the temptation to kill him with one swift strike to the temple. I stand still while my body shivers, and I fight back the tears. As Marchello sees my back, he notices the few scares from my previous lashings.

He tells the guards that he understands why I know Lebanese, that I am no stranger to the world of slavery.

A housemaid comes out to the garden and throws clothes at me, noticing that these will be the clothes I am to wear, immediately upon approval I dress.

For the next two weeks I have gotten to know the grounds and the staff. Even though Marchello is a loud aggressive man, he is rarely home and away on business. He even relaxes enough to release my shackles, so I am free to go anywhere in the property, which makes for my escape much easier. The grounds are vast with beautiful orchids, rose beds, rock islands, and statues.

The maids are very friendly, and they reassure me that I was not bought for sex but for cooking and as a lady to wear on his arm. That made me less nervous around him. After being at this mansion for two weeks and seeing how Marchello was with both female and male staff, I could see that he was gay, but in the business he had to look like a rich bachelor.

I also got to know Marchello's daughter, who was rebelling. She took to me like a daughter to a mother who had been separated for a long time. With getting to know her and become friends, I manage to get her to mail a letter to my husband and Matt.

When Marchello found out I was talking to his daughter, he beat me for he felt threatened that I would invoke Canadian woman's rights on her and that she would be damaged goods for her husband. I'm once again shackled and can't go far on the grounds.

The next day while I am hanging the clothes on the clothes line, with the other maids, I over hear them talking. They are talking about a Canadian woman who speaks Lebanese who stole a ring from the Gaston Family. And there is a warrant for her arrest.

I look down at the ground while hanging the rest of the linens hoping that the maids don't put two and two together. *This isn't happening again,* I think to myself. Why is Ryan's brother have in for me? I thought we had come to a truce and how is it Frank found out I was here?

* * *

My brother answers the phone and not one of his servants, hoping maybe Daisy got hired there. But I knew there would be no chance of that because as far as I knew my family was against foreign slave trade.

"Frank, I need a big favor from you!" I demand of him. And before he could reply, "Daisy has been kidnapped by foreign sex and slave traders. Here locator is showing her to be in your country. Until we get to Lebanon we will not be able to pin point her."

"Ryan what can I do? You know our family wants nothing to do with the Dimear family who runs this kind of trading. If she has been sold into trade, she will be untraceable. Living in rich mansions or bordellos." Frank put in causally.

179

"Look if you claim she stole our grandmothers ring like you did when I was in the country. Then maybe they may turn her into you for a reward." I tell my brother with hope in my voice.

"It might not go like that. They may cute the ring off and only return that." Frank says.

"NO! Make sure you say that you want her alive and well or no reward." I yell at him.

Frank breathes a deep sigh, "Ok, I'll do it. And I promise I will do it with Daisy's best interest. Granted your wife is a tough cookie."

And with that done, Mark, Matt and I were able to get things under way so that we could get to Lebanon to save my wife.

*　　*　　*

After all my duties were done. I am able to retire for the day, chains and all. I settle to read a book when Marchello comes busting into my room, "Who are you?" he demands in English. Shocked that he knows English, I don't answer him immediately only provoking him to get violent with me till I give in.

Once he stops shaking me, I tell him, "I'm Daisy Gaston. The ring that is claimed I stole, I did not. It is mine, and I am married to Ryan Gaston. You kidnapped the wrong woman."

For some reason I can see fear in Marchello's eyes. I know Ryan's family is powerful after being a slave to them for a week. But I can't understand why this man of great power and wealth is afraid of the Gaston family; it is clear as day in his eyes.

"I see that makes you afraid! And you should be!" I tell Marchello before he hits me and leaves me to my thoughts.

CHAPTER 15

I know I have to leave and fast. So hiding in a corner in my room trying to figure out how to break my shackles or get away with them on. Marchello's men come in with him.

Once they find me hiding in a corner, they grab me and say, "This wont hurt." I see a needle in one of the goon's hands. Freaking out, I manage to knock the men down and steal the keys only to have to still fight my way out of this estate.

Breaking free of my prison, of the gardens, I run at fast as I can. But as I'm running I feel a sharp pain in my shoulder almost throwing me to the ground. Knowing that if I fall to the ground with this pain, I will have lost all chances of getting free of the hellhole.

Jumping the wall and falling to the ground, I start to feel sick, looking over my right shoulder I see a dart. Pulling the dart out of my shoulder, I notice it to be a poison Ivy dart, one that can carry fluid. The only problem is most of the fluid is probably in my shoulder and the cause of my pain. Quickly unlocking my shackles and throwing them and the keys a side.

Knowing that I have been poisoned, I must run and put as much distance between me and Marchello's men. As I ran further and further away, my strength is weakening.

As night falls I sneak into a church before I collapse on the street. Being that I am not wearing a face veil, I might fall victim to any man. I notice a priest is closing up for the night and quietly in Lebanese I ask, "Please sir, I need sanctity. I have been wounded by a poisons dart and my strength is weakening. Might you be able to keep me secret till I feel stronger to get home to the Embassy?" And with asking him this, my voice is weakening, my pulse dropping, and my body burning up.

He comes rushing to my side and feels that I have a fever, knowing that I must be in grave danger he agrees to keep me safe and secret from anyone looking for me as long as he can.

For the next two days I suffer fevers, chills, sharp pains, and vomiting. The priest tells me it is the poison of a scorpion and I might die if I don't control my temperature. While I am suffering the effects of the poison, the Priest tends to me by medicating me, praying and any way possible.

On the third day I feel a bit better having gotten my temperature back to a normal degree, still being weak I feel I am able to get some air. My right arm is swollen and shoulder is rigid, making dressing a huge pain.

While dressing the priest rushes in my room as I'm putting my shirt on to tell me I have to leave. There are men doing a door too door search for a Canadian Lebanese lady who stole a ring from the Gaston Family. I look at my ring, and then know I have to run.

I leave out the back door into an alley and as I'm running, I run into a lady covered up in the black robe, we both tumble to the ground. She is first to speak but in English, "Watch where you are going? You bloody Arab!"

This shocks me since no one speaks English besides the woman I met when I was being kidnapped. As I get up from the ground, I look at her, dressed in black, and say in English, "Who do you think you are?" But as I look at this women, I recognize her eyes. They're of Mark's wife, Sally.

I walk up to her and ask, "Are you Mark Hodges's wife, Sally?"

Removing her veil she looks at me with emotion and says, "Yes," with tears streaming down her face. I gather she recognizes me because besides the pain in her eyes, she is happy to see me. Grabbing her wrist, I tell her, "We must leave now!"

Pulling her we head further into another alley. But the more distance we get, the sicker I feel again. Sally asks if she can take a look at me. Knowing that she is a nurse I let her, but first we must get out of the alley. She pulls me into a little shop she must work for, and takes a look at my shoulder and tells me that I need medical treatment.

Like I didn't know that, but what I wanted to know was if this shop might have something to help with the pain. She cleans out the wound and then cuts my shoulder wound some more to drain the puss and infection, which hurts like a bitch.

While she is cleaning up my wound and putting dressing on it, Sally asks, "What are you doing here? Did you get kidnapped too by Phil? Are we going to get rescued?"

In between crying in pain I tell her, "Sally I am FBI, and Mark came to me for help in finding you. I deliberately wanted to get kidnapped to help find you, but it only helps to bring down a major slave and sex cartel if we survive."

Once I am bandaged and given some aspirin, Sally asks, "So then there is a rescue mission coming?"

"I'm not sure. I am wearing a tracking device, but I don't know if the signal is being picked up. I have been in this situation before, so if we can get to the American Embassy we will be safe," I tell Sally with some hope.

Traveling by alleys in the night for the American Embassy, I feel it in my blood that we are getting closer.

Hearing yelling and not looking back we can hear many footsteps. Knowing that we are being chased, Sally and I start zig zagging in and out of different alleys.

With the sun rising, I tell Sally that it will be safe to run on the main roads. While we are running toward the Embassy and away from the men who are chasing us, I tell Sally to go ahead and warn the guards. Due to my extreme pain and ill feeling in my gut I just can't make it fast enough.

Sally makes it to the embassy gates; I am almost there when I hear Ryan's brother Frank telling me to stop that I'm in no danger and will be safe. Stopping thirty feet from the gates, I turn to look back at him only to get shot in the chest from my right.

It slams me backward to the ground, the pain from the bullet is so severe. Being weak from the poisoning five days ago I know I cannot give up. Turning onto my front so that I can get up and crawl to the gates. Seeing some of Franks men chase after the man who shot me, I don't notice Frank catch up to me.

Knowing very well that the man who shot me works for Marchello or the slave traders, I know I need to survive so that I can help bring this slavery to an end. Frank helps me up to my feet, oozing with blood lose. Frank picks me up and carries me to the gates. Where the guards are waiting for me with an ambulance to take me to the hospital.

On the way to the Hospital I pass out from the pain of the bullet shot to my chest and the remnants of the poisoning. Waking in surgery while the doctors are mending my shoulder, I know I am safe. Only to wake again in my hospital room, the right side of my chest is bandaged and I have ivy's hooked up to me.

Feeling stronger, I burst into tears when I see Matt come in. "I'm so glad to see you. There was a time I thought I may never see my family again." I babble to him while he leans into hug me.

As tears stream down Matt's face he says, "I was so scared for you when I saw you were heading into Lebanon. The fact that your tracking device was still working gave me hope."

I shake my head in disbelief. "I'm just so glad I found Sally and that this nightmare is over."

I open a file Matt had brought into the room with him. "So we were able to get Phil and some of the men working with him in Canada. We were also able to obtain paper trails of some of the women. Being that your residence was permanent for two weeks, the FBI were able to take down Marchello and his crew involved in the slave trade."

Leaning back into my pillow, I was happy to hear that Phil was captured and Marchello would also be behind bars for a long time. Now we just needed to find the missing women who were traded.

While Matt and I are talking, Frank came in to check on me. A little disappointed it wasn't Ryan, I ask him, "Why is it so many people are afraid of the Gaston family?"

I could not hear everything Frank says because I am too busy trying to understand why Ryan was banned from the country, and after spending ten years in prison I could understand his fear. Heck I felt the same fear when I saw on the video that I was returning to this godforsaken country.

But I did manage to hear Frank say, "My family used to own this town and our grandfather use to be president, so therefore with the threat of the old mafia and having family members still on the city council, most people fear us."

I shake my head because I only caught the part about the mafia, and that makes me even more afraid of his family. Before Frank left I asked him, "Would you be able to stick around and answer a few questions for the FBI?"

Frank agrees, and both he and Matt leave my room. Seeing that Ryan was not able to get into the country, I get myself comfortable for a long nap.

As I let the sleep start to take over, I feel a presents I haven't felt for a long time. My heart starts to tingle, and the hairs on back perk up. Fighting the sleep I lift my heavy eyelids only to see a very hurt man, who has conflicting anger and pain in his eyes.

"How could you betray our marriage, by being a hero only to have yourself abused. You don't feel you do enough or get enough recognition from home that you have to go running off with your ex-husband to safe his wife, while jeopardizing your own children." Ryan yells at me with much emotion behind the threat and anger.

As he moves to my bedside, I try to defend myself, but he grabs my face with both hands. Tells me I'll pay for my actions and kisses me aggressively. Then leaving me to ponder what he said.

Once Ryan leaves I cry and try to sleep, but I end up having a nightmare about the last 5 weeks. Waking up with sweat running down my body, trembles, only to buzz for a nurse so that I can get something to help me sleep. The nurse comes in and after talking to me she gives me a drug so that I can sleep.

*   *   *

I did not want to yell at her, but I was so conflicted with emotions. Wanting to hug her, kiss her and never leave her sight again. But knowing that she needs sleep, I leave her recovery room and hating myself for leaving on an angry note.

Seeing Mark and Sally hugging and not wanting to be around them, made me wish that was Daisy and I. Knowing my wife had done a great thing, by helping to find Sally but she had got herself hurt in the process. Part of the job I guess, not a part I wanted for Daisy anymore.

Joining Mark, Matt and Sally I say to them belligerently, "You two are so lucky that that bullet did not kill my wife. I don't know which one of you I would have killed first." Looking at Sally who seemed offended by my words, "I hope you appreciate what all Daisy did for you to have you found and brought back safely."

Looking down to the floor, then with tears in her eyes, Sally said, "I am so grateful that she was the one to come looking for me and the rest of the missing women. I never meant for her to get hurt, and I really never knew she was FBI or would be the one searching for me, heck if anyone would come looking for me and figure out that I had not left my husband." Sally was crying really hard, bringing Mark to her side to comfort her.

Mark looked at me annoyed that I had attacked his wife, "Why did you have to hurt her? She did not know that being kidnapped would have made it so that Daisy would be involved. If I had the resources and smarts Daisy has, then I would have gone looking for my wife instead."

After Sally went to get a cup of coffee Mark walked up to me and said compassionately, "I saw how stressed you got knowing that Daisy got involved in helping me by putting her life on the line. I saw how much pain you were in while she was getting the bullet removed and how worried you were that you might lose her. I know that you love my ex-wife more then I ever loved her. Now by seeing how much pain you were in, think of that as if she were kidnapped or went missing without a word or trace." Mark finished with tears held back and a light shoulder pat before walking off.

I had never thought how much Mark was suffering wondering what had happened with his wife. If she had been killed or just any other terrible thing that could have happened to her.

Thinking back to when I was missing for ten years and how Daisy had suffered. She was strong and I was glad she was the one to find me. If it had been me who had lost her, I think I would have gone ballistic and I know there is no way I could have found her.

Understanding Marks pain, I felt bad for yelling at Daisy. Maybe in some way she was trying to make up for the small pain she caused him by sleeping with me unintentionally. Or maybe like she said the firm was working on a missing woman's case and Sally going missing was the best thing for the case. They did find evidence of the other girls who were kidnapped and the few who did run away.

Knowing that Daisy needed to rest, I felt it best if I got some air and maybe visited my brother.

*   *   *

After managing to get 8hrs of sleep, I ate a little break feast and try to get some more sleep. But as I'm closing my eyes Ryan comes up to my bed, "I was watching you sleep then went to get some break feast when the nurse told me you were up."

I sit up frustrated that he thinks he can come in here and giving me another lecture. So before he can yell at me, I yell at him, "I want you to know that I did not plan on ending up back in this god forsaken country. I never planned on being shot or for the other things that happened. I went through 10years of being a widow and when Mark told me that his wife was missing and that he didn't feel it in his heart that she had left him. Thinking that the case would only be in Canada, and that it was a petty kidnapping. I'm sorry that I put my life and our family in jeopardy, it was never my intentions."

Before I can continue Ryan asks, "Are you done?"

I look at him with puppy-dog eyes. But then he says, "I yelled at Sally, for which I apologized for. Then Mark yelled at me, and that hit home with me. I'm sorry I was angry that you put your life on the line for another man and his wife. But that's what you have been doing for as long as you've been with the FBI. You did what you thought was right, and I understand the pain Mark felt with Sally missing."

I sit on the bed. Bringing my hands into his he says. "I also know that you too thought you lost someone you cared about and loved deeply." I try to interrupt Ryan, but am silenced by his finger as he gently puts it on my lips. "I'll finish quickly. I understand what you did and why. And I am so sorry for ever yelling at you. What you did was right, and I am so proud of you. You have more courage than I ever had. Heck I was missing for ten years. Elijah was also missing, and you found him faster than I did. Please forgive me?"

I smile with so much love. "I forgive you. Do you forgive me?"

He smiles back at me. "Yes."

"I love you so much, all I could think of when I was here was you."

Pulling me into his arms he says softly, "I love you too."

We kiss and hug for a long time, then Ryan crawled into my hospital bed, making himself comfortable. I am then able to fall asleep and a peaceful sleep at that.

Within the next few weeks, and with the help of Ryan's brother, the FBI were able to find thirty-nine women who had either ran away or were kidnapped. All but two were alive. Returned back to their families who were happy to have their loved ones back home. Most of the women were in need of therapy, but had a strong will to get past this event in their lives. The FBI providing and paying for the counselling to help the ladies. The FBI were able to get a lot of the people involved in the smuggling operation with the help of the women's statements.

My arm and shoulder got better, and my kids were so happy to see me alive and well. Ryan threw a welcome home party for me, inviting all my friends and family.

I received a metal for my bravery and courage, and on the note I knew my father was very proud of me. So I retired from the FBI making Ryan very happy, but mostly my mom and brother. After my last mission they weren't ready to lose another family member. But I knew the whole time I was in the FBI, my father was my guardian angle.

EPILOGUE

"Wow, that is an amazing story, although summed up. The fact that you were able to find your missing son, then husband and not remarry while you were widowed, then help your ex-husband find his wife and end up finding a major women trafficking operation," Jill the host said.

"Well I want to thank you for being on the show." She paused before adding, "With your busy schedule in businesses, music choreography, and taking care of your family"—she pauses again—"now that you have quite the FBI, what's in the future?"

I smile and say, "A long-awaited vacation for the family."

Looking toward one of the cameras, Jill said, "Look for Daisy Gaston's book, *One Night of Fate* in bookstores near you."

I shook Jill's hand. "Thank you for having me on your show."

The show finished taping, I talked with Jill a little more about my hectic life and then headed home hoping that everyone had their bags packed so that we could go to Australia for a month or maybe longer.

The End

Rick
403-330-5570
610-46 Ave - TOL_OVO
BOPOX 1111